CHiLD

# BOOKS BY CJ LYONS

# SAVE HER CHILD

## CJ LYONS

bookouture

Published by Bookouture in 2021

An imprint of Storyfire Ltd.
Carmelite House
50 Victoria Embankment
London EC4Y 0DZ

www.bookouture.com

ISBN: 978-1-80019-434-2
eBook ISBN: 978-1-80019-433-5

We are all in the same boat, in a stormy sea, and we owe each other a terrible loyalty.

*G.K. Chesterton*

# PROLOGUE

She woke before dawn, screaming in pain.

*No, no, no.* It was too soon. The pain stole her breath until she was gasping, swallowing any air she could get, doubled over, her hands cradling her swollen belly. *Not now, not here, not now;* the words became a bizarre mantra.

Then the pain released its grip.

She was all alone, stranded in a wilderness—a log cabin, of all things. He'd thought it was so cute, romantic, even. Most of all, safe. Their enemies would never find her here. And he had a plan. All they needed to do was follow the plan and everything would be fine: the baby would be safe, they would be rich and, best of all, they wouldn't need to spend the rest of their lives looking over their shoulders.

He was going to save her and the baby. He swore to it.

But he wasn't here.

Another wave of pain left her writhing on the floor, fighting to find any position that eased the pressure building inside her. He'd said no calls, that it was too risky and the phone was only for emergencies, only if things went wrong, but they weren't going to go wrong because he'd thought of everything and he had a plan…

Drenched with sweat, her hair falling into her face, she crawled across the cabin to the phone. She didn't care about his damn plan; all she cared about was her baby. Because something was wrong, something was very wrong.

She reached the living area. The rustic end table shifted against her weight, so she grabbed hold of the itchy plaid couch beside it, heaving herself onto it. Panting, trying to get as much oxygen to her baby as she could, she took the cell phone from the charger. She turned the screen on, to be greeted by a red light: low battery.

Low battery? They hadn't even used it—it was for emergencies only. Like now!

She glanced at the cord leading from the charger to the wall outlet and realized the plug wasn't fully in the socket. The table must have wobbled sometime during the two weeks that she'd been trapped here.

Another wave of pain had her cursing, gripping the phone so tight she thought she might crush it. This time when the pain eased, it left a strange sensation in its wake. She looked down and saw a trickle of blood going down her leg.

The baby! She needed to call for help—to hell with his rules and their enemies and bloody vows of revenge—she would not allow her baby to continue to suffer, not for another moment.

She tried to dial but realized there was no signal.

She would have to go outside, leave the safety of the cabin.

She stood, blinked back the wave of red-spotted dizziness that rushed over her, and shuffled toward the door, her feet numb against the rough wood floor. Her vision swam; the door seemed so close, within reach, then impossibly far away. But she gritted her teeth and kept moving, inching toward it, holding onto the phone with one hand, the other cradling her baby inside her swollen belly.

Halfway there, just as she reached the threadbare braided rug, pain slammed into her, so fierce that she realized the first waves had been mere ripples compared to this tsunami. It threw her to her knees, then face down on the floor, convulsing through her.

She screamed. But there was no one to hear her.

And then, like a drowning person going under for the last time, the world faded away, beyond her grasp, the light surrendering to black.

# CHAPTER ONE

Despite the August heat stifling the night, the corpse didn't smell too bad. Not yet, anyway. Detective Naomi Harper knew that wouldn't last long.

Avoiding broken glass and puddles of undetermined origins, Harper crouched on the pavement of a narrow alley on the east side of Cambria City's Kingston Towers. Around her came camera flashes and the chatter of the crime scene techs as they worked the perimeter of the scene, leaving the body to the coroner's investigator and Harper. She settled her weight on her heels as she hovered over the young woman's body.

Maggie Chen, the death investigator, pulled back the bloody length of plastic sheeting that had been found draped over the body. Harper got her first look at the victim. Tangled cornrows, blood coating her face, bruises, swelling, and obvious broken bones combined to create a monstrous profile—Harper doubted even the girl's own parents would be able to recognize her in her current state.

Harper's gaze traveled down the body, noting more bruises and damage, apparently inflicted by a brutal, prolonged beating. Mostly along one side, so probably all from a single attacker, she thought. The girl was dressed in shorts and a camisole, nothing too flashy or outrageous, but there were very few reasons why a girl her age would be in this alley at night—and they all had to do with sex.

"Any phone or purse? ID?" Harper asked Maggie.

"No. Nothing."

Damn. Then Harper noted a tattoo along the girl's wrist. "Can I get a closer look?"

Maggie stretched her gloved hand across the body, the hood of her Tyvek overalls slipping, exposing a stray strand of robin's-egg-blue hair. She raised their victim's wrist gingerly as if holding a diamond bracelet out for inspection. Except it wasn't diamonds encircling the woman's dark skin, rather an intertwined ribbon of inked calla lilies.

"Lily." Harper sighed. "Last name is…" She thought back to when she'd patrolled this sector. So many girls came and went here, the Towers seemingly swallowing them whole. Three generations and the young were still paying the price of Cambria City's failed effort at affordable public housing. "I think her name is Lily Nolan. Can't remember for sure, but she's on file."

"I'll run her prints as soon as we get to the morgue, confirm her identity." Maggie stroked the dead girl's hand before gently turning it over. "No obvious flesh beneath her nails."

"No broken nails, either." Harper nodded to the elaborate acrylic nail art adorning the girl's fingers. More lilies, done in a rainbow of bright colors with gold sparkles and diamond embellishments. The kind of nails she would have loved to have when she was a teenager—but as a minister's daughter, she'd been lucky to be allowed clear coat polish over natural flesh tones. The Reverend did not believe in "unnatural adornment."

"How could she not have fought back?" Maggie's tone was mournful as she placed paper evidence bags over Lily's hands. "She just stood there and let him do this?"

Harper didn't say anything. She was certain that during Lily's time on the street she had never fought back—not against the gang who'd turned her out, acting as her pimps while brainwashing her into thinking they were the only family who could care for and protect her; not against the johns who promised to pay more for violence but rarely kept their word; not against the drug dealers who took their payment in trade.

"How old was she?" Maggie asked.

"It's been almost a year since last time I saw her. I was working Vice." The only time that being one of the few Black women on the Cambria City's police force had served in Harper's favor, allowing her to participate in various undercover operations for the vice and drugs squad even though she was only a patrol officer. Those days were behind her now—as of four days ago. She was now finally out of uniform and off the streets, officially a full-fledged detective assigned to the Violent Crimes Unit. "I think she was seventeen."

Maggie said nothing, her silence an offering of sympathy and remorse at Lily's short life lost to the streets and the violence that stalked alleys like this one. Then she began to hum, a tune that carried both sorrow and hope in its harmony.

"What's that song?"

"Nothing. Just made it up." Maggie shrugged. "Call it 'Lily's Song.'"

"It's good. You should keep it." Maggie and her husband often performed at local open mike nights.

"Would rather not have had the opportunity to create it in the first place." They both pushed to their feet. "Where's Luka?"

Harper knew that what she was really asking was why Harper, who'd only earned her gold shield a few days ago, was here without Detective Sergeant Luka Jericho supervising her. It was a little after four a.m. on a Sunday morning, meaning the on-call team of detectives—this weekend Harper and Luka—had to travel from their homes. Luka lived across the river with his grandfather and nephew, while Harper's apartment was only a few blocks away.

"Luka's coming, but I'm primary on this one." Harper couldn't stop the hint of pride in her voice. Her first homicide that was hers and hers alone. Glancing at Lily's battered body, she quickly sobered, realizing the weight of the responsibility—this murder was hers to solve. For Lily. For Lily's family. "What can you tell me?"

"Not much," Maggie admitted. "No obvious penetrating wounds. Lack of rigor and body temp indicate possible TOD as little as a few hours ago."

"So, she was beaten, and time of death was not so long ago," Harper translated. She'd pretty much figured all of that out herself. "Did she die from the beating?"

"Possibly," Maggie stressed. As a death investigator, any of her findings needed to be confirmed by the medical examiner's postmortem. "I found track marks on her left arm, but they were all old and scarred. Once I clean her up, I can look for any fresh ones and we'll run a tox screen for drugs of abuse."

Harper glanced around the alley. There were two industrial-sized dumpsters, a small mountain of broken wooden pallets, trash spewing out of discarded garbage bags, along with an assortment of used condoms, syringes, cigarette butts—a wasteland overflowing with human DNA. A crime scene tech's nightmare. The plastic sheet the killer had draped over the body bothered her as well. "Was she killed here or dumped?"

"The blood spatter seems consistent with her broken nose and oral injuries, so my guess is that she sustained those injuries here. I haven't found any evidence that the body was moved. However—"

"That doesn't mean the other injuries weren't inflicted elsewhere, before she was brought here."

"Exactly. But gross appearance does suggest that all the injuries were inflicted contemporaneously, with the same blunt instrument, and very close to the time of death."

Harper gave Maggie an exaggerated eye-roll. "You've been spending way too much time with Ford Tierney." The assistant medical examiner was noted for his punctilious way of speaking.

Maggie grinned. "Just wanted you to look good, writing up your first report as lead detective. But, yeah, she probably was beaten and left to die here." She followed Harper's gaze around the alley. "Which, forensically speaking, is probably the worst place possible. Don't envy the crime scene techs."

"Speaking of which—"

"I'm done." She gestured to her transport team, who were waiting on the street. "We'll be out of your hair in a few minutes."

"Thanks, Maggie."

"Good luck." Maggie rested her gloved palm on Lily's head for a moment. "She deserved better."

Harper stood and surveyed her crime scene. "Don't they all?"

# CHAPTER TWO

Detective Sergeant Luka Jericho watched from beyond the police barricades at the entrance to the alley. He angled himself so that he was behind one of the halogen work lights CSU had brought in; even if Harper glanced in his direction she wouldn't see him.

She'd done a decent job so far, first making certain the scene was clear of any potential danger, then establishing an adequate perimeter and dispatching the uniforms to start canvassing for witnesses—not that anyone from the Towers would voluntarily cooperate with the police, but you could always hope. Besides, if the case ever went to court, you never wanted to give the opposing attorney grounds to suggest that the police had missed something like an eyewitness, opening the door to reasonable doubt.

Maggie followed the gurney with the woman's corpse, now wrapped in a sterile sheet inside a body bag. She motioned for her team to continue as she stopped and turned to Luka.

"How'd she do?" he asked.

"Good," Maggie answered, clearly uncomfortable with playing the role of proctor. "Asked all the right questions, even made a tentative identification, despite the fact that there was no purse, wallet, ID or phone on the body."

Luka arched an eyebrow at that. "It was someone Harper knew, then?"

"Hard to say, her face was really brutalized, but Harper recognized a tattoo belonging to a sex-trafficking victim she'd arrested during Vice operations." The disdain that filled Maggie's face had nothing to do with the fact that her victim was a prostitute. Rather, Luka understood that it was aimed at the men who'd forced her onto the street and the Vice cops who insisted on treating her like a criminal, not a victim.

"You know that bringing them in off the street is the best way to offer services and a way out without their pimps interfering," he said. They'd had this discussion too many times to count.

"Except the police always attach a price by asking these women—mostly girls—who have already had so much taken from them, to turn on their pimps, testify against them, help you do your jobs for you. Never mind the men who buy their services—"

"We charge the johns as well—"

"Yeah, a summons. One that costs less than a speeding ticket," she flared.

"The johns can't lead us to the traffickers, not with everything arranged online. That's why we need the girls to help." He wasn't even sure why they were having this debate—again. He hadn't worked Vice in over a decade; Luka's job was violent crimes, which usually translated to homicide. "Look, I'm sorry this girl ended up on the street—"

"Harper said she was seventeen, Luka." Maggie's face was flushed, whether by the August heat or her equally sweltering emotions, he wasn't sure. "*Seventeen.* She had her whole life ahead of her." She made a noise deep in her throat as if swallowing a sob. "Tossed out like garbage."

"We'll do everything we can, Maggie. Doesn't matter that it's Harper's first case as lead, I'll make sure—"

Her glare blazed brighter than the halogen lights surrounding them. "See that you do. She deserves your best."

He nodded, a solemn vow. "Call me when you get an ID confirmed."

"I will." She slung her camera case higher up onto her shoulder. "You want to make the notification or should I?"

Usually the coroner's investigator notified the family of a loved one's death. But Luka preferred to be there for cases under his jurisdiction. Not only because it was often a family member or someone intimately involved in the victim's life who was responsible for their death, but also because seeing the family's faces, hearing them talk about their loved one's life, all helped Luka to better understand the victim. For him, that was vital in forming an understanding of the crime.

"I'll do it. With Harper." Death notifications were the most difficult part of the job, and he knew Harper wouldn't like it, but this was her case now. The dead girl belonged to her.

He'd fought for Harper's promotion—she'd passed all her exams with flying colors, but several high-ranking officers had questioned her attitude. Luka had interceded and the brass had grudgingly added her name to the promotions list, assigning her to Luka's squad, warning him that any problems Harper created would be his to solve.

"She's ready," Maggie said, effortlessly reading his expression.

"I hope so," he murmured. Maggie joined her team in the coroner's van while Luka donned booties and gloves. Then he stepped past the barricade and entered the alley. Harper had been crouching, sketching the crime scene, but quickly stood when she saw him.

"Sir. They just removed the body." She sounded abashed, as if she'd already made a mistake. "I didn't want to delay—"

"Of course not." He nodded his approval, hoping she'd relax and perform like the competent investigator he knew her to be.

Luka still remembered his first case as lead. A homeless man's burnt remains had been found in an oil drum in an abandoned warehouse down by the river. With all forensics destroyed it had seemed like the kind of case that might never be closed. It had taken him months of painstaking investigation, widening his circle of suspects until he'd eventually determined that five high school kids from Cambria Preparatory Academy, an exclusive private school across the river, just outside city limits, had taken a "bum-bashing" spree too far. Despite his meticulously documented case, the DA had declined to prosecute on the murder, instead allowing all five to plead out to lesser charges. Justice often had little to do with the practice of law, Luka had learned, the lesson driving him to work even harder.

Shaking away the bitter memory, he told Harper, "Give me the bullet."

"Yes, sir." Harper used her phone to access the department's secure cloud account and pulled up photos of their victim in situ, before the body was moved. "We have an unknown female, found at approximately 3:26 a.m. by patrol officers after an anonymous 911 call. Caller was female, Dispatch said she used an unregistered cell phone. I'll be asking for cell tower records to trace any calls from the time so hopefully we can get a location."

All standard procedure. Luka examined the girl's injuries. Beaten to a pulp was an understatement. An attack like that—no way it wasn't personal. Their victim knew her killer, he was certain. "Maggie said you made a tentative ID?"

"She has the same tattoo as a girl I met while working a Vice operation. Seventeen-year-old, name was Lily Nolan. Maggie's going to run the prints, see if it's her or not. Maggie also said the blows appeared to be inflicted by a blunt instrument, but she'll have more information after the autopsy."

"Murder weapon?"

They both glanced around the alley and its abundance of possible weapons: loose paving bricks, lengths of rebar, stray two-by-fours broken off from shipping pallets.

"I asked CSU to bag and tag anything that might be a possibility."

Luka pointed to the initial photos of the body, the ones taken before Maggie began her examination. Their victim was partially covered with a blood-spattered length of plastic sheeting. "What do you make of the body being covered?"

"At first, I thought the killer draped it over her body after he'd killed her—like a sign of remorse, covering her up. Or he'd used it to move her body here after killing her elsewhere." Luka frowned and she continued, "But then I realized the only way to get that much blood on the sheet but not the surrounding alley was if he first incapacitated her—maybe with the blow to her face that caused the bloody nose—and while she was down, he threw the plastic over her and bludgeoned her in a blitz attack."

"Why?"

"To protect any blood from spraying onto him. If you look closely, you can see pattern marks from the blows. I've asked the CSU guys to compare them to our possible weapons."

He nodded, agreeing with her theory—contingent on what the medical examiner found during the autopsy. "Next steps?"

"Cell tower warrants, finish canvassing for witnesses and any surveillance cameras that might have caught our victim or our killer, confirm ID, check with Vice and patrol to see if there's been any recent unusual activity in the area, and track down any family and known associates."

It was a good plan, although Luka doubted she would get very far with any of her action items, not on a Sunday morning. Except Maggie was on the job, so that would help. "Okay. Let's get to work."

# CHAPTER THREE

Dr. Leah Wright glanced at her schedule. If they were going to do everything the kids wanted, she'd need to be in two places at once. Her daughter, Emily, and Luka's nephew, Nate, were both in front of her as they walked across the grassy field that served as a parking lot for the annual Craven County Fair. Emily and Nate had their heads together, peering at the map, planning their day. Trailing behind Leah, already bored, was Ruby, Leah's mother and reluctant childcare-helper.

She traced her finger down the list of events. Today, the final day of the fair, was devoted to children. Poultry showmanship. Junior dressage and roping competitions. Quilting bee and auction. Small engine repair race followed by a tractor pull. Candle-making class. Livestock judging. And, the highlight of the day as far as Nate and Emily were concerned: the food and arts competition judging. Followed by a pie-eating contest, chili cook-off, and auctioning the various homegrown vegetables and other food items the children had entered into competition.

Leah hoisted her knapsack higher on her shoulder and reached for her water bottle. It was just past nine in the morning and already the temperature hovered around eighty-five. August in the central Pennsylvania mountains was known for its hazy, hot, and humid days, but this summer had felt particularly stifling. Some days it was a struggle for each breath. Although maybe it wasn't only the weather. Leah's husband, Ian, had been murdered in February and now, six months later, she still woke every day expecting to see his face beside her. And then, three seconds after she opened her eyes, an awful emptiness devoured her as reality came crashing down.

The kids reached the line at the ticket booth and waited for Leah to catch up. "Ruby said if we were good, we could get funnel cakes," Emily said. "And then she said we could get kettle corn."

"And apple fritters," Nate chimed in. "Don't forget those. I promised Luka and Janine and Pops I'd bring some home for them." Nate had left Baltimore after his mother, Luka's sister, had died, to move in with Luka, Luka's elderly grandfather, and Janine, their live-in healthcare aide who kept the entire family running.

"Right." Emily was already buzzing with a pre-sugar rush, bouncing on her toes. She'd recently turned seven but still was much shorter than Nate, who was eight. "And we need to ride the carousel and the whirl-a-tilt and—"

"I want to see the horses," Nate put in.

Emily nodded. "And we need to be at our ribbon-winning. Of course."

They both nodded and stared at Leah as if she could alter physics to allow them to do everything in one day.

Leah's phone buzzed and both kids groaned when she pulled it out to glance at the message. The lab with an update on a sexual assault case she'd handled earlier in the week. It was all good news for the survivor, but Emily tugged at her hand. "You're not leaving to go back to work, are you?"

Leah smiled. "Nope. I'm yours all day long." Despite still being on call for emergencies in her position as medical director of Good Samaritan's Crisis Intervention Center, Leah's new job definitely gave her more time with Emily than her previous life as an ER physician had. Still, there were some days… okay, most days… when she missed her work on the frontlines. Although one unexpected perk of working at the CIC was its fledgling partnership with Cambria City's police department, giving Leah an occasional chance to work in the field interviewing traumatized witnesses and helping with emotionally disturbed persons; she was even taking a course in hostage negotiation.

She bought their tickets and Ruby's and they crossed into the fairgrounds. The empty field that was part of Craven Peak State Forest had been transformed into the claustrophobic cacophony of a carnival sideshow. The layout forced them down a long stretch of games and concession stands lined with vendors hawking a variety of things that no one needed, but nonetheless everyone still gathered to listen to their mesmerizing spiels and some would eventually buy. All the same useless gadgets and gizmos that they'd sold when Leah was a kid—and that she'd saved her allowance to buy, certain that the 'guaranteed to write in zero gravity' astronaut-certified pen would garner her straight As or that the X-ray glasses would grant her magical powers of observation.

It felt strange that this was the first time she'd ever come to the fair with her own mother. Ruby had left Leah in the care of Leah's great-aunt, Nellie, when Leah was eleven. But after Ian was killed, Leah had returned with Emily to live at the farm Nellie had bequeathed Leah, and Ruby had joined them, somehow inserting herself back into Leah's life. Their relationship was still strained by two decades of things not said, along with Leah's fear that sooner or later Ruby would betray Emily's trust in her, but they were making it work. Kind of. For now.

"What makes you so sure you won any ribbons?" Ruby asked the kids in a teasing tone. Emily had recreated several of Nellie's chocolate truffle recipes using the lavender and roses grown at the farm, leaving a mouth-watering aroma perfuming the kitchen for weeks as she experimented. Luka had finally given Nate his own phone, one with the best camera available, and Nate had devoured YouTube videos on using it to document his new environment. Then Luka had printed the photos Nate chose and he'd framed them.

Not wanting them to be disappointed, Leah had warned both kids that it wasn't likely that they would win anything. The Craven County Fair did not award prizes merely for participation. Emily and Nate were up against older kids who'd spent years in 4H and had generations of blue-ribbon winners to coach them.

It'd been nerve-racking, waiting all week for the judging today. She had no idea how she was going to face the kids if they didn't win something, even the lowest honorable mention. "If you don't win—" she started, only to be interrupted by Emily.

"We're winning. We're winning everything." Emily's confidence constantly amazed Leah. And reminded her of Ian. She felt a sharp stab to the heart, wishing he was there to see their daughter, hoping that maybe he was. Leah wasn't religious, but that didn't stop her from believing in Ian. If anyone could force their spirit to linger with their family after death, it was Ian.

"Blue ribbon, blue ribbon, blue ribbon," Emily chanted, taking Nate's arm and doing a quick do-si-do.

Leah glanced at Ruby, who simply gave her a smug smile. "Don't worry. It'll be fine."

Those words had never brought comfort to Leah when she was a child—mostly because they were never true. At least never when Ruby spoke them. Leah gritted her teeth and swallowed the memories, leaving a taste of bitter ash behind. "What makes you so sure?"

Ruby slowed her pace, letting the kids get a few steps ahead of them, the tinny music blaring from the stands masking her tone. "I have a certain friend who has insider knowledge. He assured me, we don't have anything to worry about."

"Really?"

Ruby nodded as the kids returned.

"Mom, can we—"

And so it began… Leah allowed herself to be tugged down the midway, her mind already reeling from the crowds and constant barrage of sensory overstimulation, but she smiled anyway. As long as the kids were happy, what was one day?

After all, it was Fair. Heralding the last magical week of summer freedom before school began. Nothing bad ever happened during Fair.

# CHAPTER FOUR

Harper wasn't certain if Luka was babysitting her or helping her. In the spring, she'd worked with his Violent Crimes Unit while still a patrol officer, so she knew that Luka got involved with all of his unit's cases, especially at the start. But this felt different. It felt like a test. Why else would a detective sergeant spend hours slogging through the heat, tramping up and down urine-stained staircases, simply to help her with the scut work of canvassing the Towers for potential witnesses? Now that she'd finally made detective, she'd hoped that the constant feeling of being judged would vanish, but no such luck.

Somewhere in the middle of their door-knock on the fourth floor, Maggie had texted, confirming Lily's identity. No driver's license, but several arrests for solicitation and drug possession, current address unknown. Lily had turned eighteen just a few days ago—the same day Harper had been promoted, she couldn't help but note, the irony only adding to her sense of frustration at such a young life taken. More than frustration: an anger that tasted bitter and raw.

As was usual with the Towers, no one had seen anything, no one could identify their victim, and no one remembered anything unusual about the night. The most they got was from an elderly man in the second-floor apartment whose bedroom overlooked the alley. He thought he heard a woman crying when he got up to go to the bathroom, but he couldn't remember what time and he didn't look out of his window; by the time he returned to bed, it was quiet.

"Maybe it wasn't a woman," he'd told Harper, squinting through thick lenses. "Could of been an alley cat. I don't know, not for sure."

She and Luka left, trudging down the graffiti-covered staircase.

"He was the best of the lot." She stifled a sigh, wishing she hadn't worn a jacket over her blouse and slacks, but she was a detective now and felt the need to look the role, even if it was hot as Hades.

They exited through the Towers' front door, brushing past youths sitting on the steps, several barely bothering to hide their drug paraphernalia. The sun now blazed over the mountaintops to the east, the air thick and heavy, promising another scorching day.

As they walked around the corner to return to the alley crime scene, Harper noted the paucity of security cameras without surprise: the gangs who ruled the Towers destroyed them as soon as they were placed, paying bounties to young kids who spotted them. Despite its location, nestled in the idyllic Allegheny Mountains, Cambria City, like many down-and-out rust-belt towns, still faced its share of crime wrought by enterprising groups of young men. While the gangs that ran the Kingston Towers and surrounding neighborhood weren't as vicious or well-organized as the more violent MS-13 or the drug cartels that plagued larger neighboring cities like Baltimore, DC, and Philly, the Towers' factions definitely contributed more than their fair share of grief to the community.

Luka stopped, hands deep in his pockets as they watched the CSU team pack up, taking one last look at the scene in the daylight. Without the harsh glare of the work lights the alley returned once more to what it always had been: a squalid, shadowy, lonely place to die.

And an easy place to potentially get away with murder, Harper realized grimly.

"What did I miss?" she swallowed her pride to ask.

He glanced at her, obviously surprised. "Do you think you missed something?"

"Luka, she was thrown away with the garbage. I really want to know. What more can I do?"

"Nothing until we retrace her steps, see if anyone had reason to kill her—"

"Yeah, yeah. The three Ps." It was the first lesson she'd learned working with him. Murder motives boiled down to passion, profit, or power. "She didn't have any cash or valuables on her, so could have been a robbery gone wrong. As for power or passion—"

"Pimp angry with her?" he suggested. "Maybe she wanted out of the life. Or she just pissed him off." Sex workers were all too disposable; there was always more supply to fill a trafficker's demand.

"Same could go for a john. Wanted more than he paid for or she was prepared to give and…" They stood side by side, the morning heat turning the odors emanating from the alley into a rancid stew too foul to breathe. She rolled her shoulders, a list of her next steps forming in her mind. "I'll start with the local girls. I know where they hang out from my time with Vice. Hopefully by then we'll have traced her next of kin."

Luka's phone buzzed—not for the first time this morning, since he was the supervisor on call for the weekend, covering not only the VCU but also the other investigatory units. "Patrol needs me to sign off on another scene. Call me when you know anything and we'll do the death knock together." He walked away, heading to his car.

Harper couldn't stop staring at the spot on the pavement where Lily's body had been found. Luka would help—as would Ray Acevedo and Scott Krichek, the other two detectives with the VCU—but this was her case, her responsibility.

She had to swallow twice as the true nature of her new job bore down on her. A person's life had been stolen. Everything Lily could have seen and done, years or decades in the future, children, partners, a family… all taken from her.

If Lily was ever going to get justice, it would be up to Harper. But was she up to the task?

Now it was 12:03 and Harper sat parked in her departmental-issue unmarked sedan debating her options. She was three minutes late for Sunday dinner; she should be rushing inside to offer apologies. Or she could throw the car into reverse and get back to work on a case that statistics said she had no hope of solving.

The August glare beat down on the Impala's windshield. Harper stared at the house she'd grown up in, a modest white-framed colonial with a roofline that paralleled that of the larger church beside it. The only home she'd ever known and yet every time she returned it was harder and harder to find the strength to go inside and face her family. Especially her father, the leader of Holy Redeemer, the Reverend Matthew Harper.

After Luka left her at Lily's crime scene, Harper had gone back to the police department where she'd pulled Lily's records and searched for known associates, made a list of people arrested at the same time as Lily, as well as the various addresses—most of them fake—that Lily had given along with an assortment of Lily's aliases. She'd also compiled the names of the people who'd bailed Lily out and paid her fines. By the time she'd finished, she couldn't even verify that Lily Nolan was the girl's real name. Typical of so many street kids, Lily had never given the same name twice and she was young enough that they had no driver's license or other official documentation to confirm her true identity.

Undaunted, Harper had spent the rest of the morning walking the streets around the Towers in a fruitless search for anyone who could possibly tell her about Lily's final hours or point her in the direction of Lily's next of kin. But Sunday mornings were about the only slow time on the streets, a chance for working girls to catch a few hours of sleep.

The entire time, all Harper could think about was Lily's birthday, four days ago. For some reason, she couldn't get past that.

Harper's own birthday was January sixth, the same date as the Epiphany, the celebration of the Magi arriving with their gifts for the Christ Child. It was a poor choice of a birthday for the adopted child of a preacher. A day to give, not to receive. A day that meant more as a biblical lesson than it did a celebration of Harper's entering the world.

As she glanced past the two silver minivans and the white Ford Expedition parked between her and the house, her father's voice rang through her head. It was her fourth birthday. *Life boils down to two choices,* the Reverend Harper had told her when she'd reached to open her first brightly wrapped present. *Only two, so it should be easy,* the Reverend continued. *Good or evil. Do you want to do the right thing, the good thing? Make our Heavenly Father smile with joy along with me and your mother? Your choice. Right or wrong. Make me proud.*

Even now, twenty-four years later, she felt the weight of the silence that had followed while she fought to understand his words, her three older brothers growing restless as the candles dripped onto the birthday cake they were poised to devour. Then came her mother's hands, squeezing Harper's shoulders as she inched her fingers toward the small mound of enticing gifts. A squeeze that warned her that it was the wrong choice.

"You look just like them," John, the youngest of the Reverend's boys had said, laying his pale white forearm against Harper's dark skin. "Mom, did Naomi come from where the Magi came from?"

"She's not a king from the Orient," Jacob, the eldest scoffed. "We got her from Philly. From a mom who didn't want her."

"Hush," Rachel, Harper's mother, commanded. "Naomi is our gift and we are blessed to receive her. Now, sweetie, what are you going to do with *your* gifts?"

Harper remembered feeling confused, torn between her desire to rip open all the bright paper and ribbons to see what lay beneath, her hope that maybe her father had taken time from his busy life of leading his flock down the path of righteousness to find the perfect gift for her, and a sinking certainty that none of these presents actually were meant for her at all.

"It's better to give than receive," Jonah, the middle son, whispered as if coaching her.

She glanced up, daring to meet her father's gaze. The Reverend said nothing, his face expressionless as he waited in judgment. Would she do the righteous thing, prove his faith in her? Or would she, as she seemed to do so often without even trying, let him down? Again.

Grimly, her lips compressed to stifle her disappointment, she pushed the gifts away. The Reverend gave the tiniest nod of approval while Rachel kissed the top of Harper's head. "Good girl. I'll add these to the pile for the charity drive." She whisked the gifts away while Harper blew out her birthday candles and they cut the cake, the boys talking nonstop, the Reverend reading his Bible, Rachel rushing around in the background filling glasses and serving.

Harper remembered how the cake stuck to her palate, tasteless and hard to swallow—not because Rachel wasn't a good baker but because Harper was so certain that, despite having made the right choice, she'd never actually be truly worthy to sit at the Reverend's table, deserving of his love.

Now sitting in a police car, August sun beating down on her, she shook her head, dismissing the childhood memory, even as she recognized that she was still struggling to win her adoptive father's respect. But she was here now, nothing for it but to go inside—especially after Rachel had called to chide her for missing the last two Sunday family dinners.

Harper secured her service weapon in the lock box bolted to the floor of the car's trunk. Technically, regulations required she carry it on her person while on duty, but her mother would not allow a handgun to cross her threshold. She had no problem with rifles or shotguns but because handguns could be so easily concealed, Rachel saw them as evil, a belief that none of her sons had been able to talk her out of. Harper hadn't even tried, her newfound detente with her family too fragile to risk. She trudged to the front door, its white paint brilliant in the sunshine, creating an otherworldly glow. As if crossing the threshold required an equally flawless soul, which Harper most definitely did not possess.

"You're late," Rachel called by way of greeting as soon as Harper stepped inside.

Harper glanced into the dining room with its table that could seat twelve. The Reverend and his three sons, all adorned in their Sunday clerical uniforms, were already seated, waiting for the women to finish bringing the food. Sunday dinner was a well-rehearsed choreography of women in motion designed to allow the four ministers to enjoy the fruits of their labor during their busiest workday. The Reverend and his sons divided ministerial duties during the work week—over the past two decades, Holy Redeemer had grown into a massive organization requiring many hands to steer it. But Sundays were reserved for a morning of preaching, family dinner, followed by an afternoon of prayer and then evening service. Harper's sisters-in-law would bring dishes ready to serve, take turns wrangling their various children, one of them eating with them in the kitchen so as to not disturb the Reverend with their noise, while Rachel would supervise, always hovering in the background until everyone was served and their appetites sated.

Harper took her customary seat across from the kitchen. She watched as Jacob's wife wrapped her little girl in one of Rachel's never-ending supply of aprons, remembering back to when it was only Harper and Rachel alone in the kitchen, exploring the mysterious world of women's work. The way Rachel had folded the oversized apron to gather the extra material around Harper's waist, crouching behind her to tie it tight and smooth any wrinkles. "There now, don't you look lovely," she'd say every time.

It'd been a long time since Harper had worn one of her mother's aprons or been invited to join her in the kitchen. Not since Harper had left college, disgracing her family.

"Sorry I'm late. I had a case," she told them. The boys ignored her, continuing to debate some new online system designed to facilitate parishioner contributions. Jonah at least glanced her way and gave her a nod of recognition.

The Reverend didn't look up from his Bible, but did startle her by asking, "What kind of case?"

That silenced the boys. Rachel stepped into the doorway, her fingers bunching up her apron, glancing at the Reverend in confusion. It was the first time he'd asked Harper about her job since she'd joined the force eight years ago. At her promotion ceremony last week, she'd invited her parents, had reserved seats for the Reverend and Rachel, ever hopeful. But nobody had come and the seats sat empty.

So now, Harper leaned forward, anxious to grasp the olive branch her father had offered. "A homicide. My first as lead detective."

"They're trusting you to solve a murder?" John scoffed. He was the closest to Harper in age but had always seemed to resent the fact that she'd been "chosen" by the Harpers when they adopted her, as if they were rivals competing for Rachel and the Reverend's love. "The police must be hard up."

"Shut up, John," Jacob said. "Someone's died. Show some respect for the dead."

Not respect for Harper's abilities to bring the dead justice, she noted.

"We should offer a prayer for them," he continued.

"Who died?" the Reverend asked, closing his Bible and removing his reading glasses, slowly cleaning them with slow, rhythmic circles. It was the silent signal for service to begin and the women emerged from the kitchen bearing steaming platters of food.

Harper was surprised he was interested enough to follow up beyond his initial perfunctory enquiry. "A young woman," she told him. "Just turned eighteen."

"Really, Naomi," Rachel chided her. "This is not appropriate conversation for the dinner table. What if the children heard you?"

The Reverend waved a hand, dismissing Harper and her victim as if his patience with polite small talk was spent. The women sat and everyone joined hands. "Let us pray," he intoned.

The Reverend didn't glance in Harper's direction during the entire meal that followed. After receiving a text summons from Luka, she left before dessert, not even sure if anyone noticed her departure. But as she approached the car, her mother ran out with a cooler of packaged leftovers.

"It's nice to see you and your father getting along so well," Rachel said.

Harper cradled the small cooler. "Yeah, five whole unsolicited words. My heart is aglow."

"Naomi Harper! Don't you use that tone about your father."

Harper hung her head. "No, ma'am. Sorry." She jerked her chin up toward the house. "It's just—I try so hard and I can't get anywhere with him."

"Your father has a lot on his mind, you know that. Not only the ministry but preparing your brothers to eventually lead—" A worried look dampened Rachel's smile. "He's doing his best."

"So am I. And speaking of doing, I need to get to work."

"Right. Your poor young dead girl. I'll keep her in my prayers."

"Actually, I've been called out to another case."

"Really?" Rachel's voice dropped to a dramatic whisper. "Two murders? In one day?"

"We get called to any suspicious deaths, so I'm not sure if it's a murder," she told Rachel as she loaded the leftovers into the car. At least she'd have dinner covered—not always a certainty while working fresh cases. "But you can only hope."

Rachel gave a small laugh. "Don't talk that way around your father," she warned. But after Naomi got into the driver's seat, Rachel leaned into the car and said in a conspiratorial tone, "But feel free to call later, fill me in."

Harper glanced up at that, almost couldn't speak for a moment. All these years she'd been praying for a chance to be welcomed back into her parents' lives. "You sure, Mom?"

Rachel kissed her fingers and touched them to Harper's forehead. "I'm sure. I want to know everything about your life, Naomi. I'm sorry it's taken so long. Will you call me?"

"Yes. It might be late—"

"That's fine. I don't sleep much. But it would ease my mind, knowing that you're safe, understanding more about what you face out there." Rachel closed the car door and stepped back. She mimed a phone and mouthed the words, "call me."

Naomi smiled and waved back, then put the car in gear and headed out. She couldn't believe how well that had gone. A weight lifted from her chest as if she'd been holding her breath for years. Rachel was only the first step—regaining her place in the Reverend's heart would take work.

Her phone rang. Luka. "We're still waiting on the coroner. How far out are you?"

The address he'd given her was up the mountain, barely inside the city limits, which placed her at an advantage since her father's home was only a few miles away. It was an exclusive neighborhood, large wooded lots with even larger mansions situated on them, a combination of historical summer homes built by the coal barons and steel magnates of the prior century and new construction by equally new tech millionaires. "I'll be there in five. What have we got?"

"Not sure. Rich guy. First responders thought suicide." But then he said the magic words that had her pressing down on the accelerator. "But at this stage, we can't rule out murder."

# CHAPTER FIVE

As he waited for their reporting witness to calm down, waited for the dead man's wife to be located, waited for a Mincey warrant to search the premises, waited for the coroner's investigator to arrive, and waited for the fire department to complete their work, Luka kept checking his phone for a message from Nate. Juggling crime scene tasks he was used to. Anxiously waiting for news about family? This was a foreign experience for a thirty-seven-year-old lifelong workaholic bachelor who was suddenly a newly minted adopted father to his eight-year-old nephew and caretaker for his eighty-four-year-old grandfather.

There could be worse places to wait. His victim, forty-three-year-old Spencer Standish, lived in a centuries-old mansion. The grounds contained the main house, the guest house, a pool and pool house, large expanses of manicured gardens along with Luka's crime scene, a stable that had been converted into a garage. Luka had scoured the area and despite the thick forest surrounding the estate he hadn't seen a single errant leaf, much less any hint of a weed daring to trespass or a blade of grass rebellious enough to outgrow its brethren.

A guy with all of this? How the hell did he end up dead, sitting inside his SUV with the motor running and the garage doors closed?

"All clear, Sergeant Jericho," the fire crew chief called to Luka as he emerged from the garage. Behind him, his men carried their industrial exhaust fans out to the drive. "Carbon monoxide levels back to a safe range."

"Any precautions my people need to take?"

"Nope, you're good to go. No signs of any other hazards, either." He joined Luka, standing beside him as the fire crew packed their gear onto their truck. "The CO levels weren't all that high to begin with. I'm not sure if they were enough to cause your man's death. Although the gas might have partially dissipated before we arrived. Plus, carbon monoxide is tricky, so hard to tell."

"You documented everything?" Firemen and paramedics didn't mix well with evidence preservation at crime scenes.

"Yep. I'll send you a full report once I'm back at the station. Need anything else from us?"

"No. Thanks. I appreciate it."

"Just doing our jobs." He nodded to the mansion on the other side of the drive. "Rich people. Never understand why someone with everything does something like this."

They shared a shrug. The fire chief strolled back to his truck.

Luka glanced at his phone one last time before heading into his crime scene. What was taking so long? Surely the judges at the fair had announced the results by now. Maybe Leah's silence meant she was busy consoling Nate. Luka thought the kid showed real talent with his newfound love of photography, but then he was definitely biased on Nate's behalf. The kid deserved a break, after losing his mother to a drug overdose and then being bullied after he moved to Cambria City to live with Luka. He only hoped the county fair judges felt the same.

He hovered his thumb over the phone screen, ready to call Leah for an update, when one of the patrol officers approached. "Sergeant Jericho? Harper just pulled up."

Luka noted the patrolman didn't use Harper's new rank, but patrol officers sometimes didn't with detectives. Besides, Harper could fight her own battles. He only hoped she'd choose them wisely—after all, not many newly minted detectives had the privilege of starting their careers in the VCU. Most had to put in their time on lesser investigatory duties like property crimes, leaving many in the department debating exactly how Harper had jumped the line.

No way in hell was Luka about to explain that the other sergeants had refused to offer her a position on their squads, despite her stellar record—including working on several plainclothes details with both Vice and the VCU. Initially, Ahearn, the commander in charge of the investigative division, had insisted that she belonged with the Domestic unit, which specialized in special victims—child abuse, sex crimes, and intimate partner violence. But Luka understood that Harper's sometimes abrasive personality was ill-suited to the needs of special victims, so he'd convinced Ahearn to assign Harper to Violent Crimes.

"What've we got, boss?" Harper's words were rushed with excitement. Despite having been on the go since before dawn, she didn't seem tired at all.

"Anything on Lily Nolan?"

She sobered. "Not yet. Still trying to locate next of kin. Tonight I'll hit the streets again, look for any friends of hers."

"Talk to Vice before you go out. They might be helpful."

"Right." She glanced at the departing firetruck. "In the meantime, how can I help here?"

He motioned to her to follow him. In the shade of a group of trees—their shadows as sharply edged as the manicured lawn—waited a man sitting on a wrought-iron bench, gazing out at nothing, tears streaming down his face. Their reporting witness. The uniformed officer standing beside him shrugged at Luka. At least the guy wasn't hyperventilating anymore.

"Mr. Hansen, I'm Detective Sergeant Luka Jericho. Can you tell me what happened here?"

Larry Hansen didn't do more than glance at Luka before dropping his gaze. He wiped his face with his palms, took a deep breath, and said, "I wasn't even supposed to be here. But I forgot my tennis racquet and I have a doubles game today." He wasn't talking to Luka as much as the air in front of him. "I have other racquets, but that one is my favorite, so I thought I'd swing by on my way to the club."

Typical distraught witness, obsessing over meaningless details to avoid talking about the crime. Luka humored the man, hoping to ease him into discussing how he'd found Standish's body. "The Porsche Cayenne parked in front of the house, it's yours?"

Hansen nodded. "No one answered the bell, but I figured I'd take a look in the pool house—Tassi and I had drinks there on Friday after our game, so I might have left it there."

"Tassi? That's Natasha Standish, correct?"

"Spence's wife." Hansen jerked his chin up, as if in sudden realization. "She's not here—she doesn't know! How am I going to face her? I can't tell her that Spence, Spence—" He turned to the garage, wide-eyed.

"We'd appreciate it if you say nothing." Luka interrupted him. "We'll contact Mrs. Standish. If you could give us her details." Both the house and the Escalade were leased by an LLC registered in Delaware, and Luka wouldn't have access to Spencer's phone contacts until the coroner's unit arrived.

"Of course." He slid a phone out, scrolled through, then handed it to Luka, who handed it to Harper.

"Walk us through what you saw and heard after you arrived, please, Mr. Hansen."

"No one answered the door, so I was walking down the drive—the tennis courts are back behind the stables, beside the pool. As I passed the stables, I heard the sound of a car running. So, I thought, that must be Tassi or Spence, lucky day, I caught them before they're going out. And I looked in the window and saw Spence's Escalade, sitting there, running, and the place was filled with smoke." He sniffed as if holding back more tears.

"Filled?" Luka prompted.

"Maybe not filled, but definitely too much. Enough to surround the Escalade, like it'd been idling there for a while. I opened the door, but only made it a few steps when I saw—" Another choking sound. "I saw Spence."

"And you—"

"I couldn't breathe." Now he sounded defensive. "I ran outside and called 911. Then I went back, hoping to help Spence, but as soon as I touched him—I knew it was too late."

"You opened the door into the garage and the driver's door of the SUV?" Luka asked. Hansen nodded once more. "Did you touch anything else?"

"Spence's neck—checking for a pulse. I might have braced myself on the driver's seat. I'm not sure, maybe other parts of the car? I was in shock."

"No problem," Luka told him. "We'll need your finger-prints—just for elimination purposes. Any thoughts as to how this happened?"

"How?" Hansen's gaze became unfocused again. "It was an accident, right? Had to be. Spence started the car and something happened before he could open the garage door." Then he met Luka's eyes. "A heart attack. I'll bet that's what it was. Poor guy had a heart attack." He sighed. "Poor Tassi. She's going to be devastated."

Luka tried to get him back on track. "Mr. Hansen, can you tell me anything about any stressors in Mr. Standish's life?"

Hansen shook his head vigorously. "No, nothing. Spence and Tassi—they're the happiest couple I know. Never bickering, not even a crossed look. And Spence loved his job. He always said it was the best of all worlds, helping people, both the haves and have-nots."

Luka exchanged a puzzled look with Harper above Hansen's head. "What does that mean? What did Mr. Standish do for a living?"

Hansen hesitated. "On paper, I guess you'd call him a hedge fund manager. But Spence was so much more than that. He found a way to make double-digit profits for his investors through packaging micro-loans to the less fortunate. Individuals, schools, churches, non-profits. It was a fantastic business model. So successful that his fund was open to investors by invitation only. Plus, they had to agree to tithe a percentage of their net profits to the charity side of the fund, but they all made so much money with Spence's investment model that no one cared. He has a brilliant mind." His lips tightened as if he were holding back more tears. He seemed pretty overwhelmed for someone who appeared to be a casual friend, Luka thought, filing away the details. "Had. Spence *had* a brilliant mind."

"Were you a part of this financial fund?"

"Not the first round—those guys made the big money. But I convinced Tassi to put in a good word for me and I'm in the second cohort. We had a fourteen percent return on our initial investment in the quarter ending in June. And all the earnings reports have been looking even more promising this quarter, so there's no way Spence could have been stressed about work." He glanced up at Luka. "No. You know what this was? An accident. Spence was a workaholic—he must have fallen asleep in the car before he opened the garage door. That must be it. A terrible, terrible accident. That's better than a heart attack—because Tassi would blame herself forever if she thought Spence was under that much stress and she didn't know it."

Luka let his contradictions slide. He'd learned it was best to observe the way witnesses tangled their own logic and then untangle it later when he had actual facts. "Do you know where we can reach Mrs. Standish?"

"Tassi? She's at a spa weekend. The Greenbriar." He glanced at the clock on his phone. "Should be on her way back already."

"Can you think of anything else that might help?" Luka liked to give witnesses a chance to expound without limiting them to a specific question.

Hansen made a show of thinking hard, then said, "No. That's everything."

"Thank you, Mr. Hansen. We'll be in touch. I'd appreciate it if you don't speak to anyone about what you've seen here. And please do call me if you think of anything else." Luka handed the man his card, then nodded to Harper.

Together they left Hansen and followed the path back to the garage. Like the main house, it was an old building, most likely built in the 1800s when Craven County's coal mines and steel operations were at their height. A time when coal barons would keep offices and homes in the city during the week, but then travel up the mountain to palatial estates where their families lived for weekends and holidays. Best of all worlds.

The garage held eight stalls, four to a side, each with their own set of double doors wide enough for a car. Despite all the windows and doors being open, it still reeked of auto exhaust. Only one stall was occupied, the one with a black Cadillac Escalade and a body behind the wheel. Maggie Chen had just arrived in the coroner's van and was photographing Spencer Standish and his death scene. When she spied Luka and Harper, she quickly put her camera away. "I expect you want me to check for a phone?"

"There's none in the car," Luka told her. "I'm assuming it's in his pocket."

They stood, observing the corpse through the open driver's door. Spence was dressed in plaid Bermuda golf shorts and a polo top. He appeared to be in good physical shape—Luka didn't observe much in the way of a middle-aged paunch despite the body being slumped over the steering wheel. His hair was blond, but his skin was rosy with pale splotches and his lips were ruby red.

"Classic carbon monoxide discoloration," Maggie told Harper, indicating the skin. "CO displaces oxygen from red blood cells."

"I'm more concerned about any other factors contributing to the cause of death," Luka told Maggie.

"Why?" Harper asked. "Do you see anything that makes you suspect it isn't suicide or an accident?"

Luka hesitated, uncertain of how to put his intuition into words. "Too early to say. At this stage, we can't take anything for granted."

Maggie patted down the body and searched Spencer's pockets. Only coroner's personnel were allowed to touch a body. "Nothing here."

"No phone?" Where was Spencer going without his phone? Of course, if he did kill himself then he wouldn't have needed it—which could mean Luka's instincts were wrong.

"If you're suspicious of something other than suicide, we could use the car's computer system to calculate exactly what time he turned the engine on," Harper volunteered.

"Good," Luka said. "I want to know if that was enough time for the carbon monoxide to kill him."

"I can build you a timeline once I get labs and the firefighters' CO levels from when they entered," Maggie said. She crouched down, examining the floorboard beneath the corpse. "I've got something." She stood and pointed. "There's an envelope down there, pretty thick. Still no signs of a phone, though."

Luka sighed with impatience. Unlike in movies, where detectives routinely grabbed any evidence they saw, he'd need to follow protocol: after Maggie's team removed the body, the crime scene techs would document where the evidence was found and bag it to maintain the chain of custody. Then, preferably back in the lab, they would photograph everything again, swab for touch DNA, and dust for prints. Only then would Luka be allowed to examine the envelope and its contents.

Thankfully Maggie was a step ahead of him. Before he could ask, she grabbed her camera and knelt beside the corpse's legs, taking a photo of the envelope. She stood and showed it to Luka and Harper.

There, easily read on the camera's digital screen, was Spencer Standish's final message to the world scrawled across the outside of the envelope:

*To whomever finds this, inside please find my full confession. To my dear, beloved Tassi—I am so very sorry. S.*

# CHAPTER SIX

Leah knew she was probably in the running for worst mother of the year, but all she wanted was to get away from the noise, heat, and crowds and go home. She was exhausted from Emily and Nate—and Ruby—all trying to pull her in different directions, talking to her in loud, fast, sugar-hyped voices. Her shoulder ached from carrying the bag with all their supplies—no way was she about to pay five dollars for a bottle of water—along with all the "prizes" the kids—and Ruby—had won. The inventory now consisted of an assortment of troll dolls, plastic cars, stuffed animals, a fake feather boa, lumps of pyrite that the kids insisted were "gold nuggets," and two goldfish in water-filled plastic bags that she had to carry by hand to ensure that they were visible and obviously alive each time Emily or Nate ran back to check on their new friends. By the time they reached the judging tent, she felt more like a pack mule than a woman.

But finally, it was almost time for the judges to announce the results for the kids' age group in the non-livestock categories. And then, please God, they could go home, where Leah had decided she'd lock herself in the bathroom for a solid two hours of soaking in bubbles and reading a book without interruption. It was a blissful fantasy, even if it would never happen. Especially not tonight—she still had budget reports to review, along with the latest batch of résumés from applicants to her new Crisis Intervention Team. She wanted people experienced enough to handle a variety of mental health emergencies, disciplined enough to operate side by side with the police, and motivated enough to want to work the front lines where anything and everything was in play.

"Mommy." Emily tugged at Leah's elbow and pointed at a stand beside the judging tent. "Look, they're selling the chickens. Can we get some?"

Nate ran up to the stand then jogged back to where they waited in line for the judging tent to open to the public. "They're not selling them as pets," he told Emily. "Sign says 'butchering included.'"

"Butcher? They're killing the chickens?" Emily's voice rose to a screech, drawing scowls from a group of older kids wearing *Future Farmers of America* shirts.

"And plucking and cooking," Nate told her.

"It'd save time for dinner," Ruby said. "How many should I get?"

Emily was jitterbugging in place, at risk of toppling Leah as she tugged on her arm. "No! Mommy, we have to save the chickens!"

"Where did you think the chicken you eat comes from?" Ruby asked in a teasing tone, ignoring Leah's glare.

"But I met these chickens! We saw them in the barn with the sheeps and the pigs and the bunnies—" She clapped both hands over her mouth and looked aghast. "Mommy, are they going to eat the bunnies? No, they can't!"

"No one is eating bunnies," Leah told her in a firm voice, hoping the thought of the rabbits would distract Emily from the idea of chickens.

"Nah, they don't eat bunnies. They cut off their feet to make lucky rabbit's feet," Nate said, dangling a white furry keychain he'd won at one of the games over Emily's head.

Before Leah could explain that the rabbit's foot wasn't real, Emily took the bait, leaving Leah as she chased after Nate. By the time they returned—Emily now in possession of the obviously fake bunny foot—the tent was open, and the line surged forward as other families with school-aged kids entered to see the fate of their children's baked goods, sewing crafts, woodworking projects, fruit preserves, artwork, knitting, photography, calligraphy, candle making… and about every other craft and skill that didn't require a blow torch.

Each group had its own display of winners, crowding the tent with cheering families as well as the occasional sobbing child—although Leah was relieved to see that, unlike the adult categories, here the ribbons were arrayed in a rainbow of colors beyond only the top three red, white, and blue ones, allowing most of the kids to win at least some recognition of their efforts. Which meant both Emily and Nate should probably leave happy. She hoped.

Not that they didn't deserve to win. Emily had tried every recipe in Leah's great-aunt Nellie's old notebooks, experimenting as if it was a chemistry lab instead of a kitchen, learning what worked and what didn't. Then she'd created her own unique variations of Nellie's truffles, combining chocolate, rose, lavender, and fruit. Her attempts at decorations were a bit clumsy, but after taste-testing dozens of Emily's throwaways, Leah could testify that her flavors were spot on. And Nate had spent hours perfecting his photography skills, at first with Luka's help, then on his own.

"This way." Emily pulled Leah's hand, the goldfish bouncing in its bag. "I see all the food stuff over here."

"But Nate's art section is on the other side. We should go there first." Emily had a tendency to be a bit forgetful of her manners— she wasn't a bully, but she did enjoy being bossy, and Leah was trying to teach her to be more considerate of her friends' feelings.

Nate, as always, was a gentleman. "It's okay. Let's see how Emily did, and then we can see how I did on the way out."

Leah realized she'd lost Ruby in the crowd. It was worse than having a third child to keep track of. Then she spotted her over near the cooking section, shaking hands with one of the judges and smiling. Surely she hadn't bribed a win for Emily? But, given

Ruby's inherent belief that no rules applied to her, she wouldn't put it past her.

Ruby waved to Emily, who ran through the crowd toward her. Leah started forward but something caught her eye. She turned, peering through an opening in the tent.

She saw a woman's face contorted in pain as she leaned against one of the two-by-fours supporting the tent's rigging. She was young—in her twenties—with long dark hair that fell forward, only allowing a glimpse of one eye and her mouth.

Nate spied her as well. "She's in trouble."

The woman raised her hand to her mouth, biting back a cry, and turned away, heading toward the trees behind the tent.

"Go," Leah told Nate, handing him the goldfish. "Tell Ruby and Emily where I am."

She edged her way past the displays and families surrounding them, heading through the slit between two edges of canvas. The fairgrounds were part of Craven Peak State Forest, a rugged wilderness expanse that encompassed two mountains, a river gorge, and a multitude of waterfalls. Was the woman running from someone at the fair? Or someone from one of the many camping areas in the forest?

Leah scanned the area behind the tent. It was filled with packing containers, trash bins, a recycling sorting area, and other detritus from the fair. No sign of the woman.

Then she heard a moan of pain coming from behind a wall of stacked pallets of water bottles. She rushed over. The woman had collapsed into a squatting position, both hands cradling her very pregnant belly, blood trickling down past the hem of her loose-fitting sundress.

"Help me," she gasped, before falling into Leah's outstretched arms.

# CHAPTER SEVEN

Luka had just convinced the lead crime scene tech to open the envelope containing Standish's confession there on scene instead of waiting until they were back in the lab, and Maggie's crew was wheeling the body out to the coroner's van when a woman's scream sounded from the driveway.

"Noooo!"

Harper was faster than Luka—although, to be honest, he was more than happy to let her be the first to greet the woman, whom he presumed was Natasha Standish. He could gain more by observing and waiting for her to calm down before asking her questions.

By the time he reached the driveway, Harper was supporting a platinum blonde in her thirties. As the widow sagged in her arms, Harper sent a pleading glance in Luka's direction. He relented and together they helped the sobbing woman over to the bench where he'd interviewed Larry Hansen earlier. Since Luka hadn't yet called Standish's wife, he assumed Hansen had—despite Luka asking the man not to talk to anyone.

"Mrs. Standish?" He offered her a handkerchief, which she immediately smeared black with make-up and tears. Harper took a step back, discreetly out of the widow's line of sight, and began to record their conversation. "I'm Detective Sergeant Luka Jericho and this is Detective Harper."

She sniffed and nodded.

"I'm sorry for your loss, Mrs. Standish."

"Tassi." Her voice was gravelly, deep and smoky.

"Excuse me?"

"No one calls me Mrs. Standish. My name. It's Tassi."

"All right, Tassi." Luka kept his tone solemn as he prepared to deliver the news of her husband's death.

But when he opened his mouth, she shook her head at him and said, "I went to the river."

"Ma'am?"

"Larry called and said Spencer was dead, so I went to the river. He was meant to be at the river. Not here. Why is he here? He can't be—this isn't, this can't be happening."

Luka exchanged a glance over Tassi's head with Harper. She shrugged, as clueless as he was about the wife's rambling.

"Your husband, you expected him at the river?" Had Standish called Tassi and threatened to kill himself along the river? There were several bridges scattered throughout the county that were known suicide spots, spans high enough over fast-moving white water that often bodies were never recovered. "When did you last hear from him?"

"No, this can't be happening," she repeated as if a mantra. Then she lurched up. "I need to see him. It's not him, it can't be." But before Luka could stand, she fell back onto the bench as if her body didn't have the strength to fight gravity.

Luka gave her a moment, then asked again, "When did you last speak with your husband?"

"He had the cancer before, fought it once—it about killed him. So when it came back, he always said he'd decide how and when to end it, not the cancer."

"Cancer?" The way the woman was leaping from topic to topic, Luka was straining to keep up. Obviously, Tassi Standish thought what she was saying was relevant and important, but Luka wished she'd leave a few conversational breadcrumbs for him to follow. "Your husband has cancer?"

She nodded grimly. Then frowned—even the furrows in her brow appeared styled by a make-up artist. "Are you sure it's him?"

"Yes, ma'am," Luka assured her. "We used his driver's license photo for the preliminary ID, and we'll check his fingerprints to confirm it."

"Fingerprints?" Her frown deepened. "Spence isn't a criminal, why would you—"

"His thumbprint from when he got his driver's license."

"Oh. Right. Of course." Despite her words, she didn't sound any less confused.

He noted that she still hadn't asked how Standish had died. "How much did Mr. Hansen tell you?"

"Dr. Hansen," she corrected. "He's our chiropractor. He said Spence was gone, that's all. I was so upset, I hung up, drove to the river as fast as I could. But Spence wasn't there…" She trailed off in confusion.

Again with the reference to the river. And she'd immediately assumed suicide. Maybe Standish's cancer diagnosis explained that, but Luka thought she'd still want to know the method her husband had chosen. Or if he suffered—the one question every family asked and that there was no good answer to.

From the corner of his eye, he saw Wilson, the CSU tech, beckoning him. "It's very hot out here and we want to know all about what's been going on with Spencer," Luka told Tassi. "Detective Harper will take you inside where you can get something cold to drink, and I'll be along shortly."

Tassi looked at him in confusion. "You want to come into the house? Why? Why can't you just leave me to bury my husband in peace?"

"Ma'am, in cases of unexpected deaths—"

"But Spence's death *was* expected. I mean, the man gave his life to this community. Do you know who he is? He single-handedly established the Craven Relief Foundation, uses his position to ensure that his clients donate handsomely to it. Do you have any idea how many children have gotten medical care because of Spencer? Not to mention families with food on their table and roofs over their heads? Why do you insist on prying into his private life?"

Luka did a double-take. Tassi's demeanor had gone from confused and shocked to privileged entitlement in the space of a few heartbeats. She seemed to read his reaction, because she covered her face with her hands and slumped down on the bench, which made him wonder if she really was as frantic and upset as she appeared. "Harper, I think Mrs. Standish needs to get out of this heat. Could you please help her inside where it's cooler?"

"Of course." Harper slid her arm around Tassi's shoulders and helped her up. "C'mon, Tassi. We'll get you someplace more comfortable, give you some privacy."

Tassi kept her eyes almost completely shut, leaned her weight against Harper—who at five-eleven towered over Tassi's petite form—and clutched her arm as they shuffled toward the main house.

Luka joined Wilson inside the back of the CSU van, thankful for the air conditioning running at full strength. "What have you got for me?" he asked the tech, knowing Wilson would never interrupt an interview without good reason.

"I was able to open the deceased's envelope without compromising any evidence. I took photos of the contents—figured you'd want to read them before you talk with the widow. It's pretty damning."

"Wife was just saying what a pillar of the community Spencer was," Luka muttered as he leaned over the tech's laptop to read Standish's confession.

"If by 'pillar' you mean someone building a Ponzi scheme using a charity foundation as its base, then yeah, sure."

Luka scanned through the images and realized they weren't actually a confession, so much as evidence: pages of financial transactions from a variety of accounts, both local and offshore. It would take hours to go through and verify them all—hours that would need to wait until banks and brokerages were open for business to confirm the data. Standish had been moving millions around, but one thing was clear even from a quick glance: most of it hadn't stayed in any investment account or charity foundation for long; instead it had been funneled back into Spencer Standish's own pockets.

"There was also this," Wilson told him, scrolling through to another photo. "Kinda puts everything else in perspective."

It was a handwritten note on personal stationery, written in the same distinctive scrawl as the note on the front of the envelope:

*Dear Detective or whoever is investigating my death,*

*Please know that I fully regret and repent my crimes. I would blame my failing health, but the truth is that I intended to steal whatever I could from those arrogant bastards. Not for myself, but to help others. I thought that if I could dispense the money via the foundation, then even if I was caught, it would still have done some good.*

*But then the market got tight and Tassi needed—well, it doesn't matter, because I could never say no to Tassi. She's not involved in any of my crimes and has no knowledge of them whatsoever. She's innocent.*

*I take full, complete responsibility and confess that I was the sole perpetrator of the crimes you'll find detailed in these documents.*

*I'm so sorry. I'm a weak man and unworthy of forgiveness.*

*I can't bear the thought of the pain an arrest or long, drawn-out trial would cause Tassi, so this is the only way. I'm sorry.*

*Spencer Standish*

Luka read the note again and skimmed over a few of the financial statements. Just enough to know the right questions to ask Mrs. Standish until they could get a full forensic accounting of Standish's business, charity and personal finances. He called the judge on duty for the necessary warrants, forwarded Standish's confession, and swore an affidavit.

"You'll want the house, the office, and all financials for both husband and wife?" the judge asked.

"They live on a sprawling estate with several outbuildings, so the entire property and all vehicles, electronics—"

"Yes, so I see. And we'll freeze all financial accounts. Are you planning to involve the federal authorities?"

"Probably. We need a chance to examine the evidence first."

"Of course, of course." The judge hesitated. "I think we're okay here, but I should disclose that I've had dealings with the charity foundation. In fact, you'll be hard pressed to find a judge who hasn't."

"How's that, Your Honor?"

"We and our spouses have participated in several charity events to raise money for them. As did the local bar association, the medical association, Cambria City College—"

In other words, Standish had tainted pretty much Craven County's entire upper strata. The people with money or influence or both.

"Bottom line," the judge finished, "is you're going to have some very upset people knocking on your door wanting answers, Detective Sergeant. You'd best prepare yourself."

Luka held his irritation in check. He hated when cases got political. "Thanks, Your Honor. I appreciate it."

He hung up and caught Wilson's eye.

"This is going to be a red ball, isn't it?" the CSU tech said with a frown. "You know we can't rush—"

"I know. Do the best you can." Luka sighed. "I need to call Ahearn." The commander would want advance warning of the political tsunami headed their way.

"Good luck with that. I'll have my guys finish here and we'll take the SUV to the garage for complete processing."

Luka nodded and left the air-conditioned confines of the CSU van, the outside air hitting him like a blast wave. He tried Ahearn but there was no answer, so he left a voicemail. Then he crossed the lawn and climbed the porch stairs to enter the Standish residence.

It was as opulent on the inside as he'd expected, although mostly due to the lavish construction materials and ornate architecture. The foyer was empty of any personal items and when he stepped through the archway into the spacious front room, he saw that it was furnished only with a few tasteful antique sofas and chairs grouped into conversation areas. There were few personal effects, making the house feel more like a property staged for sale than a lived-in home.

Harper and Tassi were huddled together on a loveseat, Tassi weeping into Harper's shoulder and Harper awkwardly attempting to comfort the widow. Luka hid his smile as she pleaded silently with him to rescue her.

"Detective Harper, could you fetch a glass of water for Mrs. Standish?" He offered Harper a lifeline. She nodded gratefully, disentangled herself from Tassi, and leapt from the sofa, heading to the rear of the house.

"I know this is difficult, Mrs. Standish," Luka started as he chose a chair at right angles to the loveseat where Tassi was now curled around its arm, her tears staining the silk upholstery.

"It's Tassi, please," she corrected him with a sniff.

"Tassi. If you're up to it, I'd love to hear more about Spencer. When did you first move here?"

Before she could answer, the front door banged open and a blond man in his fifties strode past Luka as if he wasn't even there, taking the seat Harper had vacated. He wore a black suit and clerical collar and Tassi immediately turned, wrapping her arms around him.

"It's all right," he told her. "I'm here now. Don't say another word. Let me handle everything." He patted Tassi's back, then looked past her to Luka. "Detective Sergeant Jericho, I presume? I'm Reverend Matthew Harper."

# CHAPTER EIGHT

The pregnant woman moaned and pulled her knees to her chest, an instinctual posture of impending birth. Leah knelt beside her.

"Breathe through it, breathe." She demonstrated. Once the contraction had passed, she said, "What's your name?"

The woman didn't answer right away. She took a few deep breaths. "Beth."

"Beth, I'm Leah. When's your due date?"

"Next month. It's too soon—" Another contraction cut off her words. Leah didn't need to glance at any clock to know this baby was coming. Now.

"Beth, I'm a doctor. I'm going to help you and your baby. First, I need to get us some help." The fair would have an ambulance and crew stationed on site. Leah glanced toward the tent, ready to summon someone from inside, but Beth grabbed her arm.

"No. Don't go."

Ruby and the kids came running out of the tent. "What's going on?" Ruby asked. But then she quickly took in the situation. "Kids, stay back."

"Get the ambulance over here," Leah told her as another contraction writhed its way through Beth. "I need more hands." She'd soon have two patients to care for, one of them a premature baby. Ruby nodded and shepherded the kids back into the tent. Leah grabbed a bottle of water and used it to rinse her hands, then reached into her bag for the small bottle of hand sanitizer. All she had by way of supplies were basic items: an Ace wrap, some Band-Aids, a clasp knife, an Israeli trauma dressing. She'd been anticipating scraped knees and twisted ankles, not a preemie.

The contraction passed and Beth fell back against the stack of bottles. "Are you allergic to anything? Taking any medicines? Have any medical problems?"

Beth vehemently shook her head to each question. "I feel like I need to push," she gasped.

"Don't push, not yet. Try to breathe through it. I'm going to examine you, see how close the baby is. Is that okay?"

Beth nodded.

"Your ultrasounds all normal, no signs that the baby is breach?" Although with a preemie, they could flip positions. Leah ran through the neonatal resuscitation protocols in her mind—it'd been a long time since she'd delivered a baby. Usually if a woman made it as far as the ER, they could get them to Obstetrics in time to give birth up there. "How many weeks did they say the baby was?"

Beth clenched her teeth, although Leah had her hand on her belly and didn't feel a contraction. Finally, Beth answered. "Missed my last few appointments. Thought I'd have time—" Another contraction cut her off. They were coming even faster. Leah glanced around; where was the damn ambulance? She really didn't want to deliver a preemie without access to oxygen and proper equipment.

Then she realized: who came to a county fair alone? Much less a pregnant woman venturing into the sweltering heat of the crowds. Beth carried nothing with her—no bag, no trinkets from the arcade games, not even a water bottle. Her dress had no pockets, therefore no phone or wallet, either. Where had she come from? Why was she alone?

"What's your full name, Beth? Tell me who I can call for you. Family?"

Beth just shook her head, lips pressed tight. The sound of an engine came from around the corner of the tent and the ambulance appeared. *About time*, Leah thought, grateful that the baby had waited. The rig pulled up and the rear doors opened. Ruby, Nate, and Emily all hopped out, followed by a medic, who was joined by his partner. Ruby herded the kids to the far side of the wall of bottles, thwarting their efforts to see what was going on.

"Had to show them how to find you back here, didn't I?" Ruby said before Leah could voice the question.

"Thanks. Please get the kids home. I need to stay with her."

Ruby didn't argue, thank goodness—but Leah knew she'd pay for it later. Ruby always collected on her debts.

"What've we got, Doc?" the first medic asked as his partner pulled the gurney close.

"Uncertain gestational age, I'm guessing approximately thirty-four to thirty-six weeks. Contractions less than two minutes apart, urge to push, some spotting, no med history but also no recent prenatal care." As she gave them the report, Leah helped Beth onto the gurney and the other medic strapped her in as another contraction hit.

"I need to push," Beth cried out.

"Breathe, Beth. Give us a sec to get you into the ambulance," Leah told her, ignoring the medics' panicked looks. They were only EMT-basics, not trained in advanced life support. Like most Pennsylvania EMS services, Craven County relied on volunteers, so it wasn't always possible to staff every shift with full-fledged ALS paramedics.

"You are coming with us, right, Doc?"

Leah nodded, her focus on Beth as they jostled her into the back of the ambulance. The first medic joined her while the other got in front to drive. "Get her on the monitor, hand me the OB pack, let's get some O2 going." She grabbed a pair of gloves and slid them on, immediately feeling more in control of the situation despite the bumpy ride as they drove over the grass, heading out to the dirt road leading to the two-lane highway twisting down the mountain to Cambria City.

Under the oxygen mask, Beth heaved in breath after breath as Leah examined her. The medic prepped the neonatal resuscitation equipment and stood by, ready to hand Leah whatever she needed. When she examined Beth, the baby was already crowning, a head of dark hair pulsating with Beth's movements.

"The baby's right here," Leah told Beth. "Try hard not to push for a moment while I check." Everything looked good; the amniotic fluid was clear except for a small amount of blood—not unusual. "Do you know if it's a boy or girl?"

"Girl," Beth said between gasps. "They thought it was a girl."

"Well, won't be long now before we know for sure." Leah glanced at the medic and he nodded his readiness. They bumped over a curb and the road got smoother. Good timing. "Beth, when the next contraction comes I want you to push for a count of ten, okay?"

Sweat pouring into her eyes, hands gripping the gurney's rails, Beth nodded. Leah grabbed a towel and a pack of gauze, hands at the ready. She kept one hand on Beth's belly and felt the contraction before Beth made a sound.

"Okay, push, push, push!" Leah urged as the baby's head emerged. Then she saw the bulging, gelatinous umbilical cord that connected the baby to the mother's placenta. The cord had wrapped itself around the baby's neck. "Wait. Stop. Breathe but do not push."

"What's wrong?" Beth cried out between gasps.

"Just hang on." Leah carefully teased the nuchal cord over the baby's head, taking care not to pull too hard—the baby was still depending on its blood flow, not to mention the risks of hemorrhage to Beth if it tore. Once the head was free, she swiftly suctioned fluid from the baby's airway. "Okay, now push."

Beth blew her breath out as another contraction hit. Leah slid her hands around the baby, guiding the shoulders, turning it to make the passage easier. It was a good size for a preemie—but

Beth had been so uncertain of her dates that it was possible the baby wasn't as early as Leah had supposed. The head and shoulders were delivered by the time Beth collapsed back, gasping for air.

"One more push like that and we're done," Leah coached her even as she took advantage of the few seconds between contractions to suction out the baby's mouth and nose again. Another contraction hit and the baby slid out into Leah's waiting hands.

No meconium, color a bit dusky, she noted as she suctioned again then dried and stimulated the baby with the towel. The baby took a gasp, breathing on its own, but still not crying.

"Is she okay?" Beth gasped. "Why can't I hear her?"

"She's a he," Leah told her with a smile as she continued to rub the baby's back, hoping to coax a gusty cry to finish clearing his lungs. The medic attached an oxygen monitor and checked the baby's pulse, but Leah knew they'd both be good—the baby's color was pinking nicely and she could feel his heartbeat beneath her fingers. She clamped and cut the umbilical cord, grabbed a clean, dry towel and wrapped the baby, bracing herself as the ambulance sped around a curve.

"Does he have a name?" Leah took the medic's stethoscope and listened for herself. Despite how quiet the baby was, his lungs sounded clear, no heart murmurs, everything looked good. She hefted him, guessing his weight: a good size—he was probably close to full term.

"No name. Not yet. Can I hold him?"

"Better than that, I want you to put him directly against you; skin to skin is the best way to keep him warm. We'll keep both of you on the monitor until we can get you to the hospital, but everything looks good so far." She held onto the bedrail to keep her balance as she maneuvered up to the head of the gurney.

Beth gasped and tears appeared as she reached for her baby. "It's you," she whispered as she cradled him against her breast. "I've been dreaming of you for so long and now you're finally here."

Leah blinked back her own tears at the sight of the mother and baby. Deliveries always got to her, the miracle of life wrought through pain and blood and fear and ending in hope. She glanced at the medic and saw him swiping away his own tears with the back of his shirtsleeve. He gave her a sheepish shrug and she grinned in return.

She checked Beth's vitals and massaged her belly, hoping that the placenta could wait until they got to the OB floor—delivering it was always a mess.

"Now that things are calmed down," the medic said, pulling out his clipboard. "I need a little information for our record. Let's start with your name."

Beth kept her head bent over the baby, arms tightening around him as if she was afraid he would be taken from her.

"Beth?" Leah touched her arm. "We're trying to help you. Can you tell us your full name?"

Beth shook her head, her gaze still fixed on the baby, lips pressed tight.

Leah and the medic exchanged glances. "Beth, this is all confidential. If you're scared of someone or running away, it's okay. We just want to give you and your baby the best care possible."

Beth looked up, meeting Leah's eyes with an expression that was more than fear; it was sheer terror. "No. I've said too much already. They'll find me. I can't let them find me." She clutched her baby tighter. "Can't let them find us."

# CHAPTER NINE

Harper heard her father's voice and came to an abrupt stop, almost dropping the glass of water she held. The glass was made of crystal so thin and elegant that it probably cost more than her take-home pay. Wouldn't that make a lovely impression of competence, smashing it to bits simply because she was startled? But then, what would the Reverend think of her fetching water in the first place? Would he assume that Luka didn't trust her with real detective work, that she was only here as a token? It was what a lot of the patrol officers she'd left behind would think. She could deal with them making false assumptions, but not the Reverend.

She forced herself to take a breath. She was an adult now, a professional—just like the Reverend. She had a job to do and the fact that it was practically her first day and her father would be watching her do it, well, all that fell under the category of "suck it up and deal." After all, a man was dead and it was Harper's job to do whatever it took to see that he received the justice he deserved.

Harper took another breath to steady her nerves and strolled back into the living room to hand Tassi the glass of water. She acted as if it was the most natural thing in the world for her father to be present at a death scene—which it actually was, given his profession. Although she'd never thought of any of his parishioners dying in a manner that would draw the attention of the police. Given how traumatized Tassi appeared to be, it was good that the Reverend had come to offer her spiritual comfort.

Tassi clutched the glass with both hands, staring into it, while Harper stepped over to join Luka. The Reverend stopped midsentence, his gaze barely pausing on Harper before he turned to Luka, angling his shoulders to exclude her.

"Sergeant Jericho, do you really think it's appropriate to assign my daughter to a case where we might be forced to play an adversarial role?"

"Adversarial role?" Luka said. "Reverend Harper, I thought you were here to offer spiritual support."

"Clearly Tassi is in no condition to answer any of your questions. The fact that you seem oblivious to that makes me think I need to advise my client to assert her constitutional rights."

"Client?" Luka glanced at Harper, obviously hoping for a translation.

"My father is more than head of the church," Harper explained. "The Reverend also acts as an attorney for many of his parishioners."

Luka turned to the Reverend. "You're a lawyer?"

The Reverend drilled Luka with a stare but Luka didn't flinch.

"My father insisted I learn a trade that would be of benefit to our congregation, as has been customary in our family for generations," the Reverend explained. "I am both a doctor of divinity and a doctor of jurisprudence, specializing in family law. My sons have followed our family tradition—" He avoided even the slightest glance in Harper's direction, a not-so-subtle reminder of her choice to rebel against the Reverend's wishes. "My oldest, Jacob, has a master's in communication, Jonah is a licensed social worker, and John is a certified financial planner."

Luka's expression didn't change as he absorbed this information, but his posture shifted slightly, and Harper knew he was preparing to alter his tactics. "Family law. So you wrote Spencer Standish's will for him?"

"Yes, as well as creating the family trust he established so that Tassi will be taken care of after his death. With Tassi's permission,

I can provide you with copies—save you the time of obtaining a court order."

Tassi nodded, her gaze fixated on the depths of the glass she cradled. She didn't seem to care that the men were speaking over her head as if she wasn't even there. But Luka did, motioning to the Reverend to join him in the foyer where Tassi couldn't hear. Harper hesitated; she knew she was probably meant to remain with the widow, but couldn't resist the opportunity of watching the two men she respected most square off.

"Did you also know about his deathbed confession?" Luka asked in a low voice. "It was dated yesterday and reads as if his language and word choice was scripted by legal counsel."

The Reverend seemed disappointed by the question, his expression disdainful. "I'm afraid that falls under the umbrella of attorney-client privilege. As do any specifics we might have discussed while drafting Spencer's will or trust. I would have expected a senior officer such as yourself to know that."

"What about the charity foundation?" Luka persisted. He didn't realize it, but Harper knew that Luka's refusal to accept the Reverend's answer would only anger her father. But then she looked more closely—maybe Luka did realize it. Maybe he hoped to use that anger against the Reverend, get him off balance. She leaned back, taking it all in. No one confronted or challenged the Reverend. Ever. "It would be on public record if you were involved in its creation. I trust you wouldn't waste my time—"

"I was not involved in the foundation's creation. Spencer and Tassi established it themselves soon after their arrival here. However, as you'll see as soon as you bother to glance at the foundation's letterhead, I am on the board." Somehow the Reverend implied that the fact that Luka even asked the question meant he was less than competent. "Along with most of Craven County's leaders."

"Of course." Luka nodded as if acquiescing. But Harper saw the gleam in his eye and knew it was all an act. "Well, in that case, since Mr. Standish's confession implies that his crimes may be linked to improprieties in his charitable foundation, then it's you who might have a conflict of interest if you continue to represent Mrs. Standish. Everyone on the board or connected with the foundation will need to be questioned."

"I sincerely doubt that, but we can approach a judge." The Reverend offered his rebuttal. "And you will of course need to assign my daughter duties elsewhere."

Harper couldn't help but stare at her father, but his gaze never shifted in her direction. Why was he so concerned about her involvement in this case? The Violent Crimes Unit would treat Standish's death as suspicious until the coroner ruled. If Standish did kill himself, then the VCU's investigation would end there. Standish's other crimes, given the level of financial malfeasance and fraud Luka had alluded to, would no doubt be investigated by the state police and the feds. Was the Reverend embarrassed by his possible entanglement in Standish's crimes? Did he fear she'd think he was a fool to have been manipulated into lending his good name to a corrupt charity? She blinked, suddenly feeling disoriented. The Reverend worried about what his wayward daughter thought of him? Surely not.

Luka gave her a studied look and she finally caught up to what was really going on—not the family-forgiveness fantasy she'd concocted. No. The Reverend was smart enough to know that if he couldn't use family connections to help him, then his best bet was to make sure those family connections also couldn't hinder his cause by sharing insights with his enemies.

Making it very clear whose side he saw Harper standing on, and it wasn't the right side, the family's side. In his eyes, she was now an opponent, not a daughter.

Before she could say anything, her phone sounded. It was a text from one of the patrol guys in the Kingston Towers sector who'd spotted a few working girls back on the street. Not urgent news, but it gave her a way to exit gracefully, avoiding allowing her father to use her as a pawn in his power struggle with Luka. Plus, Luka had things handled here, while she was the only one actively working Lily's case. *Her* case.

Pointedly ignoring her father, she turned to Luka, holding up her phone. "Got a lead on our earlier case. You good if I head out to follow up?"

He nodded. "Keep me updated."

"Yes, sir." She walked toward the door, shoulders back, chin high, wanting her father to see how professional she was. Maybe the Reverend didn't trust her to draw the line between family confidences and her job, but she needed him to know that at least Luka respected and trusted her. She wasn't sure why it was so important to her, but it felt like more than saving face. It felt like crossing an important threshold from childhood to adulthood.

If only her father also saw it that way. "Call your mother, Naomi," the Reverend said in an off-hand tone as she reached the door, as if he'd only now noticed her presence. He knew she'd seen Rachel an hour ago, so his words were clearly meant more to illustrate how unimportant her career was compared to her family obligations. "It's cruel of you to make her constantly worry when she doesn't hear from you."

Harper stifled her sigh. So much for being treated like an adult, much less an equal.

# CHAPTER TEN

Luka watched Matthew Harper's expression as he dismissed his daughter. There was more going on there than normal parent-child relationship friction. Harper was intensely private when it came to her past. The only things Luka knew about her family were that she'd been adopted and that her father and brothers were all ministers. Was there some reason why Matthew wanted his daughter off this case?

Or perhaps it was a simple diversion, intended to distract Luka from some essential truth. It was too early to say, and Luka definitely wasn't rushing to judgment.

"Mrs. Standish." He focused on the widow. "I've requested a search warrant for your home and your husband's office." Usually he'd start with the wife's statement before sorting through financials, but Matthew was right—Tassi was in no condition for a formal interview. And, given that the widow had already summoned her attorney, Luka didn't want to give her any opportunity to remove evidence. "We will, of course, provide you with a written copy, but it would expedite things if you could give me the keys?"

Tassi shook her head, bewildered. "Search? Where? Here? Why? Whatever are you looking for?"

"Your husband left a letter implying that he was involved in some financial impropriety," Luka explained. "We need to secure any documents, electronics—"

"Spence would never!" Tassi exclaimed, bolting to her feet so quickly it caught Luka off guard. She pointed a finger at the door. "I want you out of my house. Now!"

Luka waited a beat, expecting Matthew to calm his client, but instead he gave Luka a challenging look. "Surely this can wait, Detective. You can see how traumatized Mrs. Standish is."

"I'm afraid it can't wait." Luka kept his voice low and gentle. "We'll try to expedite things to minimize any inconvenience, Mrs. Standish."

"But, I don't understand—I don't know anything."

"I'd like to start with your husband's cell phone. Do you have any idea where it is?"

Tassi's arm, still pointing past Luka, began to tremble. She dropped it to her side. "Phone? At the river, in the water... No. None of this makes sense. None of it." Her voice was barely above a whisper and she still faced the door, speaking to the air past Luka's head.

"Can you explain that to me, Mrs. Standish?" he tried to coax her. "Why were you expecting to find your husband at the river?"

More tears. She covered her face with her palms and collapsed back onto the loveseat beside Matthew. In any other circumstances, Luka would attempt to provide whatever comfort possible, but given that Tassi had chosen to call her spiritual counselor to attend to her, he nodded to Matthew to take over. Matthew folded his hands around Tassi's and whispered something. She looked up and they bent their heads in prayer, lips moving in unison.

Luka's phone buzzed. He crossed the massive room until he reached the hallway leading to the rear of the house. Matthew and Tassi were still in sight—across a basketball court's length of hardwood floor, plush rugs, and antique furniture. Luka still found it strange that there was only a single wedding photo framed above the fireplace. He answered his cell. It was Commander Ahearn, head of the Investigative Division.

"Is it true?" Ahearn began without greeting. "Spencer Standish killed himself?"

"Maybe." Luka explained about the suicide note and confession. "The wife is a bit scattered, can't really get anything from her right now, so I'm headed to his offices to take a look."

"Your eyes only for now. Spencer worked with a lot of highly placed men. Pillars of the community. We don't need their names dragged through the muck, not when we're not even certain what happened."

"The wife mentioned some kind of cancer—"

"There you go, man wasn't in his right mind."

"Yes," Luka replied, "but the firefighters said the carbon monoxide levels weren't very high when they arrived at the scene."

"You're not sure it was a suicide?" Ahearn asked, sounding thoughtful, weighing the political ramifications of each possibility, deciding which would be more advantageous. "That could open a can of worms best left buried. You'd best be certain of your facts. I want you to report everything directly to me. We need to stay in front of this." As usual Ahearn didn't bother digging very deep into the treasure trove of clichés he loved to mix and match.

"I could use more people." Luka's gaze drifted down the end of the long hallway, doorways situated on both sides. It might take days to complete even a cursory search of the mansion and grounds.

"Pull in whoever you need, I'll authorize the overtime." Authorize and overtime—two words seldom heard in the same sentence when coming from Ahearn. "Whatever you need to speed this up—and keep it quiet. I'm headed to the house. I want Mrs. Standish to understand how seriously we take this, give her the department's condolences in person. And I'll handle any press when the time comes."

Fine with Luka. "Thank you, sir. I'll have Ray Acevedo and Scott Krichek meet you here. They can be trusted with the search of the home, with minimal disruption for the widow." Ray was Luka's second-in-command, more street-ready rough-and-tumble than Ahearn probably would like, but Luka trusted Ray to get the job done right. While the less experienced but more polished Krichek could hone his natural kiss-ass tendencies with Ahearn and the widow.

Luka called Ray and Krichek to fill them in and spoil what was supposed to be their Sunday off, then returned to Tassi and the reverend. "My team will be over to conduct the search of the house," he told her. "Until then, I'll be leaving an officer to stay with you."

Tassi barely managed a nod of understanding. And yet there were no more tears. He couldn't be certain how much of her reaction was true grief and how much was embellishment. It would be interesting to talk to more people who knew her, get a better feel for her personality. Since he couldn't interview her immediately, the least he could do was to be prepared for when Matthew, as her attorney, allowed him to speak with her.

"Where are you going?" Matthew asked as Luka headed to the door.

"Spencer's offices." Luka didn't really need a key; the warrant would allow him to pick the lock or call a locksmith to make entry.

"Then I'm going with you to observe." Matthew rose, Tassi's hand dropping from his arm to the loveseat in a languid motion that felt rehearsed. "That would be best, save you from worry, right, Tassi?"

"If you say so, Matthew. I can ask Larry to come over."

Larry as in Larry Hansen, the neighbor who found Spencer's body. Luka had had a feeling he'd been holding something back during their conversation—were he and Tassi closer than mere tennis partners? He'd let Ray know to keep an eye on them both and they'd definitely need to look deeper at Hansen. And how odd that Matthew, given his role of spiritual advisor, seemed more concerned about protecting Tassi's legal interests—a curious conflict of interest. Luka would have assumed that consoling a parishioner in their time of grief would supersede any legal duties, but presumably Matthew justified it as protecting Tassi's overall future? Or was he simply more interested in seeing what evidence Spencer Standish had left behind?

Matthew had said he was on the foundation's board—perhaps he was more involved than a name on a letterhead?

The minister passed Luka to head to his vehicle, a white Lexus SUV with a tasteful Holy Redeemer insignia on the side. Clearly ministering to a congregation in this upscale neighborhood paid handsomely. Or were Matthew's dealings with Spencer the source of his wealth?

Luka juggled phone calls as he drove, including arranging for Sanchez, one of the department's cyber techs, and a pair of uniformed officers to meet him at Standish's office. The same address was listed for both Standish's financial firm and the charity foundation. Luka was surprised to see that it was a small storefront in a strip mall, sandwiched between an empty Radio Shack that had gone out of business years ago and a nail salon. The store's windows and glass door were covered with butcher's paper and there was no sign. Clearly Standish didn't meet prospective donors or investors here.

The patrol units were waiting when Luka arrived. Matthew Harper had also already arrived and was arguing with the officers to allow him access, but they stood their ground. "Where do you want us, Sergeant?" one asked.

"Let's see what we're dealing with, then we'll divide and conquer." Luka turned to Matthew. "If you have the key, now's the time to give it to me. Save your client a locksmith bill."

The reverend reluctantly pulled a small keyring from his slacks and handed it to Luka. "Those should give you access to everything."

"Who gave them to you?" Luka hadn't seen Tassi hand Matthew anything at the house.

"Spencer. When we last met."

Luka noted that he still wasn't saying when or where. "Wait here."

Matthew bristled, moving to follow Luka. "I have a right—"

"To observe. After we clear it." Luka strode forward to the patrol officers standing beside their cars. He knew them both. Morton, the senior of the two, had joined the force a few years before Luka. And Azarian—Luka had been his field training officer. Over a decade ago. Suddenly Luka felt old. He greeted Morton, "Thought you were going for your sergeant stripes."

"Passed the test, waiting for an opening. Why? You ready to retire yet, old man?"

"Think I still have a few years left in me." He explained the situation as he eyed the parking lot. A silver minivan was parked in front of the nail salon, alongside an old Camry and a Ford Escort that had seen better days. Anchoring the corner of the strip mall was a gas station with a convenience store and a few cars also sat at the farthest row of parking spaces—employees, probably. Other than the nail salon, this end of the strip mall was quiet. "Morton, you're with me."

They left Azarian with Matthew and approached the office door. Luka selected the most likely key from the ring Matthew had given him and was rewarded when it fit the lock.

As soon as Luka opened the door, the afternoon sunshine spilling inside the dark interior, he sensed something was wrong. He snapped the lights on, illuminating a long, narrow space filled with desks, computers, and office equipment. There was no movement inside the room, but there was a wall about three-quarters of the way down, dividing the space and blocking his view. The door to the rear area was open. There were no lights on, but he had the sensation that he'd just missed movement.

"Go outside, head around to the rear exit," he told Morton. Luka drew his weapon and sidled forward, edging his way through the maze of desks and office paraphernalia. A small rattle echoed through the empty doorway at the rear. Someone was there, hiding in the dark. "Police," he called out. "Come out, show me your hands. Now!"

Luka heard a louder noise, the sound of a heavy door being opened. He ran from the lit area through the open door into the dark rear of the store in time to see the fire exit door close. He stumbled through the darkness, pushing the door open and hoping that Morton had made it around the back of the building in time to block their fleeing subject.

Luka raced out into the narrow alley behind the building. A noise came from his left and he spun toward it. A dumpster careened toward him. He dove out of the way, landing on a small pile of broken glass, inches away from the speeding dumpster before it slammed into the brick retaining wall that formed the far side of the alley. Pain bit through his left shin as he rolled to a sitting position, scanning the space where the intruder must have pushed the dumpster from. There was no one to be seen. His man had vanished.

Morton arrived, his passage blocked by the dumpster that had stopped on a diagonal.

"Call it in," Luka shouted, his voice fueled with frustration. "You see anything?"

Morton radioed Azarian, instructing him to cover the far end of the alley. "Nothing. There was no one my way." He pivoted the dumpster far enough that he could get through to Luka. "You okay? You're bleeding."

Luka stood, holstered his useless weapon, and examined his hands. They were scraped up, but there was more gravel and grime than actual damage.

Azarian appeared at the far end of the alley and jogged down to join them. "No one. They're gone." He pointed to Luka's leg. "Sarge—"

Luka glanced down. A large shard of broken glass protruded from his shin. It wasn't until he saw it that he realized that it actually hurt. A lot. Adrenaline gave way to a rush of queasiness as blood trickled out from under his pants leg and onto his shoe.

"Aw hell," he muttered as he sagged against the retaining wall. The last thing he needed was to waste time with a trip to the ER. Maybe they could deal with it using one of the squad car's first-aid kits. But Azarian's wide eyes and suddenly pale lips made Luka look again. The glass protruded at an awkward angle as blood oozed out around it. He tried taking a step but that produced a wave of blood and pain that stole his breath and he slumped down onto the retaining wall.

Luka caught his breath, pulled his phone free and dialed Ray. "Change of plans…"

Since walking was out of the question, Azarian retrieved a wheeled office chair from Standish's place and he and Morton wheeled Luka through the offices and back out front to where Matthew was pacing, talking to someone on his phone. He hung up when he saw Luka. "What happened?"

Luka ignored the question, the same way he was trying to ignore the five-inch shard of glass protruding from his leg. He might have succeeded except it throbbed with every heartbeat. "Did you see anyone run past?" he asked Matthew. "Would have been from that direction."

"Man or woman? What did they look like?" Matthew asked.

A flush of momentary embarrassment heated Luka's face as he realized he had no idea. The damn dumpster had blocked his view. Then he noticed that the gray minivan was gone from in front of the nail salon. "Did you see who left in the van?"

"A woman. Middle-aged. I didn't pay much attention, but she wasn't running. She walked out of the nail place."

Luka nodded to Morton, who headed into the nail salon to question them. The sun was beating down on the pavement, heat waves shimmering around him and he had the fleeting thought that the plastic wheels of the chair might melt. He used his good foot to scoot the chair back inside Standish's office, grimacing as it bumped over the threshold. Matthew followed.

"Don't touch anything," Luka ordered him, uncomfortable having a civilian so close to evidence.

Azarian returned with a first-aid kit. "Medics are on the way." Behind him entered another man, Sanchez, the tech from the cyber squad, carrying a briefcase of tools.

Sanchez's eyes scanned the office, and without needing any direction from Luka, he found an empty desk and got to work, starting with photographing the scene, documenting the serial number of each electronic device. A vehicle pulled up outside. Luka looked up, expecting to see the ambulance, but instead it was a black Tahoe, similar to those driven by federal agents. Had Ahearn called them already?

A man wearing dark gray slacks and a navy polo emerged. He was tall, an inch or two taller than Luka's own six foot one, had the physique of someone who never missed a day at the gym, and the swagger of a fed. He crossed into their crime scene, took his sunglasses off as he assessed the situation, dismissing the other men to address Luka. "Where's Spencer Standish?"

# CHAPTER ELEVEN

Leah accompanied Beth and her baby up to the Obstetrics floor where the Labor and Delivery nurses bustled both her patients away, clucking and fretting over the mess. L and D nurses hated out-of-hospital deliveries. Not only did they disrupt their well-established protocols but there was always a concern about complications for both mother and child.

Leah cleaned up and went to the nurses' station to chart her role in events surrounding Beth's delivery. As soon as she finished her dictation, the ward clerk approached her. "Dr. Wright, you came in with the woman who delivered out of hospital. Do you know her name? I'm trying to register her in the computer."

"Beth."

"Right." The clerk waited, but Leah didn't have any more information to give her. "Beth what? She wouldn't talk to me and the nurses said she wouldn't give them a last name either. But I need to register her—"

"Sorry, Beth is all I have." Leah wondered at Beth's refusal to give a name. To the ward clerk it was an administrative inconvenience, but there was so much more going on. Clearly Beth was traumatized, fearful about the safety of herself and her baby. Was someone after them? Why?

"I'll put her in as Beth Doe," the clerk muttered, obviously unhappy. "The people in Utilization Review can figure it out tomorrow when they're back."

"Has this ever happened before?" Leah couldn't remember ever encountering an ER patient who refused to give a name. Even the street people could usually be coaxed into providing some form of ID or a proper name—especially after the ER nurses got them a warm meal and a chance to shower and change. "Is it against the law?"

"Never happened to me," the clerk said. "If she used someone else's name or insurance that would be fraud, but using no name? I honestly have no idea." She returned to her desk and computer, leaving Leah to wonder.

Maybe Beth was a victim of domestic violence? In this day and age of social media and internet tracking, shelters had to be especially cautious, often keeping their locations secret to the point of meeting potential new clients off site. What if Beth had been on her way to meet a shelter volunteer when she went into labor? After all, pregnancy was the second most deadly risk factor for intimate partner violence—the first being leaving the relationship.

Leah's team in the Crisis Intervention Center partnered closely with the domestic violence programs. But she couldn't go behind Beth's back and try to access confidential information. What could she do to help Beth? Because, no matter what Beth was running from, it was clear she needed help.

After she finished her charting, she stopped at Beth's room. The OB had delivered Beth's placenta, the nurses had bathed her, and they were carefully monitoring her for any postpartum complications since they had no records of her medical history. Beth appeared exhausted, her face almost as pale as the snow-white sheets that cocooned her.

"Just wanted to look in on you before I left," Leah told her, taking the visitor chair beside the bed. "How are you feeling?"

Beth glared at her, lips pressed tight and for a moment Leah thought she wasn't going to speak. Then she said, "They took my baby."

"They usually bathe the newborns, check them for any problems, give them vitamin K and warm them up. I can go see how long it will be, if you want."

Beth nodded, her eyes closing tight as if, by avoiding seeing the world around her, she could deny it entirely. Leah knew the feeling of yearning for the rest of the world to simply pause, give her time to catch up. After Ian's murder, she'd been so terrified that something might happen to Emily. The constant vigilance and fear had taken their toll—and she was still paying the price with sleepless nights and anxiety.

"Everything changes when you have a child to protect," Leah said in a soft tone.

Another nod from Beth, but at least this time she opened her eyes, even if she was staring at the ceiling, her hands tugging the sheet higher up as if the thin cotton was a shield against reality.

"So many decisions, choices," Leah continued. "Your son. Does he have a name yet?"

Beth shook her head slowly, a silent tear slipping down her cheek. She didn't bother to wipe it dry.

"Is there anyone you want me to call? Your son's father? Grandparents? A friend?"

"No. No one." Beth slumped against the pillow. With the sheet tucked up beneath her chin, she looked so young and vulnerable. "He's gone."

Before Leah could ask anything more, a soft knock came at the door and the nurse poked her head inside. "I wanted to let you know that your little boy is fine. He was a little chilly, so we have him under the warming lights, but let me know when you're ready to visit him and I'll take you to him."

"He's okay?" Beth asked.

The nurse smiled. "He's just wonderful. Now, don't try to get up on your own, not with that IV. Call me, okay?"

Beth nodded, her gaze distant again. The nurse waited a beat, then shrugged at Leah, and left.

"Beth," Leah said. "It's only the two of us. Please, tell me. Why are you so afraid? I can help, I want to help."

Eyes still closed, Beth shook her head. "No, you can't. No one can."

Leah sighed, waited to see if the younger woman changed her mind, then stood. She slid one of her cards for the Crisis Intervention Center from her wallet and wrote her cell phone number on the back. Then she tucked it into Beth's hand. "Please. Call me if you need anything. Even if you just want someone to listen. I promise you, I can help."

Beth's only response was to squeeze her eyes shut even tighter. But she kept the card, so Leah counted that as a step in the right direction.

She walked down to the nursery and watched the nurses through the observation window. Beth's baby boy was under warming lights and his nurse was checking a heel-stick blood sugar test. The monitor at his Isolette showed good vitals. When the nurse had finished, shucking her protective gown and washing her hands, Leah tapped at the window to get her attention. The nurse smiled and a minute later unlocked the door to invite her into the charting area. "Checking on our new addition?"

"Yeah. I just saw the mother. How's he doing?"

"Good. Quiet, though. I'll take him to mom as soon as his temp is stable."

"She wasn't sure of her dates, said he was a month early—"

The nurse shook her head. "Not so early. On exam, I'd put him at thirty-six to thirty-seven weeks."

"That's good." It meant much less risk of complications, even without prenatal care and an unconventional delivery. "What's your take on mom?"

The nurse hesitated. Once babies were delivered, the nursery team cared for both mother and child as a family unit, facilitating bonding. "Not sure yet. She seemed in shock."

"Denial is more like it." Leah explained how Beth had hidden at the fairgrounds. "She was terrified. I think she was running from someone. But she won't talk to me."

"Then no way will she talk to the police. Let me try—and if I can't get anywhere with her, we'll put a call in to social services." The nurse sighed. "Think she's incompetent to make decisions about herself and her baby? Should we get psych involved?"

"I don't think she understands that by not talking she's actually making things harder on herself."

"Even though she's fine, they both will probably be here a few days. We'll need to wait on cultures for the baby." Observing babies at high risk for infection for forty-eight to seventy-two hours in the hospital was standard procedure. "Plus, I'm not sure we can even discharge her or the baby since we had to register her as a Jane Doe—well, Beth Doe."

"Could you let me know how it goes? Or if I can help—or one of the CIC's staff." Leah's position as medical director for the Crisis Intervention Center gave her access to the best-trained social workers and interviewers in the county. It was the reason that they'd forged their new partnership with the police, to assist with vulnerable witnesses and victims as well as offering forensic, trauma-based interviews.

The nurse nodded. "I'm seven to seven today and tomorrow, so I'll call you after rounds in the morning. Hopefully she's only in shock, needs a little time. Knowing her baby is healthy will help as well."

"Thanks." Leah left, going through the multiple secured doors that made the nursery floor the safest area in the hospital. Only nursery staff and parents wearing special electronic wristbands paired to their infants could take a baby beyond the ward without triggering an alarm. Even hospital staff like Leah needed to use their keycard to gain access and civilians needed to be buzzed in by a ward clerk monitoring the entrance.

Beth and her baby boy would be safe here. It was what waited them beyond Good Sam that had Leah worried.

# CHAPTER TWELVE

Harper pulled up alongside the patrol car waiting in the high school's empty parking lot and rolled down her driver's side window, cursing the heat that flooded her car—it had taken the entire drive down the mountain to get the interior temperature half-bearable. "What do you have for me?"

The uniformed officer, a guy named Tommy Narami, lowered his window. "Saw a few of Freddy's girls over at the Burger Chef."

"Anyone on this list?" She showed him the names of other girls arrested alongside Lily.

He propped his sunglasses on top of his head and flipped through her sheaf of booking photos. "Yeah. These two: Heidi and Tina. A couple of Freddy's boys are with them, but I don't think they'll give you any trouble."

Harper made a small noise of disgust. Of course Freddy wouldn't trust his girls out on their own—not because he was worried about their welfare; more likely he wanted to make certain the girls weren't ripping him off. "Thanks, Tommy."

"No problem. Call me you need anything."

Harper drove away, already thinking through her approach. It was too dangerous to talk to Heidi or Tina directly—that would lead to Freddy's unwanted attention and could place the girls in danger. But if the girls were in a group, and Freddy's boys were right there, she could work with that, leave an opening for anyone who had information to contact her when they were safely alone.

She pulled up alongside a fire hydrant in front of the fast-food joint and observed the group through the plate-glass windows. Five girls, including Heidi and Tina. Because their pimps were paid via online apps, the girls carried little to no cash, so Harper wasn't surprised to see that there weren't any food containers on the table, only a collection of large soda cups. Drinks were the cheapest item on the menu and the girls would make them last until it was their turn to venture out to the curb and flag down potential customers. Working girls were always underfed and hungry, which gave Harper an edge—thanks to Rachel.

She went inside, taking a moment to pause and appreciate the miracle of modern technology as the air-conditioned chill greeted her. Tommy was right: the girls were "protected" by two corner boys sitting at a front table, filling their faces with burgers and fries. Barely old enough to shave, yet they thrust their chests out and dropped their hands to the waistbands of their baggy shorts, giving Harper the stink-eye. She flashed her badge and ignored them, even as they got on their cells, calling their boss, no doubt.

The counter staff ducked their heads, knowing that if they asked her to remove the loiterers, they'd pay the price later. Harper gave them a nod, reassuring them that she wasn't there to cause any trouble. She carried her cooler over to the girls. They were slouched along the seats lining the booth, pretending to ignore her.

Harper set the cooler on the table with a loud thud. "You guys hear about Lily?"

Two of the five gave an automatic nod, but quickly flicked their gazes away. As if anything outside the smudged and dirty window was more interesting than Harper.

"I'm trying to find her family. Let them know she's passed." Harper figured Lily's family was a safe topic even if the corner boys reported their conversation to Freddy. "You guys hungry?" She opened the cooler, unleashing her secret weapon: Rachel's roast with all the trimmings. The aroma overpowered even the weakest of them and while the corner boys looked on with envy, their greasy burgers forgotten, the girls dug in like locusts.

One girl, Heidi, edged over so that Harper could slide into the booth beside her. Harper sat quietly as the girls devoured the leftovers, passing the containers around, their guards dropping as their bellies filled. Tina sat across from Harper. She was the oldest of the group, in her thirties at least, and studiously avoided Harper's gaze, keeping her expression stony and distant. No joy coming from that direction, Harper thought, so she focused instead on Heidi. "You doing okay?"

"I remember you," Heidi said. "Picked me up last winter, got me a coat and boots."

"Heidi, right?" Harper said as if she didn't remember. The girl had been freezing, close to frostbite standing on a corner one icy night. "Thought they sent you to juvie."

"Suspended sentence. Judge sent me home to Lancaster, but couldn't deal with my dad—" She rolled her eyes. "So now I'm back. At least Freddy takes good care of me."

And yet it was Harper who'd bought the girl a coat from the Goodwill. It always shocked her to be reminded of how brainwashed the girls were, how they believed that they were loved, respected, and cared for. The drugs helped erode their inhibitions, of course, and addiction kept them anchored by invisible chains, but the psychological manipulation was more powerful than any drug or fear of violence. All she could imagine was that their lives at home were so bad and their expectations about love and family were so warped that they wouldn't know the real thing if they ever found it.

"You knew Lily? She ever mention where home was?"

"Nope." Heidi filled her mouth with a biscuit and Harper turned to the others. None of them knew where Lily came from, just that she wasn't from Cambria City. Harper carefully edged the discussion into the previous night, but everyone denied seeing Lily.

"Good thing, because Freddy'd kill her he saw her poaching his territory."

"Besides," another chimed in. "Thought she left the biz. Like, last year or something?" This garnered a chorus of nodding agreement.

"Maybe jail?" someone suggested.

"Not for that long," another girl said. "Rehab?"

"You cook this yourself?" Heidi asked. "Like every day?"

Harper smiled as she gathered the empty containers and returned them to the cooler. "My mom did. Sunday dinner. Me? I live out of my microwave."

The girls nodded. "Tell your mom thanks—and you can bring more anytime."

"No, she can't," one of the corner boys shouted from their table. "Hey now, there's cars waiting, you all need to get back to work."

The girls muttered, until the two youngest were nudged from the booth, adjusting their tube tops and hair as they strutted past the corner boys and out the door. Harper realized she wouldn't get anything more out of them, not with the corner boys there, so she stood to leave. She slid a few cards for the shelter her brother Jonah ran onto the table—on the back she'd written her own cell number. "In case you ever need anything."

The girls studiously ignored the cards, but she hoped one or two might take one. As she walked to the restaurant's door, Heidi passed her, heading to the restroom. The girl glanced over her shoulder at Harper, who made sure the corner boys weren't watching and then followed.

Once Harper had closed the door behind her, Heidi said, "Sorry, I couldn't say anything before. But have you tried Macy? She and Lily were real tight. They used to work for Freddy but took off last year, which is why he'd be super pissed off if he found Lily back here, working his territory."

Macy Holmes. She was on Harper's list, had been arrested once with Lily. "Any idea where I can find her?"

"Works for Philly now, over on Second usually."

"Thanks." Harper reached for her wallet, but Heidi stopped her with a gesture.

"No cash. Freddy will find it and think I've been holding out on him. But maybe another meal sometime? I haven't had cooking like that in a long…" Her expression turned wistful, eyes blinking back tears, reminding Harper that she was only a kid. Then Heidi cleared her throat, her features hardening once more. "Well, never had cooking that good, I guess. Anyway, hope you find Lily's folks, let them know about her. She was always real nice to me."

Harper handed her one of Jonah's cards. "There's always a hot meal waiting for you at the Pierhouse Shelter—my brother runs it, just tell him I sent you. I'll bet he could help you find a job or a safe place to live, if you ever—"

Heidi scowled, then spun on her spiked heels to inspect her features in the mirror. "Got a job. Besides, I could never leave Freddy. He loves me, takes care of me." And with a wave of her hand, she dismissed Harper.

# CHAPTER THIRTEEN

Luka eyed the newcomer with suspicion. The man had the bearing and arrogance of a federal agent, yet he hadn't identified himself as one. Had Ahearn called him in? But if so, then why was he asking for Spencer Standish—shouldn't he already know Standish was dead?

"This is an active crime scene, sir," he told the man, feeling at a distinct disadvantage sitting below him, one leg still dribbling blood despite the gauze Azarian had packed around the shard of glass. He would have loved to have seen the shard gone altogether, but basic first-aid principles said never to remove an impaled foreign body because of the risk of causing hemorrhage or further damage. "May I see some identification?"

The man considered this, then slid a hand into his rear pocket and withdrew a thin wallet. He opened it and held it down at Luka's eye level, but he didn't look at Luka; instead he was watching Sanchez. "Foster Dean. DEA, retired." He snapped the wallet shut, returned it to his pocket. "Where's Standish?"

"And why is a *retired* drug enforcement agent interested in Mr. Standish?" Luka asked.

"I'm here to help, Detective—"

"Detective Sergeant Luka Jericho." Luka let that hang for a moment. "Help how?"

Dean started to step past Luka but stopped when every cop in the place—even the cyber tech, Sanchez—alerted, all turning to stare at him. Dean wasn't old enough to have gotten his full twenty years in, so he must have left the DEA for another job—or because he was asked to leave.

"Where is he?" Dean snapped, his focus now solely on Luka. "Do you have him in custody?"

"I'm afraid Mr. Standish is not available," Luka answered, playing along to see what Dean knew. Although he had the feeling that the abrasive former fed wasn't going to volunteer any information, despite his offer of assistance.

But then Dean surprised Luka. "You don't even know who you're dealing with, do you? For starters, Spencer Standish isn't his real name. His real name is Scott Spencer." Dean scoffed. "I could tell you a lot more, but I'd like something in exchange. Do you know where he is?"

"Why are you so anxious to locate him?" Luka asked.

For the first time Dean appeared uncertain, his gaze assessing Luka like a poker player debating whether to fold or bluff. "I work as a private security consultant. My clients were victims of a Ponzi scheme Spencer ran back in Colorado. I've been searching for him for almost three years, since he fled Denver."

The timing fit with Spencer's arrival in Cambria City. Luka nodded his agreement. "Okay, Mr. Dean. Tell me what you know about him and I'll tell you where Spencer is."

Dean glanced at Luka's leg and the shard of glass. "It's a fairly long conversation. How 'bout you tell me where to find Spencer and, once you're patched up, we'll talk. I'll tell you everything." As if to punctuate his words, an ambulance pulled up to the curb out front. Luka tried to hide his grimace—talk about poor timing.

"Wait outside and we'll discuss this further," he instructed Dean in a voice loud enough to get Azarian's attention. The burly officer sidled over to stand beside Dean, his body positioned so that the other man had no choice but to step outside to give the medics room to roll their gurney inside.

The medics worked efficiently, gathering Luka's details as they took his vitals, cut away the bottom of his trouser leg, bolstered the gauze supporting the shard to further stabilize it, applied a splint to immobilize his leg, and lifted him onto the gurney.

"I'm needed here; can you finish treating it yourselves?" he asked them, reluctant to leave the crime scene or Dean, his only witness.

"Sorry, no can do," the first medic told Luka. "It's pretty deep, embedded in the muscle, and we can't risk taking it out in case any blood vessels are damaged. Believe me, you want to be in the hospital if that happens."

"Not to mention it's gonna hurt like hell without the good drugs," his partner quipped.

"How long can we wait?" Luka persisted, noting that Matthew Harper had sidled outside and was speaking with Dean. There was no way Luka could stop them, but he didn't like the idea of the two of them joining forces. He needed information and so far all Matthew had done was to prevent Luka from obtaining any, under the guise of client confidentiality and Tassi's emotional distress. Damn convenient for the pastor-attorney to be able to use both professions to guard his client's secrets.

"Dirty foreign body?" the medic answered. "Wait longer than a few hours and it means a trip to the operating room and increased chance of serious infection. Wouldn't risk it, if I were you, Detective."

Luka knew they were right, but he also couldn't risk losing Dean's information. "Okay, give me a few minutes and then we can go."

Before he could invite Dean back inside, Morton returned from the nail salon. "Hard to get much out of anyone," he said. "But they did confirm that a woman in a gray van came in to have her nails done. Said she didn't have an appointment, waited for a few minutes, but then left again."

"Did they get a name?"

"Nope, sorry. And no CCTV inside—but I have a call into the owner of the property to gain access to his security footage. That will cover the entire shopping center plus he owns the gas station on the far corner."

"Good. I'll get my team working on court orders for any other nearby businesses that have cameras." Luka nodded to Dean, beckoning him in, ignoring the medics who were standing by, filling out their paperwork and pretending not to be eavesdropping. "Mr. Dean, time to talk."

Dean rolled his shoulders back, making himself appear even larger and more intimidating. Luka knew that whatever Dean told him it wouldn't be everything the man knew. He could see it in the way the man's gaze grew distant as he decided what story to tell.

"Spencer is originally from Ocean City, New Jersey. Used to run some low-level scams in Atlantic City, but drew attention from the wrong crowd."

Luka wondered if that meant criminal organizations or the police.

"Then he fled out west. Six years ago, he surfaced in Denver as a supposedly legit hedge fund manager. Lived the lifestyle of the rich and famous, cozied up to old money and new, made a lot of charity contribution pledges, said he had so much money that he didn't need any more, was instead devoting his financial talents to helping charities raise capital. Put his money where his mouth was by creating a charity foundation that doubled its capital in fifteen months."

Sanchez hovered at the edge of Luka's vision, obviously anxious for a word, but Luka didn't want to stop Dean, not while he was being so forthcoming. "Anyway," Dean continued, "returns like that had everyone knocking on his door, begging him to manage their investments. Charities, private foundations, individuals. But he told them all no."

"Baiting the hook," Luka surmised. Classic setup for a scam—and people always fell for it.

"Exactly. Next quarter, his foundation posted even better returns and his wife let it slip at a charity gala that he had a system that was foolproof."

"How involved is she?" Luka asked.

Dean frowned. "We never found any proof that she was involved. But after that, he began to increase his client base."

Basic rule of any con: get the mark to beg for the privilege of having his money stolen. Conmen thrived on their victims' greed and often used the defense that honest men could never be swindled. A self-serving lie, but all too often it allowed them to skate away from their more serious offenses, especially when victims realized they'd appear either complicit, incompetent or stupid if the con was revealed to the public.

"So your clients were victims of Spencer?" Luka asked.

"You know I can't tell you that. Let's just say they have a compelling reason to find him."

Dean had only revealed what Luka would have discovered with a thorough background check. But he had saved Luka time, so Luka gave him what he wanted. "Spencer's dead."

Dean didn't even blink. Instead, he smirked. "Are you sure about that? He faked his death three years ago, an apparent drowning during a fishing trip. No body was ever found, and he laid low for almost a year before showing up here as Spencer Standish."

Sanchez beckoned again and the medics were checking their watches, anxious to get going. Luka didn't want to keep them from answering other calls, but he knew Dean had more to offer. Then he saw an unmarked white Impala pull up beside the ambulance. The calvary had arrived. Ray and Krichek here to relieve Luka.

"Thanks, Mr. Dean. But we're sure. Spencer's corpse is in our morgue—I sent him there myself." He nodded to the medics that he was ready to go. "Wait here, please."

The medics wheeled him outside back into the broiling heat. Ray and Krichek greeted him on the pavement as he waited for the medics to open the ambulance doors.

The two couldn't be more different: Krichek, the ultimate hipster, never far from his mushroom coffee or a wisecrack, had joined the VCU a year ago, a transfer from property crimes. The kid had a few rough edges—a fondness for puns and conspiracy theories to start—but showed promise if he didn't allow his own ambitions to sabotage him. While Ray, despite being five years older than Luka, would happily end his career without ever seeking promotion. He'd come up through the ranks working undercover for Vice and Drugs, and still, even in his Sunday suit, could be mistaken for a grate man. But he was the smartest cop Luka knew and, despite being slowed down after getting shot in the leg six months ago, there was no one Luka would rather have beside him if things went south.

"Fancy new accessory you're sporting there, boss," Krichek quipped, nodding to the glass protruding from the swath of bandages.

"Yeah, I think you're taking this body piercing fetish a bit far," Ray added, but his gaze was fixed on Luka's face, checking to make sure that he was all right.

"Only hurts when I laugh," Luka said. "Anything at the house?"

"Ahearn's there. Widow took a sedative, so nothing more from her. Has a neighbor—that Hansen guy—sitting with her. So far nothing on the search—" Ray glanced at Krichek.

"Place is weird," Krichek took over. "Downstairs like something out of a magazine, upstairs, most of the rooms were empty."

"And their bedroom? Cheap furniture and boxes." Ray shrugged. "Either they never unpacked after they moved in—"

"Or they were getting ready to run," Luka finished. Which meant Tassi might not be as innocent as she acted. "Any sign of Spencer's cell?"

"No," Ray answered.

"I'm waiting to hear back from the carrier to ping its location," Krichek added. "When's Harper getting here? She should be helping with the scut."

"She's working her own case." Luka gave Ray a quick rundown of what he'd found so far at the office—including their dumpster-wielding intruder. Krichek went into the office to start work. "Dig into Dean, see if you can get him talking. He knows more than he's sharing. And Matthew Harper—" Luka glanced around the parking lot. Matthew's SUV was gone.

"Harper? As in our Harper?" Ray asked.

"Her father. He's Standish's—or Spencer's—attorney. And minister."

Ray groaned, immediately realizing the complex implications the reverend's presence presented. "Think he knows who Spencer really was?"

"No idea, but we'll need to formally interview Tassi. But first we need as much intel as we can get about how involved she was with her husband's scams." He beckoned to Sanchez, who stood behind Ray, bouncing from one foot to the other like a kid. "Sanchez, what did you find?"

"That's what I wanted to tell you," the tech said in a rushed voice. "Every hard drive has been purged. Like military-grade level, completely overwritten not once or twice but at least a dozen times. I'll take another look in the lab, but chances are, we got nothing."

Ray swore.

"Okay then, we'll just have to do it the old-fashioned way," Luka said. "Walk and talk. Someone's got to know something. Starting with the widow. I want her in my office tomorrow."

"Ahearn won't like it," Ray said. "She's got a lot of friends in high places."

"He'll like it if we can close this quickly and quietly. You and Krichek dig up everything you can so we'll be ready for her." He thought for a second. "Do a full background check on Dean and invite him in for a formal interview as well."

The medics had loaded Luka into the back of the ambulance when he waved Ray back. "Let's ask Leah Wright to help us with Tassi's interview. That way no defense attorney can claim that we ignored her emotional distress."

"You got it, boss. Have fun in the ER," Ray said as he slammed the ambulance door shut, the vibration making Luka wince. Funny how he hadn't noticed the pain at all while interviewing Dean or discussing tactics.

He felt embarrassed about being forced to abandon his crime scene—even if it wasn't his fault. He made a list of priorities: obtaining any camera footage of their intruder, full background checks on everyone involved, tracking down the financials to verify the documents Spencer had included with his deathbed confession, getting the postmortem to the top of the ME's schedule, reviewing Spencer's SUV's black box, finding his missing cell phone, talking with the Denver authorities as well as anyone possibly involved with Spencer's current Ponzi scheme… and that was all mere preparation for his interviews tomorrow.

As always it came back to the three Ps: profit, passion, power. If what Dean said was true, then there were a lot of people who could lay claim to all three motives for wanting Spencer dead. Had the man killed himself to avoid their retribution?

That question led to more: how complicit was Tassi? And, even if she somehow was ignorant of her husband's misdeeds—which Luka sorely doubted—how far would Spencer's victims go to get their money back? Would they assume Tassi knew where it was?

Now that Spencer was dead, was his widow in danger?

# CHAPTER FOURTEEN

As Harper returned the cooler to her car and headed over to Second Avenue to find Macy, she couldn't help but feel frustrated by her inability to convince Heidi to accept a way off the streets. But she also understood the girl's wariness—she was under-age, so if she left Freddy's protection, she'd either need to make it on her own on the street or she'd be forced into foster care. A kid like Heidi could easily be swayed to choose the devil she knew in Freddy and his so-called love.

Halfway down Second, Harper spotted a skinny blonde sheltering in the shade of a doorway. Macy. Lily's friend was only a year older than Lily, Harper remembered from Macy's arrest report. How was it that she was getting older and these girls were getting younger and younger every year? As if there was a never-ending supply to replace the ones used up, burnt out, or dead.

What would it take to change things? In a country that could put men on the moon, surely there was a way to break the endless cycle of girls and women being used, abused, and tossed away like garbage? Like Lily had been. She flashed on the image of her body, battered and bruised beyond recognition. What was worth doing that to someone, anyone?

Harper knew nothing of her own mother's circumstances, but after joining the force and seeing the realities and lose-lose choices that women faced, particularly pregnant women, she couldn't help but wonder if her mother had given her up in the hope of Harper avoiding a similar fate. Harper couldn't even begin to imagine the strength it took to make that kind of sacrifice, to lose a child forever in the hopes that you were giving them a better life. The thought made her send a quick prayer of thanksgiving for the mother she had never known, as well as the family that had made her one of their own.

She parked the car across the street from where Macy stood. As she crossed the road, she caught Macy's eye. At first the girl turned away, shoulders hunched as if denying Harper's existence. But by the time Harper reached the doorway, she'd turned back around and was slumped against the wall in a belligerent posture, her glare containing more attitude than seemed possible for a stick-thin, five-foot tall—without the five-inch heels—teenaged girl.

"Hear about Lily?" Harper started.

Macy's jaw tightened. "Yeah. We all did."

"I haven't seen her around in a while. Know who she's been hanging with?"

Her shoulders jutted up in a knife-edged shrug. One spaghetti strap of her sequined top slid down, but Macy ignored it. "Thought she got out."

"When'd you see her last?" Harper assumed a relaxed posture, holding up her own side of the wall.

The August heat was doing little to mask Macy's body odor. Harper caught a whiff of an acrid garlicky tang—and it had nothing to do with what Macy was eating and everything to do with the meth she'd been smoking. Probably why she was clutching her tiny purse so tightly.

When Macy didn't answer, Harper aimed a pointed glance at the small, sequined bag. They both knew what would happen if Harper took a look in the bag—an arrest for felony possession was a lot harder to walk away from than an arrest for solicitation. Not to mention that it was Sunday, so she would be guaranteed a one-to-two-night jail stay before she could be arraigned and bail set. Withdrawal from meth? Not something Harper would wish upon her worst enemy.

Another shrug, this one more tentative. Which Harper translated as Macy acknowledging that she had seen Lily recently, but wasn't going to talk without incentive.

"Want some coffee? A bite to eat?" There was a diner down the block. It wasn't much to look at, but they served breakfast all day and night. "I'm starved."

"Should be working."

"C'mon. My treat."

Macy wrapped her arms around her chest, edged a glance beyond the doorway.

"Who you working for these days?" Harper asked. Heidi had said Philly, but when Harper had checked with Vice that morning, getting up to speed on current intelligence on local traffickers, she'd seen that he'd been arrested last month for assaulting a customer and was still in jail. Which meant either Macy was trying to go indy—a dangerous choice, being on the street without protection—or someone had taken over Philly's stable. Harper took a long look up and down the block, making sure no one saw Macy talking to her. If a pimp saw a cop alone with one of his girls, there'd be a price to pay—for the girl.

"No one. Just myself."

"Is that safe?" Harper was certain that Macy was lying about answering to a man—whether she called him a pimp or not. For some reason, the girls on the street loved to boast about their independence, even while under the thumb of men who laid claim to their time, any money they made, and their bodies. It was as if their feeble protests of freedom blinded them to the fact that they were modern-day slaves: replaceable, forgettable, disposable.

"Gotta know how to take care of yourself is all." Her words ran together, a bit blurred, making Harper wonder how high she was.

"Who was Lily working for?" Harper asked.

"Lily? No one."

"Do you know where she was staying?"

Macy blinked slowly and shook her head, wobbling on her heels as they left the doorway and headed toward the diner. Clearly on something more than meth.

Harper steadied her with a hand on her arm, noting the track marks there—old and new. "You okay?"

"I'm fine." Macy yanked her arm away from Harper. "Just fine." Tears seeped from her eyes, smearing her make-up. She stopped, leaned against a shop's display window. "Lily. Why'd she do it? Why'd she come back?"

Bingo. "When did you see Lily, Macy?"

Macy shook her head, the tears streaming even harder. "She thought—she said—"

A neon orange Mustang slid to the curb, honked once. Macy whirled away for a moment, palms swiping her face, then turned back, a wide smile stretching her features—a smile that didn't make it anywhere near her eyes. "Gotta go."

"Macy, wait—"

"It's not what you think," Macy said, her tone almost pleading. "He's my boyfriend, loves me."

The driver honked again, this time a short, angry burst. Macy rushed over, yanked the door open, and fell into the front seat. Before Harper could do more than take down the plate, the car sped away.

Nothing she could do except run the plate and see if it led to anyone with warrants. That could give her leverage enough to pull Macy's boyfriend in, allow her a chance to speak with Macy alone, in private.

Frustrated, Harper stalked across the street, back to her car. She plopped her weight down into the driver's seat and slammed the door. It was as if Lily Nolan was invisible, already vanished from everyone's memory. And if that was true, how was Harper going to find her killer?

# CHAPTER FIFTEEN

After Luka arrived in the ER, the first thing the doctor did was to send him to X-ray to determine how deep the glass had penetrated. The next thing was to wait while they gave him a dose of antibiotics via an IV and prepared to remove the damn thing, starting with cutting off most of the left leg of his slacks. Which gave Luka plenty of time to sit on his bed, comparing what he could see of the glass sticking out of his now naked leg with the X-ray on the computer beside him that revealed the jagged point beneath the skin, digging into his muscle. The doctors and nurses hadn't seemed very impressed once they had decided that no blood vessels were damaged and a trip to the operating room wouldn't be necessary, but seeing the complete picture in vivid white against black of the X-ray impressed the hell out of Luka. Imagine if he'd landed on his back or belly, or God forbid, his neck.

After a thousand worst-case scenarios flitted through his mind— including a few minutes of self-flagellation for not catching the guy, or at the very least seeing enough of him to identify him—he spent his time trying to figure out what the shard of glass could be part of. Not a soda bottle. His glass—given that it had taken up residence several inches inside his body, Luka felt possessive of the inconvenient piece of glass—was too tall and the curve too wide. Liquor bottle? Or wine, perhaps? How about a pickle jar?

Random thoughts but far better than worrying about things beyond his control—like his open cases, now in the capable hands of his team. Ray would call him if anything broke in the Spencer case, while Harper was hard at the frustrating and usually fruitless work of locating cooperative witnesses in the Lily Nolan murder. Which left Luka bored and restless, his imagination spinning out possible theories—less than theories, actually, since he had no facts or evidence—about Spencer's life as a conman and whether his death had been suicide, a bizarre accident, or murder. Luka's gut said murder, but he needed the autopsy results to back him up. Otherwise Ahearn and the powers that be might close his investigation, allowing the feds to take over to pursue the financial crimes. Although, with Spencer dead, he was certain the case would be a low priority—after all, unless they found evidence that Tassi was involved, there was no one left to prosecute.

Which actually gave Tassi a pretty good motive to get rid of her husband—especially as it sounded as if, thanks to the Reverend Harper's legal skills, her money was protected from any claims against Spencer. He made a note to follow up on her alibi and financials.

His musings were interrupted by the arrival of two doctors dressed in surgical garb and a nurse. As the first surgeon explained what to do, the second, obviously junior, surgeon followed his instructions while the nurse made sure they didn't screw up. Which was why Luka appreciated nurses so much. They had to dig deep and do several layers of stitches through his muscle—mattress sutures—so in addition to the local anesthetic they gave Luka nitrous oxide to breathe, which might have colored his perception of events. It definitely made time go faster and although he felt tugging and pulling, he really couldn't complain of any pain.

Once they were finished, Luka was surprised to see that it was almost seven. He felt as if he'd wasted most of the day because of this side trip to the ER. As he waited for the nurse to return to remove his IV and finish dressing his wound, he heard a knock on the open door.

"Luka?" Leah said. "What happened?" She stepped inside and saw the X-ray displayed on the computer screen. "Ouch. You doing okay?"

"Better now. Just waiting for discharge. What are you doing here?" Then he remembered—she was meant to be at the fair with the kids. "Did something happen? Is Nate okay?"

"He's fine. We had a bit of an adventure at the fair—a pregnant lady went into labor and I had to deliver her baby. I'm waiting on Ruby and the kids to come pick me up, since I rode here in the ambulance."

Luka realized he also didn't have a ride home—Ray would have taken his departmental car to return to the station. "Me, too."

"What happened?"

He started out feeling more than a little embarrassed but by the time he'd finished the story, Leah had sunk into the chair beside his bed and was listening in rapt attention. "Luka, you were so lucky. What if he'd had a gun?" They both knew there was no easy answer to that. "Did you call Nate? Or Pops? Tell them you were injured?"

"No," Luka admitted. He'd thought about it but had no clue how to handle it. This whole idea of family waiting at home for him was still new. "Didn't want to worry them. Figured once they saw I was fine, it'd save them getting upset."

"Luka." She sighed. "It doesn't work that way. You can't take a shortcut past emotions. And Nate really needs honesty from you."

"And I'm honestly fine. So where's the problem?" He changed the subject. "How'd he do? At the fair with the judging?"

She looked sheepish. "I have no idea. Had to leave before we found out, and I haven't had a chance to call them." She gave him a look of consideration. "Actually, I could use some advice. The woman who gave birth, she was all alone. No phone, no wallet, no ID, and she won't tell anyone her name. She appeared out of nowhere—I think she was running from someone. She seemed terrified."

"Going into labor all alone would do that."

"Yeah, but this is more. She said she was frightened someone would find her. Like she was running away from someone. And even now, her baby is fine, but she's refusing to talk to anyone. We had to register her as a Jane Doe."

Luka knew that Leah had excellent instincts. "You want me to see if I can find out who she is?"

"I'm not sure. Getting the police involved might make things worse, spook her. But if she is in trouble—" She blew out an exasperated breath. "Perhaps all she needs is a good night's rest in a safe place. I'll try again tomorrow morning."

"There's not much we could do unless social services think the baby is in danger. Then we could get a court order to force her to give us her identification, maybe also fingerprints. But even that doesn't mean we'd be able to find out who she is."

"Yeah, that sounds way too confrontational. If she's a victim of domestic violence or the like, I don't want to scare her off. There has to be another way."

"If you think of anything, let me know. And I might also need your help." He explained the crime scene he had been at that morning, about Tassi and how scattered she'd been. Not to mention her possible motives for murder. "Could you interview her? See if there's signs of mental distress or—"

"Or if she's faking it?"

"Exactly. She might be complicit in her husband's crimes; she could be trying to hide from any responsibility." He frowned. "But she did just lose her husband. If she's innocent, I don't want to ignore the impact that kind of trauma could have on her mental status."

Leah's phone buzzed. "Ruby and the kids are out front. Okay if I bring them back to see you?"

He shrugged, trying to look nonchalant. She left, returning a few minutes later with Ruby, Emily and Nate. Ruby hovered in the doorway, while Emily rushed over and reached up on tiptoe to give him an awkward hug. "Luka, what have you done?" she admonished him, her gaze fixed on the plastic-and-Velcro brace the nurse had sequestered his leg inside.

But it was Nate who had all of Luka's attention. The boy hung back, his expression blank.

"I'm fine," Luka told him. "Fell on some glass, is all."

Nate gave a jerk of his chin in acknowledgment, but his expression remained guarded. Luka remembered the social worker in Baltimore telling him that Nate had once, during one of the brief periods when his mother had regained custody, returned home from school to find the apartment empty. It wasn't until two days later that he'd even known she'd OD'd and had been in the hospital.

"I should have called you," Luka said. "I'm sorry."

Nate considered that. Luka ignored the others to beckon Nate closer. Hesitation slowing every step, Nate moved to Luka's bedside. Luka wrapped his arm around the boy's shoulders, drawing him as close as possible. Letting him know that he really was okay. "See, it's nothing. Only a few stitches."

"Did it hurt?" Nate asked, his gaze fixed on the thick swatch of gauze visible between the Velcro straps.

"Actually, I didn't even know I was hurt until I looked down and saw it. Then the doctors gave me laughing gas, so I didn't feel a thing."

Ruby handed Leah a set of car keys. "Can you get this lot home? I've got a date and these two have about frayed my last set of nerves." She left before giving Leah a chance to answer.

"Where's the baby, Mommy?" Emily asked. Then she spun back to Luka. "We had a baby at the fair!"

"Was she okay?" Nate added. "That lady?"

"She's fine and she had a beautiful baby boy," Leah reassured him. "And you were a big help, getting the ambulance for me." Nate's smile widened and his posture relaxed.

The nurse came in with Luka's discharge instructions and a set of crutches. The kids happily critiqued his clumsy efforts as he tried them out on the way to the parking garage and Leah's car.

Once Luka was situated in the front passenger seat, already despising the crutches Leah stowed in the rear cargo compartment, he called Ray for an update. "Anything new on our searches of the Standish house and office?"

"Nothing yet. Sanchez is working the electronics from the office and the widow is still sequestered," he said, in a tone implying finger quotes around the final word. "Turns out the neighbor is a chiropractor and also her doctor, so he gave her another sedative. As if she wasn't already loopy."

As they spoke, Luka noted Nate's disapproving scowl in the sideview mirror, reminding him that he was supposed to be off duty, doctor's orders. "I should go," Luka said for Nate's benefit. "Need me for anything?"

"Nope. Even Ahearn finished his schmoozing and took off. Only grunt work left until we can get the cell records and financials once the banks are open in the morning."

"Still no sign of Spencer's phone?"

"We got the carrier to do an emergency location ping, but nothing. My guess is someone removed the battery."

Which implied someone trying to cover their tracks, since a GPS ping should work even if the phone was turned off. One more strike against Spencer's death being a possible suicide, despite all appearances.

"What about the ex-DEA guy, Dean? Did he give you anything more about what Spencer was up to in Colorado?"

"Took off right after you left. Said he'd be in touch, whatever that means."

What it meant was that Luka was now more curious than ever about the former fed's involvement. Ray read his mind. "I've got Krichek working on a background check."

"Good. Anything else?" Luka asked. Behind him, Nate's scowl tightened.

"Get some rest. I'll call you if we need you."

Luka hung up as they pulled out of the parking garage. Leah hesitated at the stop sign, but it was Nate who asked the question. "Are you coming home?" His tone was guarded, but Luka heard his undercurrent of need. "Or going back to work?"

Luka twisted in his seat to face the boy. "No more work tonight. I want to hear all about the fair. Did you guys win any ribbons?"

Nate beamed but beside him Emily suddenly scowled and kicked the back of Leah's seat. "Hey," Leah told her. "Cut that out, I'm driving."

"I won't!" Emily shouted. "How come you're no fun, not like Daddy? If he were here we could've won all the prizes! He would've taken time off work to help us win."

"Calm down and tell me why you're upset," Leah said, even as Luka cringed at Emily's outburst. Nate buried all his emotions, so Luka hadn't yet needed to deal with a tantrum. Emily's face was dark and twisted, a storm ready to break, making him hope he never had to.

Instead of talking to Leah, Emily kicked out furiously, tears streaming from her face. "I hate you, I hate you, I hate you!"

# CHAPTER SIXTEEN

A quick check of the Mustang's registration revealed that Macy's new boyfriend-slash-pimp, an eighteen-year-old named Darius Young, had no outstanding warrants and neither did Macy. Which limited Harper's options as far as curtailing their activities so that she could speak to Macy again. The Bill of Rights was pesky that way, keeping Harper from doing whatever she wanted to in order to close a case.

As she walked the streets surrounding Lily's death scene, trying in vain to get anyone to talk about Lily, Harper was well aware that it was more than the Constitution limiting her efforts. These kids who made their living on the streets—and they were all young enough to be considered kids—risked their lives simply by talking to Harper. She thought of the girls she'd tempted with her mom's cooking and hoped they hadn't suffered for speaking out, even if they were only sharing tidbits of gossip.

Feeling drained by the heat and the fact that she'd learned nothing new that would help her locate Lily's family or her killer, she decided to try one more avenue of information—her brother Jonah, who ran Holy Redeemer's outreach programs.

Jonah's mission was located in an old hotel building near the wharf, only a few blocks from the Kingston Towers where Lily's body had been found. A hundred years ago, the Pierhouse had catered to itinerant dock workers, and with each subsequent generation of owners it had fallen into more disrepair until finally the last owners had donated the building to Holy Redeemer as a tax write-off. Jonah had brought it up to code and now the building, rechristened the Pierhouse Mission, functioned as soup kitchen, food bank, day care, counseling clinic, and homeless shelter.

Harper parked behind the building and entered through the rear entrance. Clouds of steam floated past her as soon as she opened the door to the sweltering hot kitchen. Steaming vats of vegetables were being stirred by volunteers clad in aprons and hairnets, while others took baking sheets stacked with chicken from the commercial-sized oven, perfuming the air with a savory scent that made Harper's tastebuds take notice.

She found Jonah in the walk-in refrigerator taking inventory, but he wasn't her only brother there—so was John. John was only a few years older than she was and all their lives they'd clashed. Rachel had once told her that John resented Harper for replacing him as baby of the family, but given that both Rachel and the Reverend doted on John and gave him anything he asked for, she'd never understood his animosity.

"C'mon, Jonah," John was saying as Harper entered the refrigerator, blessing the chilled air after the humidity of the kitchen. She stopped inside the door, not wanting to interrupt their conversation. "It's only for a short while. I'll pay you back long before you need to access your operational capital."

"No. I can't risk it," Jonah answered, his pen bobbing in the air as he counted sacks of oranges. "What do you need the money for, anyway?"

"Nothing, it's no big deal—a little robbing Peter to pay Paul so we can take advantage of some high-yield investments."

"Well then, I guess, how about you invest a little less?"

"That's not how it works. This is for the church's future security."

"Yeah, but I have to make sure I have enough money for the security of this mission. Do you have any idea how many people count on us?" He turned to face John and spotted Harper at the door. "Hey, li'l sis, what are you doing here? Don't tell me anyone died?" Given his vulnerable clientele, Harper knew he was only half-joking.

"Well, actually. The case I mentioned at dinner?"

"The one you ran off for?" John asked.

"No. My case. Lily Nolan." She held her phone out to Jonah, Lily's picture filling the screen. "I thought you might know her? She worked the streets around here until a year or so ago, then no one saw her again. Not until this morning when her body was discovered."

"Bless her soul." From Jonah's lips, it sounded like an actual prayer. He had a way of making pronouncements like that sound honest and authentic. Unlike John, who was clearly paying mere lip service when he spoke in a religious tone. But maybe Harper was jaded and had misjudged her brother as a hypocrite—after all, the Reverend trusted John with the church's finances and their mother doted on John as "the best of them all."

Jonah studied Lily's photo carefully while John fidgeted, obviously irritated that Harper had interrupted. As if talk of investments took precedence over a murdered girl.

"I'm trying to locate next of kin, anyone who knew her," Harper said.

"If you're going to talk about dead people, I'm out of here." John started for the door, but turned back. "I'll call you, Jonah. We really need to discuss this more." He swung the heavy steel door shut.

"What was that all about?" Harper asked. John had seemed even more intense than usual. But he always was when he talked about the church's finances. He was responsible for ensuring Holy Redeemer's future—and the Reverend never let him forget it.

Jonah glanced at the door with a frown. "Not actually sure. Mom wants me to give him access to the mission's accounts, some kind of special investment?" His attention returned to the phone. "Lily. I remember her. I don't think she's been around lately. But she had a close friend, Macy is her street name. Have you tried her?"

"Our chat got cut short when her pimp put her back to work. When did you last see Lily?"

"A year, year and a half ago?"

Finally, a break. "Please tell me you have records."

He smiled down at her. "I have records. C'mon." He set down his inventory clipboard and together they left the refrigerator and headed through the kitchen to his office, a tiny windowless room lacking any air conditioning. Harper's palms quickly slicked with a sheen of sweat. Jonah's office was a mess, crowded with lost and found items, stacks of donated books, toys, and toiletries, bags of clothing—the one closest to her was overflowing with winter coats—and boxes simply labeled *Misc.*

"It was good to see you at dinner today. I was glad you came. I think Mom and Dad were as well." Jonah was the only one who got away with calling the Reverend "dad."

"Yeah, I'm trying. They don't make it easy, though."

"You mean Dad doesn't—"

"Would it kill him, just once, to acknowledge that my job is important, too?" She almost clapped a hand to her mouth. To voice such rebellion out loud? Unheard of. Jonah glanced at her in surprise and they both chuckled.

"One thing is for sure," he said. "You're not that timid little girl that we could sweet-talk into doing almost anything."

"You sweet-talked. Jacob and John always bullied and black-mailed. Or locked me in the manger until I repented my sins and gave in." The manger was a space hidden behind a false wall in the oldest part of the church, now used to store the Christmas nativity statues and other miscellaneous seasonal items. Originally designed as a safe room to shelter the church's holy relics and valuables, it was a cramped, cobweb-filled, low-ceilinged closet saturated with the overwhelming scent of the creosote that had permeated the original building's logs. A forgotten space that the church had expanded around and absorbed—forgotten except by bored young boys intent on harassing their little sister. "Not to mention letting me take the blame anytime we got caught."

"Dad always took it easy on you, at least compared to us guys. We had to be toughened up, prepared to take on the mantle of responsibility that comes with saving souls." His impression of the Reverend had her smiling. But then she remembered why she was there. Lily.

He shuffled through the maze of debris to his desk and turned on his computer. Harper stood in the doorway, careful not to move too much for fear of causing an avalanche. Over his shoulder, she could see the icons and folders filling his computer screen—it was as messy as his office space, but he didn't seem to notice as he found what he was looking for with only three clicks. "Lily Nolan. Here we are."

"I can get a court order if you're uncomfortable sharing—"

"If she weren't dead, I'd ask you to. But helping you find her family? That's a blessing." Typical Jonah, an eternal optimist, assuming that Lily even had a family who cared enough about her to grieve her passing. Harper couldn't help but wonder where Lily's family had been during her time on the street—much less what had caused her to leave home in the first place.

"She stayed here early last year. We helped her get into a recovery program." He squinted at the screen and she wondered if he needed reading glasses. He was only thirty-four, but bad eyesight ran in the family and Jonah was the only one of the boys who'd avoided glasses as a child. "No emergency contacts or next of kin listed, I'm sorry."

Harper sighed. Of course not. "How about a phone number? Her phone wasn't with her, but if I can locate it I'll be able to access its contact list."

He scrolled down. "No, she left it blank."

"Can you give me the name of the recovery program? They might have something in their records." She'd need a court order to get the information, but it was her best bet given the other dead ends she kept hitting. Along with another chat with Macy. Somewhere far away from Macy's new boyfriend.

Jonah nodded and scribbled the information onto a sticky note. Their fingers touched as he handed it to her. "Want to stay for dinner?"

She took the note and shook her head. A dinner invitation from Jonah meant standing behind a hot counter serving food before eating leftovers herself. After her long day—not to mention an even longer night ahead working the street for leads—she deserved a real meal. Which translated to ordering takeout and eating it while sitting at her desk, writing up warrants for Lily's rehab records and catching up on anything Luka needed. She gave him a wave as she headed out the door, her mind already on her next steps. "Thanks, maybe next time."

"Then I'll see you next Sunday!" he called after her.

Harper pretended she hadn't heard—she wasn't sure how much more family she could take this week—and let the door swing shut behind her.

But then, almost as if her visit with Jonah had tempted fate, her phone rang: Rachel.

"Your father needs your help and I expect you to give it," she said before Harper could even say hello.

"Help?" The Reverend never asked anyone for help. Never. Of course, he wasn't actually asking, was he? He was letting Rachel do his dirty work. "With what?"

"You need to tell your father what the police found out. About Spencer Standish. It's important."

Harper snapped, "My work requires just as much confidentiality as his does."

"A covenant with God is different, and you know it. Besides, he'll never need to know you said anything. You can tell me and I'll slip it to him, pretend I heard it from women gossiping—or

Spencer's wife, Tassi. That woman—" Harper could practically hear Rachel's eye-roll.

"The Reverend is acting as Tassi's attorney, so he has access to more information than I do at this point."

"But he's so worried—I'm worried for him, Naomi. I've never seen him this way. Please, if you find out anything, you have to tell me. Help me protect him. It's what families do."

Rachel's answer to every argument. If a child misbehaved, it was wrong because it disrespected the family, meaning the Reverend. If their behavior reflected poorly on the family—for example, if they attended the religious college where generations of Harpers had excelled with honors and they were expelled—then they were responsible for bringing dishonor to the entire family. A crime punishable by virtual exile.

Harper should know, because she was still serving her sentence, a decade later. Well, on parole at least, given that Rachel, thanks to Jonah's urging, had been allowing her to attend Sunday dinners for the past few months. But being allowed back also meant being expected to place the family's needs above her own, no matter what.

She sighed. She should never have dared to hope. She was better off on her own anyway—hadn't the last decade proved that?

"Sorry, Mom. No."

"Naomi Harper, I expect you to grow up and stop being so rebellious. We are your only family and we deserve—"

"I can't. Please don't ask me—I can't." Harper hung up before Rachel could make her feel more of a traitor than she already did.

# CHAPTER SEVENTEEN

Luka glanced over to see Leah blinking back tears after Emily's outburst. Emily's words had hurt her more than the little girl could ever know. The grief of missing her husband was obvious—as was the even deeper pain that she might have failed her daughter.

He searched for words but found none. When he checked the sideview mirror, he saw that Nate had buried his face in his phone, although he occasionally flicked a glance at Emily, waiting for her to calm down. Once her sobbing eased, Nate put his phone down and took her hand in his, saying something in a voice too quiet for Luka to hear, but which made Emily nod and seemed to soothe her.

By the time they reached Jericho Fields the car was filled to bursting with a silence wrought with grief and guilt. Nate tumbled out of his seat and ran around to Emily's side of the car to help her out of her booster seat. Rex, the scraggly mongrel that Nate had saved from an abusive home several months ago, came galloping up to greet the kids, ignoring the adults as unworthy of his attention.

As the children played with Rex, Leah sat still in the driver's seat, both hands clenching the steering wheel as if it was taking all her strength not to let go of her emotions. After a long moment, she sniffed, then finally turned to face Luka.

"I'm sorry about that," she said. "But you should know, Ruby said that Nate won a special honor with his photo of Pops. Plus, she said one of the judges teaches art and gave Nate her card, said you should call her."

Despite his sadness over Leah's pain, Luka couldn't help the pride that swelled his chest. "He won?" he stammered, not realizing until that moment how worried he'd been that the rest of the world wouldn't see Nate's talent and potential like he did.

"Ruby said the judge wants to invite Nate to her classes or something. Anyway, I'm sorry I wasn't there to see it myself—and that Emily is acting out."

"I guess that's normal at her age." He tried to sound as if he actually knew anything at all about seven-year-old girls. He glanced at Emily and Nate, the dog between them. Nate was on his knees while Emily stood, their foreheads practically touching as they spoke. She was so petite and Nate was so tall that Luka marveled at the study in contrast the two supplied. So very different and yet also both children of violence and grief, struggling to find their place in a suddenly uncertain and frightful world. It was good they'd found each other.

"I'm not sure we'll ever find our new normal, not since Ian…" Leah's voice drifted off. "Every time I think she's doing better, making progress, something else sets her off. Anyway, I'm sorry. Nate should be proud of his accomplishments and I know, once she's calmed down, Emily will tell him that and apologize."

Luka imagined how proud Pops and Janine would be when they heard that Nate won a prize. And a teacher was interested in his work. First time putting himself out there and the kid hit a home run—how amazing was that? But then he looked more closely at Leah, saw the dark smudges below her eyes and the rigid tautness of her neck muscles. It'd been six months since her husband was murdered and he'd thought she was doing okay, despite the challenges of juggling a new job with single parenthood. But clearly, she was still struggling. "Everything okay?"

"Me?" Her shrug was a study in nonchalance. Luka wasn't fooled, but also knew she wouldn't talk until she was ready. Nate was the same way, always needed time to mull things over for himself before he could share anything with the outside world.

"I'm fine." She left to retrieve his crutches. Together, they joined the kids.

"Emily, I think you have something to say to your friend before we go," Leah said in a firm, parental tone.

Emily instantly appeared chagrined and remorseful. She touched Nate's cheek with her palm and gazed directly into his eyes. "I'm glad you won. Your pictures were very good—I would have given you the blue ribbon instead of the white one."

"And—" Leah prompted.

"And... I'm sorry I didn't win like I told my daddy I would." Emily leaned back, crossing her arms over her chest, daring Leah to try to get anything more out of her, such as admitting that her tantrum was uncalled for.

Leah's spine grew rigid. "How about apologizing to Nate for screaming in the car when you should have been celebrating with him?"

Emily frowned at Leah, her lower lip protruding in a stubborn pout. "I won't. And you can't make me."

Leah's lips tightened and her face flushed. Luka realized that as hard as he had to work to help Nate, what he faced was nothing compared to what Leah was dealing with after the trauma Emily had been through.

Nate saved the day by hoisting his bag and hugging Emily goodbye. "See you tomorrow, right?"

"Yes, sir," Emily said with a smile. "We only have a week left before school!"

Emily hopped back into the car while Nate walked toward the house, leaving Luka leaning awkwardly on his crutches. "Thanks for the ride," he said.

Leah bit her lip, her expression blanking—the same way Nate's did when he was overwhelmed. "Good night." She secured Emily in her booster seat, then climbed back into the car and drove down the lane.

Luka hobbled inside. Pops and Janine were so thrilled by Nate's tales of the day at the fair, including the lady with the baby and winning his prizes, that no one asked for any details about Luka's injury after he said he fell onto a piece of glass, allowing him a respite.

Nate gave him the card from the photography judge. *Viola Reed, Fine Art Photography*, it read. He flipped it over to where she'd written a note: *Your nephew shows promise, I'd love to teach him. Please call me.*

Curious, Luka left the others as they celebrated Nate's victory and went out to the back porch to call the photographer. He leaned his crutches against the wall and sat on the porch swing, hoping to catch any hint of a breeze.

"Ms. Reed?" he said when she answered the phone. "This is Luka Jericho. I'm Nate Jericho's uncle. You sent him home from the fair with—"

"Mr. Jericho, I'm so excited that you called." Her voice was warm, her accent local, reflecting the hills and valleys surrounding them. "Nate shows such promise."

"I'm sorry I wasn't there at the fair. I had to work." He felt the need to explain, to make sure she knew Nate had his family's support.

"Of course. Well, I won't keep you from your family or Sunday dinner. I only wanted to extend an offer—but you'll need to decide fairly quickly."

"Offer?"

"In addition to my freelance photography business I also teach art at the Cambria Preparatory Academy. You've heard of it?"

He rolled his eyes. The exclusive private school boasted of its rich and powerful alumni. "Yes. Actually, I was thinking of it earlier today." He didn't explain that it was because the kids responsible for his first murder case were students at Cambria Prep.

"Well, I'm on our fine arts scholarship committee and one of our elementary school pupils had to relinquish their spot in the fall class. I'd love to offer their scholarship to Nate."

Luka stared at the phone, certain he'd heard wrong. "Nate? But you don't know anything about him."

"I know he's a promising young artist and I believe his talent could flourish here. Give me your email and I'll send you all the pertinent information. And then we could schedule a tour for this week? I really do hope you'll consider allowing us to have some part in shaping Nate's future."

He gave her his contact information and she hung up. When Luka glanced up, he saw Nate standing in the doorway, Rex at his side. He was staring at him with that all-too-grown-up expression that said he saw and understood more than Luka wanted him to.

"I'm sorry Emily yelled at you earlier," Luka said. The phone weighed heavy in his hand. This wasn't his decision alone. Nate's life had been much too tumultuous and chaotic; he deserved some say in his future. He patted to the seat beside him and Nate joined him on the porch swing, while Rex curled up at their feet. "What would you say if you weren't in her class this year? You'd still be friends, see each other, but—"

Nate shook his head, cutting him off. "Emily isn't mad at me. That's not why she was yelling."

"It's okay, Nate. Emily will get over how she feels. You don't need to make excuses or blame yourself."

"No, you don't understand." He balled his fists in frustration as he searched for words. "She's not mad." He pulled out his phone, shoved it at Luka. "Here. Look. Can you see it now?"

Luka studied the image, a candid shot taken of Emily during her meltdown in the car. "You're right. She's not angry—"

"She's sad." Nate sighed in sympathy with his friend. "It wasn't me she's yelling at. She wanted to win first prize. Because she's always won first prize. At school with tests, when she did stuff with her dad. So she just, just…" He faltered, his vocabulary not keeping up with the complex emotions he was attempting to describe. "She wanted that feeling again. Like she had with her dad. Like he wasn't gone."

Not for the first time, Nate's perception stunned Luka. The boy saw and understood more than most adults. "She misses him." Luka took another, closer look at the photo. He recognized Emily's expression as the same one he'd caught on Leah's face whenever she dropped her guard or thought no one was looking. "She wants things to go back the way they were." He turned to Nate. "Is that how you feel?"

Nate seemed startled, unused to any adult asking about his feelings. "I miss my mom. But I don't feel the same as Emily does about her dad. It's... different, because I never really knew my mom—every time I got close to her, she'd be gone and I'd be back in foster. So maybe it hurt like Emily hurts but a long time ago when I was only a kid. Not now."

"So, you're not sad like Emily?" Luka hoped he was mirroring Nate's feelings correctly. After six months seeing a grief counselor, this was the first time Nate had opened up. Luka didn't want to say or do anything that might close him back down.

"No, sir." Nate sounded hesitant and Luka kicked himself for pushing too hard.

"That's okay," Luka tried again. "Maybe you feel a little mad—like you did when I didn't call you about getting hurt like I should have?"

Nate jerked his chin in what could have been a reluctant nod.

"Growing up," Luka continued, "I was the big brother and it wasn't cool being friends with girls back then, especially not your little sister. So your mom and me, we were the kind of brothers and sisters who fought all the time. Know what I mean? We still loved each other but we were always yelling and arguing. And when she died, I felt really bad because we had another fight that same day."

Nate's head still hung low but his gaze crept up, almost meeting Luka's. "You loved Mom, right?"

"I still do. Love her with all my heart."

"But you're mad at her, too?"

"Yep. Furious. That she's gone, that she left without saying goodbye to me or Pops or you." He blew his breath out. "I miss her so much, but some days that only makes me even more angry with her for making me feel this way." He paused. "You ever feel like that?"

Nate bit his lip and nodded.

"Guess we're in this together, then. Think Emily kinda feels the same? Like she's sad, so sad the only way to let her feelings out is by acting mad? Even at her best friend?"

Another nod. Nate flicked the phone's photo stream, and this time Leah's face filled the frame. "I think Dr. Wright feels like that sometimes too. But she never lets it out, keeps it bottled up inside." He met Luka's gaze. "She's like me that way."

"What helps you to feel better?" Luka asked. "Does talking with Dr. Hannah help?"

A shrug. "I guess. Maybe. Talking to you, too. But mostly I guess what makes me feel good is taking my pictures—like I'm saving memories for Mom, you know? Playing with Rex, teaching him stuff so he can be a good dog and forget where he came from, I like that, too. And I like helping Emily when she's sad. Making her laugh again, that feels good." He turned his face up, searching Luka's. "Is that okay?"

Luka couldn't resist hugging him. "It's more than okay. Remember how you saved Rex from those men who were abusing him? You were his hero."

Nate pushed him away and rolled his eyes. "Nah. I'm no hero, not like you. But maybe. Someday. Someday I can grow up to be like you."

Warmth flooded Luka's chest and he found himself blinking fast. "Know what? You're gonna be a hero—in your own way. I'm sure of it."

"But—can a hero ever feel afraid? Cuz I do. All the time."

Luka flashed to the expression on Nate's face when he'd seen Luka in the ER. "Can I tell you a secret? So do I. But that's a good thing, because no one is born brave or a hero. We learn how to face our fear; that's how heroes are born."

"But how? How do you do that?"

Luka considered. "I think of the people I love. You, Pops, my parents, your mother." And Cherise, his first love, lost so many years ago. "I think all courage comes from love. So if you start out loving people, letting them in your heart, then you're already most of the way there. Does that make sense?"

"I guess." Nate yawned, not bothering to cover it. Rex, ever vigilant, saw it and ambled over, ready for his before-bed walk around the house. The scruffy mutt rubbed his head against Nate's leg, nudging him toward the porch steps.

"Get some sleep." Luka gave Nate another quick hug. He pocketed Ms. Reed's card. "We'll talk more tomorrow." After he had checked out Cambria Prep. And broken the news to Leah that Nate might be going there without Emily.

He grabbed his crutches, his leg screaming for him to go lie down. *One step at a time*, he thought as he limped inside. One step at a time. It was the best he could do.

# CHAPTER EIGHTEEN

Emily was silent during the few minutes it took Leah to drive them from Jericho Fields to Nellie's farm. Leah didn't mind. She was so embarrassed, angry, guilty, worried—she was so many things that she needed time to sort through her own emotions that Emily's outburst had wrought. Every time she thought things were finally getting better, that life was approaching some semblance of normality despite Ian's absence, every time, despite Leah's best efforts, something like this would happen. She was exhausted by constantly trying to act normal, by watching Emily like a hawk, trying to protect her, to do the work of two parents.

But now it was clear. Leah was failing her daughter. And Ian.

Tears blurring her vision, she parked the car in front of Nellie's house. No matter how long Leah lived here, this would always be her great-aunt Nellie's house. Even now, as the sun set behind it, painting the sky above the mountain a gentle lavender that clung to the treetops like a downy quilt, the large white farmhouse anchored its surroundings. As if whispering to anyone who needed to hear: *I'm here, I'm not going anywhere, you're safe here.*

The summer night echoed the words—although, somehow to Leah's ears they were in Ian's voice, not Nellie's—and Leah knew what she had to do: she had to make Emily hear and understand them as well. Fumbling her seatbelt, Leah climbed out of the Subaru, grabbed a tarp from the back, then finally gathered Emily from her car seat. She carried Emily on one hip, like she had when

Emily was a baby, tossed the tarp onto the lawn with her other hand and sat down, Emily in her lap.

Emily was crying again, rocking and flailing her arms as if attempting to exorcise all the emotions that so overwhelmed her. Leah wrapped her arms around her daughter and rocked along with her, saying nothing, simply providing a secure anchor.

Finally, Emily went limp in her arms. Stars showered the sky above them. Leah lay back, nestling Emily beside her. "I'm sorry you didn't get a ribbon," Leah started. "You worked very hard and should be proud—"

"I did get one," Emily snapped. She sat up, dug something from her pocket and thrust it at Leah. "See. It's fake." And cheap, Leah saw as she uncrumpled the nylon streamer that was fraying along its edges. "It's not like the real ones. Miss Ruby gave a judge money to give it to me. I saw." Her voice broke. "That's what made me so mad. Then Miss Ruby made me thank the judge, like I'm stupid or something!" She wailed at the heavens.

"You know Miss Ruby loves you, right?" Leah said in a tone that she hoped hid her own fury and frustration at Ruby's misguided attempt to make Emily feel like a winner. Ruby would never understand the power of real accomplishment—to her the ribbon would always be the point, what the rest of the world saw and used to judge you. Ruby could never understand that real winning was the work, achieving your vision. And that it didn't matter if a judge saw it or not. But how to explain that to a seven-year-old?

Emily sighed. "Miss Ruby loves me. I love her. But sometimes, she treats me... Not only her, Ms. Driscoll, the teachers and kids at school—why does everyone treat me like I'm different, Mommy? They either treat me like a baby because I'm small or tell me 'you're acting too big for your britches, Emily,' like Ms. Driscoll, or say I'm weird or strange or they can't play with me or..." Her voice edged into tears again, but this time she intertwined her arm in Leah's, squeezing tight, and was able to control them. "I wish Daddy were here. He made me feel smart. We learned things—together. And it was fun. Not like school."

"Even with Nate there?" Leah asked. The vice-principal, Ms. Driscoll, had left her two voicemails demanding a meeting to discuss separating Nate and Emily in an effort to "curb Emily's rambunctious, disruptive behavior." So far, Leah had ignored them. But she only had a week left of summer vacation—and the only thing making school at all tolerable for Emily was Nate's presence in her class. Which meant Leah had to prepare to battle Ms. Driscoll—in her mind, Cambria City's equivalent of the Wicked Witch of the West.

"Nate makes things better," Emily said. "But then I get him in trouble—by accident. And then the kids or teachers pick on him and it's not fair." She blew her breath out in a sigh that made her sound even older than the centuries-old farmhouse beside them. "It's not fair. Daddy should be here. I should have won a ribbon because my truffles were excellent tasting—even if they weren't pretty with all the decorations the other candies had. People shouldn't judge on what they see on the outside but on what's inside."

Leah suppressed a chuckle. If only... "Your dad would be very proud of you, teaching yourself how to make your truffles, experimenting with flavors."

"I did it exactly like he taught me. Imagine one change at a time, then try it and see how close to your imagination you come. It's like when we wrote computer games. We had so much fun." Another long-suffering sigh. "If he were here, I wouldn't even need to go to school. He could teach me everything."

This was exactly what Ian had argued for before they enrolled Emily. He'd volunteered to cut his work hours in order to home-school her, but Leah had wanted her to have the chance to socialize with other kids her age. It was one of the few arguments during their marriage that Leah had won—and now she wondered if she'd been wrong about everything.

They lay in silence, the stars multiplying as the night grew darker. So many stars. "You know your dad's up there, watching over you. Always. Even when you can't see the stars, they're always still there."

"Just the sun hides them. And the sun is a star, too. And we have stars inside us, right? Because of the elementary—"

"Because of the elemental particles," Leah corrected. "Atoms, like the carbon that builds your muscles and bones and that made the flowers and trees and—"

"And diamonds! Daddy taught me that—I read it in one of his books."

"And diamonds. All those particles, they came from stars."

"So Daddy came from the stars. And now he's back with them?" She nestled closer and Leah wrapped her arm around her, hugging her tight.

"Exactly."

"Mommy, can it stay like this always? No more school, Nate can come and play—"

"Not sure when Nate would want to come and play. You owe him an apology. For acting out when it was his turn to celebrate. That made his hard work and winning his prizes seem not as important and special as they are."

"I'll tell him I'm sorry. Maybe we can throw him a party? I can make truffles."

"Maybe. Except for that, you're grounded. It's okay to share your feelings, but kicking and screaming when I'm driving the car isn't the right way."

Emily considered that. "Yes, ma'am. So I'll be grounded tonight and then Nate can come tomorrow and we'll use Daddy's computer to look at all his pictures from the fair. I want to see more of the baby lady."

"The baby lady?" Leah asked with trepidation, praying that Ruby hadn't allowed Nate to capture photos of Beth in labor.

"Yeah. I remember seeing her a few times. Near the horse barn and at the corndog stand and near the Ferris wheel—that they said I was too short to ride. That's not fair."

"Wait, so you saw Beth earlier? What was she doing?"

Emily shrugged one shoulder. "Talking on her phone. She was angry. Then she threw it."

Leah sat up. "Beth had a phone and threw it out? Do you remember where? Was it into a trash bin?" She could ask Luka to send an officer out to retrieve it before the trash was hauled away.

Emily shook her head. "No. It was into some trees. I'll bet Nate took a picture. He takes pictures of everything." She tugged Leah back down. "Look at the stars, Mommy. Can you teach me how to take pictures of the stars? Then I can teach Nate. That would be fun, wouldn't it?"

Leah suppressed her urge to search for Beth's phone—and identity—forcing herself to relax and concentrate on Emily. After all, how many more nights like this would they have before Emily grew too old to cuddle with her mother and share all her secrets?

First thing tomorrow, she promised herself. She'd deal with Beth and the kids and the dreaded Ms. Driscoll and the budget due at work and the bills to be paid… they could all wait until tomorrow. Tonight Emily needed her.

# CHAPTER NINETEEN

Harper had spent the rest of the night trying in vain to find anyone who saw Lily before her death or knew how to contact her next of kin. She'd bought numerous coffees and burgers for street kids and even tried to wheedle intel from the few pimps and drug dealers who protested at her scaring off their customers.

She'd learned that Lily hadn't been on the streets for a while. She had first shown up in Cambria City when she was sixteen, lasted a little more than a year working for Freddy, most of it spent in a haze of oxy and then heroin addiction, before vanishing sometime last year. Harper hadn't been much older herself when she'd been thrown out of college and her family's affections. She remembered the constant fear of navigating life on her own: juggling bills because her scant waitress's wages wouldn't allow her to pay them all at once; depending on the kindness of strangers to tip her well—sometimes forced into playing a role, rewarding their not-so-subtle harassment with a bitter smile.

As much as she'd like to think her survival was the result of some special hidden strength inside herself, Harper knew that it was as much about luck as anything else. Hearing the vague accounts of Lily's short-lived time in Cambria City left Harper wondering what more she could have done to help Lily during their several brief encounters. She'd steered Lily to Jonah's mission and, from what he said, she'd taken advantage of the services he'd offered, and yet, somehow, she'd still been lost: another anonymous victim of the streets.

No one admitted to seeing Lily recently; most assumed she'd died of an OD last year. No one knew where she came from, who her family was—or where they were—or, worse, seemed to care. Other than Macy, that was. But Macy was nowhere to be found Sunday night, so Harper eventually headed home for a few hours' sleep.

Monday morning, after showering, changing clothes and grabbing a bottled protein shake in lieu of breakfast, Harper headed back out. She had an extensive to-do list, including requesting a court order for Lily's rehab records and continuing her search for Macy. First, though, she had a far worse duty to attend to: observing Lily's autopsy. On her way to Good Sam she called Maggie Chen to let her know she was running a few minutes late.

"Didn't Luka tell you?" Maggie said. "He still wants you here, but not for the Lily Nolan case."

"Why?" Harper felt a fool, out of the loop on her own case. "Did you already finish? What did you find?" Lily's autopsy was her last chance to find any evidence Lily's killer might have left behind.

"Haven't had a chance to start. Lily's autopsy has been rescheduled."

"Rescheduled? To when?"

"To follow. Which means whenever the medical examiner has time to get to it. After we finish the Spencer Standish postmortem."

Harper bit her lip, trying to curb her anger. "Some rich idiot dies and my victim is dropped to the bottom of the list? Who's the ME assigned? I want to talk to them."

"It's Ford."

Great. Ford Tierney would never upset his schedule simply because Harper asked. He was the most rigid, punctilious, and brilliant of the three forensic pathologists who worked with Craven County's coroner as well as the other four surrounding counties, none of whom could afford their own qualified medical examiners. Consolidating their unique, specialized services saved money, provided faster results, and was a huge help to law enforcement—especially as they happened to be quartered at Good Sam, making them especially convenient for Cambria City's police department. But covering such a large swath of the state meant they were always juggling which case took priority. And clearly a prostitute killed in an alley took a back seat to the suspicious death of a millionaire who'd confessed to a Ponzi scheme.

"Can you at least give me any preliminary results from Lily's case?" Harper hated to beg, but something was better than nothing. She couldn't afford to lose momentum now, not when she had so little of it to start with. No witnesses, no exact time of death, not even a next of kin to interview to learn where Lily had been for the past year and why she had suddenly resurfaced back in her old neighborhood.

"Writing it up now, but it's not much," Maggie told her. "Tox screen negative—"

"Wait." Harper had assumed there would be traces of drugs in Lily's system. "Nothing? No oxy or heroin?" Lily's previous drugs of choice.

"Not even alcohol. She was clean."

So Lily hadn't returned to the streets because of a relapse. If she hadn't needed cash to fuel her addiction, why had she returned? "Okay. What else?"

"There's no evidence of recent sexual activity," Maggie said. Which also meant Lily hadn't been working the streets—so what was she doing in an alley at three in the morning? "Oh, and Ford will need to confirm, but from the X-rays it looks like the lethal blow was a blow to the back of the head. From the bruising, I'd guess it was one of the first blows, if that helps."

"Are you saying the majority of her injuries were inflicted after she died?"

"Yes. Again, preliminary, we need to examine the tissue, but yes. She was dead or at the very least unconscious after sustaining the lethal blow."

They were both silent for a moment. "That's an awful lot of rage." Harper couldn't help but visualize the beating Lily had taken. "I mean, it must have taken several minutes to beat her like that."

Maggie's voice dropped. "I counted over twenty blows based on the external contusions. All from the same weapon. The wound patterns suggest it was one of the wooden slats from the alley, if that helps."

Harper knew it was almost impossible to lift fingerprints from rough lumber and there was no way the CSU budget would cover testing every length of wood for touch DNA, given that there'd been a dozen or more in the alley. Besides, with the amount of traffic that the alley saw, any DNA they found could be explained away as transfer from an innocent bystander.

"So she was punched in the face, then hit on the back of her head—" She stopped. *One step at a time*, she heard Luka's voice of caution. "Was the blow to the head inflicted with the same weapon as her other injuries?"

"Looks like it, but we'll need microscopic comparisons to be sure."

Which meant they needed the autopsy completed before Harper would have more than a working theory—but at least it was progress.

"Did you locate next of kin yet?" Maggie asked.

"No. She didn't have a driver's license, and every time she was arrested she used a slightly different name: Lily, Lilian, Lili with an i, Nolan with an a, i, or e, and Dolan—"

"With an a, i, or e," Maggie finished for her. "These kids, they leave their families for a reason. They aren't looking to be found. With no official government ID, it's like they don't even exist."

"I know. I ran her photo and details through every missing persons database, but so far no matches."

"She'd only be in the database if someone cared enough to report her missing," Maggie said.

"Right now, that's just you and me."

"Maybe it's good that her autopsy is delayed."

"Why's that?"

Maggie hesitated. "We don't have space to keep unclaimed bodies for long, so it means the clock hasn't started, since we haven't completed our examination."

Suddenly the protein drink Harper had gulped was threatening to turn rancid. "Do me a favor? Call me before that happens. I can't stand the idea of her being cremated, her ashes tossed in the back of some storage closet."

"You know I'd never let that happen."

"Thanks, Maggie."

"No problem. I'll call you once we have Lily's autopsy on the schedule. I'm headed home now, but you'll have Ford and Joel there for the Standish case." She hung up.

Harper kept driving. Hopefully she could get some work done on Lily's case while she was observing the Standish autopsy—there was always a lot of downtime while the medical examiner did all their routine stuff, especially when the ME was Ford Tierney.

She thought back to the first cases she'd worked with Luka when she was still a patrol officer. What would he say when faced with a case full of dead ends and no active leads? He'd tell her to start with the victim: understand the victim's life and you'll understand why they were targeted, how their world and the killer's intersected. Even if she knew nothing of Lily's life now or before she initially arrived in Cambria City, she could still try the rehab facility where she'd been last year. Except it might take hours to days to get a court order for medical records.

Her phone rang. Rachel. Harper cursed—she really didn't have time to deal with one of her mother's guilt trips. She'd already told her that she wouldn't betray her badge to get the Reverend inside information on the Standish case. She almost ignored the call, but finally relented. Maybe Rachel was calling to apologize.

"Are you all right, Naomi?" Rachel asked. "You didn't answer when I called back last night."

So. No apology for asking Harper to compromise her morals. Only denial that anything had happened at all. Typical Rachel. "Sorry, Mom. I got tied up."

Rachel paused as if waiting for Harper to say something more, but Harper had no idea what. Surely Rachel wasn't expecting Harper to be the one to apologize. "So what are you doing?" Rachel finally asked. "Following a juicy lead? Tailing a perp?"

Her attempt at slang left Harper smiling. "You've been watching too much TV."

"Don't tell your father; he thinks I never watch anything that's not rated PG. But it is rather exciting. Can you tell me anything?"

For the first time, Harper realized exactly how boring her mother's life must be. Especially now that all the children were out of the house and the Reverend no longer needed her help running Holy Redeemer. Funny, she'd never thought what it must be like to live in the shadow of a larger-than-life man like the Reverend. What had her mother wanted for herself? Harper knew Rachel had never gone to college—had she ever thought of a career or any life other than the one she had?

For some reason Harper thought of Lily. Rachel and Lily's lives couldn't be more different, yet she had an intuition that both felt trapped by their circumstances. She shook off the idea—how could she possibly compare Rachel's life of privilege to Lily's life on the streets?

"Right now, I'm actually on my way to the morgue—" she answered Rachel.

"Your prostitute killed in the alley, of course." Rachel sounded disappointed. Harper was about to explain that she was attending the Standish autopsy, but then she realized that was exactly the kind of information Rachel was trying to wrangle. Was she actually interested in Harper's life at all? Was she merely bored and looking to Harper for distraction? No, Harper didn't believe that. Rachel was acting as she had Harper's entire life, doing whatever was needed to help the Reverend succeed.

"Sorry, Mom. I don't really have time to talk."

"Well, perhaps you could come to dinner or call me later? We'd love to hear more about your big case. It was even on the news last night." Her mother didn't say it, but it was clear: all she really cared about was Spencer Standish's case.

As she hung up, Harper couldn't help a wave of anger. Why was it that no one placed any value on time spent solving the murder of a teen prostitute? Lily had had her whole life before her; surely she meant as much as some middle-aged corporate conman. Or at the very least, she deserved not to be forgotten, her killer allowed to walk free.

Well, Lily had Harper on her side, if not the rest of the world. No way in hell was Harper about to give up on her. Not today, not tomorrow, not ever.

# CHAPTER TWENTY

In his prior life as a childless bachelor—aka six months ago—Luka would have been at his office hours before dawn after a weekend on call. In fact, he might never have bothered to go home other than for a quick shower and change of clothes.

Now, here he was, having an actual sit-down breakfast with his grandfather and Janine. He was exhausted—the leg had kept him awake all night and he'd been up all of the night before that working cases. He deserved to simply sit for a few minutes and enjoy a cup of Janine's excellent coffee along with her equally excellent eggs and sausage. But despite his throbbing leg and the damn crutches that hurt his arms, Luka itched to get to work.

"What are we going to do about Nate?" Janine asked as she joined him and Pops at the circular table. This table was where all the important decisions regarding Jericho Fields had been made for two centuries, from new types of apples to cultivate, to planning Luka's wedding before his fiancée had been killed. They'd also planned Luka's parents' funeral here—him, Pops, and his gran. Then after Gran passed, and then after Luka's sister, Nate's mother, died, it'd been just him and Pops alone at this table. But now it was the place where they discussed the family's future: Nate. "School starts next week. And you know that vice-principal, Driscoll, is going to make his life hell."

Pops made a small grunt of disgust. "I say we teach him how to fight back, give those bullies a taste of their own medicine."

"Which will get him expelled," Luka said.

"Or arrested," Janine added. "Did you see how they took a six-year-old away in handcuffs, put him in a jail cell, all because he had a tantrum? Ever know any six-year-old who never had a tantrum? They didn't even try to understand why he acted out."

"Was he Black?" Pops asked.

"Yes."

"That's all they need to know. Don't care about the rest. Probably claimed he was a danger to the teacher or other kids, that he was out of control—"

"Isn't that the definition of a child having a tantrum?" Janine retorted. She was in her fifties, her own children raised and gone, the daughter, granddaughter, and great-granddaughter of Polish coal miners. And she didn't put up with crap from anybody. "Last year he had Emily with him, but this year Driscoll assigned them to separate classes."

"It'll be like he's starting over again," Pops said. "He won't know any of those kids. Hard enough the first time around; at least he met Emily." In the spring when Nate had first arrived, the school had made him repeat first grade because his schooling had been erratic down in Baltimore. But he'd worked hard over the summer and he'd shown real progress, and they'd decided he could skip ahead now, and rejoin his age group in third grade.

"And it was Emily helping him over the summer who got him caught up," Janine put in. She was certain Emily and Nate shouldn't be separated, but Luka wasn't so sure.

Leah had agreed to let Emily skip ahead to third grade, despite the fact that she'd be the youngest in the class. Better to keep them together, Leah had said, and at the time Luka agreed. Nate needed friends. Nate was such a great kid, but because he'd been working so hard on academic progress over the summer, Luka hadn't been able to enroll him in sports camp or any activity where Nate could socialize with other boys his own age. Now he worried that having Emily there was a crutch and Nate wouldn't even try to find other friends.

"Yeah, but he needs friends his own age." Luka remembered his own third grade. Back then, girls had cooties and were to be avoided at all costs. So where would that leave Nate if he hung out with a girl, especially a girl who was a bit quirky and who didn't always fit in, like Emily? Luka loved that about Emily, but as their encounters with Ms. Driscoll had proven, being quirky wasn't always the best way to avoid trouble. And the last thing Nate needed was more trouble in his life. The boy had been through enough.

Pops made a noise. "Notice how it's our problem figuring out the best thing for a Black boy who the principal doesn't want associating with a white girl? I'll bet Driscoll didn't dump this on Leah. I'll bet she never calls her about Emily being disruptive."

Luka didn't have an answer to that. "I don't care. As long as he's getting the best education possible. Which means, we should take Viola Reed's invitation of a scholarship to Cambria Prep seriously."

"Token Black kid—those snobby rich boys will eat him for lunch," Pops said. "Or get his ass arrested when they push things too far. And you know the parents and teachers won't tolerate anything from Nate. He'll be on his own."

"It could be a great opportunity," Janine put in. "If they're offering a full scholarship, might be worth a look. If he stays there through high school, it could mean a better choice of colleges, put him on a career path he might not have otherwise."

"I'll call her, learn more," Luka said. "And I have a meeting set up with Ms. Driscoll and Nate's new teacher later this week—if we don't decide to move him to Cambria Prep."

He eyed the clock on the wall and sighed. As much as he'd rather stay here and figure out Nate's future, he had cases that wouldn't solve themselves. Time to get to work.

As if on cue, his phone rang. He glanced at it, certain it would be Harper, upset that he'd asked Maggie to reschedule Lily Nolan's autopsy, but was surprised to see that it was Leah.

"Morning," he said when he answered it.

"How's your leg?" Before he could answer, she continued, "Remember that patient I asked for your help with?"

"Your Jane Doe who almost had her baby in front of the kids? Yeah, she's pretty unforgettable."

"I couldn't say more last night, not with the kids there," she started with a rush of words. "But Nate may have taken some photos of her at the fair and Emily said she saw her throw a phone away. Emily's grounded because of how she acted last night—and I apologize again about that—but do you think it would be okay for Nate to come over today so she can look at his photos? Emily remembers exactly when and where—"

"You know that photographic memory of hers is going to get you in trouble someday. But yeah, fine with me."

"Great, thanks. I've been up all night worried about her—Beth, my patient, not Emily. Well, Emily, too, but that's different. Why wouldn't she tell us her name? Who was she running from? I thought if the kids can pinpoint where Beth tossed her phone, we could get it, check her contacts, see who she is and if she needs help—"

He'd grabbed his crutches and was hobbling across the room and so almost missed the implications of what she had said. "Wait, slow down. Who exactly is *we*? Because if it's me, then I have no authority to—"

"I can't shake this feeling of dread. My worry is that Beth's a victim of domestic violence, on the run from someone. Luka, if you'd seen her face—" She finally took a breath. "We need to help her."

Luka frowned. "Technically she hasn't committed a crime—unless the hospital wants to prosecute her for not paying her bill, but that wouldn't be until after she was discharged." He thought about it. "I could speak with her if you think it would help."

"Would you mind? The nurses were talking about getting a psych consult, but she's definitely not psychotic or delusional, she's good old-fashioned scared witless. She needs to know she's protected and that her baby is safe here, then she might open up. After that, we can get her into a shelter or whatever help she needs."

"Leah. I know you're worried about Beth and her baby, but you need to understand that I can't force her to talk. She's hasn't committed any crime that I know of and, even if she had, she'd still have the right to say nothing."

"I know, I know."

He could sense her anxiety threading through her words and couldn't help but wonder how much was actually driven by Beth's predicament and how much was about Emily and her tantrum last night.

"When do you think you can get over here?" she asked.

"You're already at Good Sam?"

"Yes." She sounded a bit sheepish. "Came in early to see Beth, but her nurse said she was sleeping, so I'm in my office."

He glanced at the clock. It was too early to have any preliminary results from the Standish autopsy, but maybe by the time he'd finished talking with Beth? It'd be good to have some information to prepare for his interviews with Tassi and Foster Dean scheduled for later today. He'd been hoping to get some paperwork done, follow up on his other open cases, but... "I'm on my way."

"Thanks, Luka. I owe you."

# CHAPTER TWENTY-ONE

Leah hung up the phone, able to take a deep breath for the first time since she'd arrived at her office before seven this morning. She'd woken with the sun—not that she'd slept more than an hour or so, not that she ever slept through a full night since Ian had been killed. But last night was different. Usually she was tossing and turning, worrying about Emily, about what she could be doing better, remembering how Ian was such a natural at parenting, thinking about how much she missed him…

Last night she couldn't stop thinking about Beth. The haunted, driven look on her face when Leah had found her. Her words kept echoing through Leah's mind every time she'd closed her eyes: *Help me. I can't let them find me. Can't let them find us. Help me.*

Who was Beth, and who was she running from? Leah had to know; she couldn't shrug it aside. Of course, Luka was right; Beth didn't have to tell them anything. If she didn't, then Leah would have to find another way to help—maybe by finding Beth's phone. But she was hoping Luka would be able to get Beth talking. He had an easy way about him, at once gentle and understanding but also strong and protective.

While she waited for Luka, she tried to distract herself with work. After Ian's murder, she'd left the ER with its evening and overnight shifts to take the job of medical director of Good Sam's Crisis Intervention Center. While she still did some hands-on interventions herself, like providing forensic interviews for the police, the vast majority of her new job had turned out to be managing a near-constant budget crisis.

When she took over the department, it quickly became clear that they'd need additional funding. Thankfully, her assistant had a nose for finding grant money that would allow the CIC to continue its victim advocacy work here at Good Sam as well as providing mobile crisis response teams staffed by psychiatric social workers and specially trained EMS providers. Now that the money had been earmarked, it was Leah's job to find people to fill those positions, hence the early morning arrival at the office to go through the résumés and decide who to interview.

The current staff functioned well together, so Leah needed to find people who would fit in with them. But she also needed the type of person who would be able to function independently on the streets alongside the police. It was a tricky balance—as she'd seen herself during her early days working with Luka's team—and required the right personality.

"I need to talk to them all," she muttered as she clicked from one perfectly formatted résumé to the next. Words on a screen were meaningless; she needed to meet them to see if they had the right skill set, to tell how they might react in a crisis.

A knock on her door startled her. Luka poked his head inside, leaning on his crutches. "Your assistant wasn't here yet, so—"

"Thanks for coming. I really appreciate it." She closed down her computer and stood. "How's the leg?"

"Hurts like a sonofabitch if I stop to think about it or if I move it or anything touches it or the wind blows the wrong way. Other than that, it's fine."

"Translation: noncompliant patient refuses to take his pain medication or follow doctor's orders to rest."

He rolled his eyes at her. "Thought I was the one doing you a favor?"

"Sorry, sorry. You're right." Leah led the way to the elevator and up to the OB floor. The Labor and Delivery area was buzzing with activity and the waiting room was overflowing with anxious family members.

"Her name's Beth?" Luka asked as Leah used her keycard to get them through the secure doors separating the nursery and postpartum wing from the rest of the floor.

"That's what she told me." They passed the large, glass-walled nursery. Leah glanced inside—no sign of Beth's baby under the warmers. Which meant he was stable enough to stay in Beth's room, a good sign. The nurse covering the nursery seemed busy, so Leah decided she'd check the baby's chart after they saw Beth.

They reached Beth's room. The door was shut and a "Mother nursing" sign hung on the doorknob. Leah knocked softly, then when there was no answer, she rapped louder.

Luka shifted his weight nervously from one crutch to the other. "Maybe we should come back later," he said, eyeing the sign with trepidation.

"You can face down men with guns, no problem, but a mom nursing her baby makes you nervous?"

He shrugged. "I don't want to make her more anxious, is all. A strange man—"

"Let me check on her and we'll see." Leah edged the door open and peered inside. The lights were off, the room dark. "Beth? It's Leah. I wanted to see how you—"

No answer. The room felt empty, and as her eyes adjusted, guided by the small red lights that marked the call buttons at the bedside, she realized that Beth wasn't there. Leah snapped the lights on. The room was vacant, with no signs of Beth or her baby other than an IV bag, its tubing dangling on the floor, leaking into a puddle.

She rushed to the bathroom. Empty. Then back out to the hall where Luka waited. "They're gone."

"How? The hospital has a security system for newborns."

She started toward the nurses' station and he followed, his crutches thumping against the linoleum.

"Perhaps she's taking a walk, stretching her legs."

"I didn't see her baby in the nursery."

"How could you tell? They all look alike."

They reached the nursery. Leah rapped on the glass and the nurse on duty looked up from her chart. Using her keycard, Leah opened the locked door. "Have you seen Beth Doe? Or her baby boy?"

The nurse frowned. "They're in her room."

"No. I was just there."

"Hang on. She's not mine and things are crazy around here today—worse than a full moon." She checked the computer. "Yeah, Katie's note says the baby's temp was stable so she took him to mom's room to nurse. Said they showed good bonding, baby latched on no trouble, and she left them after answering mom's questions." She glanced up at Leah. "That was over two hours ago."

Luka stepped forward, swinging his jacket open to reveal his badge. "Can you check the baby's location using its monitor bracelet?"

The nurse clicked a few more keystrokes then relaxed. "He's right where he should be. Room 616."

"We just came from there," Leah told her. "They aren't there."

"They have to be," the nurse protested. "You must have the wrong room." She summoned a nursing assistant via the intercom. "Watch things for me, will you? I'll only be gone a second." Then she beckoned to Leah and Luka to follow her. She strode down the hallway until she reached Beth's room. Leah and Luka joined her inside. "I don't understand. The computer says both mom and baby are here. Right here."

Luka pulled back the sheets from the bed. Nestled in the center of the mattress were two monitor bracelets. "Call security. Lock it down." He glanced up at the nurse, whose mouth had dropped open. "Lock it down. Now."

# CHAPTER TWENTY-TWO

Harper didn't understand why everybody hated it when Ford Tierney was assigned to do the postmortem on their cases. She liked the man. Yeah, he took forever, but he always gave you a straight answer once he'd taken the time to verify all his findings. And, while he never wanted to talk about the circumstances of a case—the science should speak for itself, he said—he never seemed to mind when she asked questions. Maybe because she never challenged him, instead merely sought to understand.

Still, Harper wished she was anywhere else but here, sitting in the small observation area elevated to give a bird's-eye view of the gruesome proceedings as the assistant medical examiner conducted his examination of Spencer Standish's body. She wanted to head to Lily's rehab facility in person but instead she'd had to rely on a phone conversation. She'd been on hold for twenty minutes, so she hung up and tried again, hoping to get someone other than the snippy administrator she'd first spoken with, who'd seemed unhappy with Harper's promise of a court order to follow, if she could just give Harper Lily's next of kin information now. This time another woman, who identified herself as a volunteer manning the front desk, picked up.

It was Harper's first bit of luck on Lily's case. The volunteer was young, bored, eager to chat, and oblivious to patient confidentiality statutes. Yes, she remembered Lily—one of their success stories. And did Harper know, Lily had only come to rehab because she'd almost died of an OD and her best friend had brought her and promised to go through the program with her? It was so sad that Lily ended up clean and sober, finishing her program, while the friend had been kicked out after trading sex for drugs with another patient.

"Do you remember the friend's name?"

"Sure. Macy. Like the Thanksgiving parade with all the balloons."

"I'm trying to contact Lily's family," Harper said. "To inform them of what's happened. I can send you a court order to release the information, but that will take a little time. Could you—"

"Let me look." Harper could hear her keyboard clicking, and she waited patiently for a few moments. "No, sorry. Lily listed Macy as her emergency contact and Macy listed Lily. Guess they only had each other as family. Better than a lot of folks we see, though. I don't understand how so many people can find themselves so alone, with no one."

Harper did, but she didn't say anything to jade the volunteer's hopeful outlook on life. The girl was still young; she'd learn in time. "Thanks, you've been very helpful."

"I'm sorry about Lily."

Harper ended the call and turned her attention back to the autopsy. Tierney finished going over Maggie's notes and the timeline she'd constructed using the firefighters' data, comparing the garage's carbon monoxide levels to what was in Standish's blood. "Maggie's right," he said after checking a few calculations. "This man did not die of carbon monoxide poisoning. His blood levels are much too low."

"If it wasn't the carbon monoxide that killed him, could it have been something related to his cancer?" she asked.

"Cancer?"

"Yes. The wife said he'd been treated in the past, but it had come back."

Tierney tutted over the blood work, shaking his head. "There is nothing abnormal here except his cholesterol is a bit high. What kind of cancer?"

"Wife didn't say."

"Hmmm… Well, let's let the body tell the story. The body never lies." It was the kind of pompous pronouncement that Luka found irritating, but Harper felt strangely reassured by the prospect of answers and a concrete way to find them that didn't rely on unreliable witnesses.

It took almost two hours of slicing and dicing before Tierney had finished his dissection of the body, leaving only Spencer's head still intact. "I don't think this man ever had cancer," he finally said, his voice crackling through the speaker in the observation room, getting Harper's full attention.

"Never? As in he doesn't have it now—"

"Never as in, there's no sign of past disease, but what is even more suspicious is there is no evidence of any treatment. And he certainly does not have cancer now."

"His wife acted as if his cancer was terminal. If he didn't have cancer, then why kill himself?" She was musing out loud, puzzling through the facts and assumptions. Just because the scene looked like a suicide, didn't mean it was a suicide.

"I can't speak to that as I haven't found the cause of death yet." He turned to his assistant, Joel. Tierney was constantly snapping at him, expecting him to somehow read his mind and know what he needed next. Harper could tell that he would have preferred if Maggie never got a day off work. "Did you find the films yet?"

Usually Maggie would take full body X-rays in any suspicious death case and have them ready for Tierney to examine before he started working with the body. But there'd been some screw-up somewhere and today Tierney was forced to examine the body while waiting for his X-rays.

"Yes, sir." Joel snapped to attention and flicked a large computer screen on. "Here they are." He moved to prepare the head and neck for dissection, cleaning and covering the rest of the body, while Tierney reviewed the films.

"Well, now. Harper, look at this." He tapped the computer and an enlarged view of the skull films appeared on Harper's screen in the observation area. "See this?"

Harper sent a silent prayer of thanks to Maggie. In the spring, when she'd first been assigned to Luka's squad and had been lost in a sea of forensic knowledge that she'd never had to use out on the street, Maggie had given her informal tutorials. Tierney traced a thin black line that threaded the otherwise white bones of Spencer's upper neck.

"A fracture?" Harper hazarded a guess and was rewarded with a nod from Tierney. She touched her own neck in the same area, immediately below the base of her skull. "Cervical spine—that's bad, right?"

"For this gentleman, worse than bad. Fatal. Both odontoid processes, extending into the body of the second cervical vertebrae."

"Is that what killed him?" Harper asked. A broken neck—she hadn't been expecting that. Neither had Luka—although he had suspected that Spencer hadn't killed himself, she remembered.

"Unless I find another injury, yes." He whirled back to the cadaver and grabbed a scalpel. "Let's see if I'm right." As he slid the knife around the face, prepping to reflect the skin back over the scalp to reveal the skull, Harper averted her gaze—she hated this part.

"With his neck broken like that, would he have been paralyzed right away? Or might he have lived long enough to make it to his car, turn it on?" Because someone *had* started the car—the question was, could it have been Spencer himself? Perhaps this was all an accident, only Spencer had succumbed to his injuries before he could leave the garage? But if so, why did he have his suicide note and confession with him?

Unless someone else had placed them there. The widow would be a good bet, given that the confession exonerated her. Who else stood to profit from Spencer taking the fall for conning all those people? Except, so far, her alibi seemed to check out.

Tierney waited until he had the brain and spine exposed and could determine the extent of the damage before answering her question. "If you're hypothesizing that he managed to walk to his car, open the door, climb in, and turn it on—no, in my opinion there's little possibility he could have managed any of that. I think he would have dropped where he was injured. The injury would have killed him approximately ten to fifteen minutes later without medical intervention. In my opinion," he repeated in a tone that suggested that his opinion was as good as fact. Which, knowing Tierney, it probably was.

"How would a fracture like that happen?"

"A rapid deceleration injury combined with the angle of impact. We see this type of injury in diving accidents, pedestrians—especially children—struck by automobiles, slip and falls, such as where a person lands hitting their occiput on a step or curb."

A step. Like the running board below the SUV's driver's door. "What killed him?"

He glanced up from his probing of the neck bones. "That's the unfortunate part. You see, if he'd received prompt medical attention, the fracture could have been stabilized and he might have survived. But as it was, a spinal injury that high, the accompanying swelling would have eventually compressed the nerves that control the muscles of the rib cage and diaphragm. Basically, his breathing would have become more and more shallow until, eventually, he asphyxiated."

Suffocated, she translated. A horrible way to go. "But if he was paralyzed as soon as he fell, then someone else must have placed him in the car." Unless... "Any signs that he was moved after he died?"

"No. All indications are that he died sitting up in the driver's seat."

Meaning, Standish hadn't been alone in the garage. Someone had moved him into the car and made his death appear a suicide—

all while he was slowly suffocating to death. "So, we're talking premeditated murder."

Tierney met her gaze through the glass separating them. He gave her a grin that suggested she was asking the right questions. "Excellent reasoning, Detective. Find your answers and you find the person or persons who left this man to die."

# CHAPTER TWENTY-THREE

"Code indigo, nursery," the calm yet authoritative tones of the hospital operator sounded from every speaker. "All personnel, be advised, code indigo, nursery."

"I take it that's us," Luka said, as he waited, on hold with hospital security. Good Sam's campus encompassed several buildings connected by a maze of tunnels, two parking structures, and three off-campus parking lots. It was a big area to cover with only a handful of personnel.

"Code black is anyone with a weapon, code silver is for a missing dementia patient, and code indigo is a missing child," Leah told him. They sat together inside the locked nursery where she was going over Beth Doe's chart and was on hold with the social worker who had visited her last night.

Leah held a hand up and turned her focus to the phone. "This is Dr. Wright. I need to talk to you about Beth Doe. You did a consult on her."

Luka was still on hold, so Leah put her phone on speaker. "Why?" the social worker answered, sounding hurried. Luka glanced at her name in the chart, it wasn't someone he recognized from his work with Leah's Crisis Intervention Team.

"Your note says she refused services."

"Right, because she did. What's this all about?" Now the social worker sounded defensive.

"I need to know exactly what you saw and what she said. What was her affect? Did she mention a plan, a home, any friends or

SAVE HER CHILD                    149

family she'd be contacting? What safety net does she have to help her with the baby? Was the baby in the room? How were they interacting?" Leah spit off the questions in rapid fire, clearly annoyed. "You know, basic foundation of any social work consult."

"My God, it's her, isn't it? She's the code indigo."

"And you might have been the last person to see her." Leah was exaggerating; they already knew the nurses had seen Beth after the social worker, but sometimes a bit of melodrama loosened tongues. "By the way, I'm here with Detective Sergeant Luka Jericho of the Violent Crimes Unit. He's also waiting to speak with you. We're up in the nursery; when you get here, we'll buzz you in." Because of the lockdown, most of the hospital keycodes were deactivated.

The social worker blew her breath out. "I'm on my way."

While they waited, Luka read the nursing notes. "They were getting ready to discharge mom even though the pediatricians wanted to watch the baby another day? How does that work?"

"Blame it on insurance," Leah replied. "They only cover twenty-four hours after delivery, then the mom is kicked out unless she has complications. But if we have room available, the nurses are really good at finding ways to let mom stay; they call it 'nesting.'"

"A woman just gave birth and you kick her out on the street?"

"It's either that or the hospital won't get paid anything for violating the insurance guidelines. And what good does it do anyone if no one can use the hospital? I mean, no wonder our infant and child mortality rate—not to mention the number of women who die of pregnancy and delivery complications—is the same as most third-world countries. It's not because doctors and nurses are stupid or we don't want to do our jobs; it's because politicians and business people are lining their pockets with money meant to go to patient care. The insurance companies have skimmed everything they can from the health care industry and there's nothing left."

She took a breath and Luka held up his hand to indicate that he was no longer on hold. The security chief had been rambling for a few moments, but since none of what he said was helpful, Luka had barely listened.

"These are vulnerable missing persons," he told the chief. "I need you to pull the video of any vehicles leaving campus, as well as all entrances and exits over the last two hours." He hung up before the chief could sputter a protest.

Two hours. Beth and her baby could be anywhere by now. He turned to Leah. "If Beth had provided her details, had insurance to pay, followed all your hospital procedures except she left with her baby before the paperwork was done, would you consider her or the baby at risk? Enough to warrant a manhunt? Because with us already two hours behind, that's what it will take—we'll need more than my people, we'll need state police, maybe even the feds, public service announcements, which means getting the press involved as well."

Her glare was answer enough, but he needed more. "I'm playing devil's advocate, here, but to my knowledge Beth hasn't broken any laws. So unless I can prove to a judge that she and her child are at risk—"

"Luka, she was terrified," Leah protested.

"Of what? Of who?"

"I don't know." Frustration creased her forehead. "What about an Amber Alert for the baby?"

They both knew she was grasping at straws. Amber Alerts were only issued when you had descriptions of the suspects and their vehicle. Otherwise, they only served to alarm the public and alert the subjects that the police were searching for them. "An Amber Alert for his own mother? We have no evidence that anyone else is involved or that they've been kidnapped—"

"We have no evidence they weren't."

"We also have no evidence that Beth wasn't delusional. Possibly her fears were a result of a mental illness, not based in reality?"

Leah directed her sigh at the phone where she'd hung up from the social worker. "We should know that—if the social worker did a proper consult."

"And we have no evidence that the baby is at risk, being with her? You said so far everything looked fine, the pediatricians were monitoring him, right?"

"Yes, but…" She trailed off. "I can't prove anything, but Luka, trust me, I know, I just know. This isn't a case of a woman who mistrusts doctors or modern medicine. She was truly, genuinely terrified. She didn't just leave. She *ran*."

"There's not much I can do, legally. But I'll review the hospital security footage, see if we can identify how she left, if she used a vehicle. And if she was with anyone."

"It's been two hours. She could be anywhere. If she has a car, she could be in Pittsburgh, Philly, New York, DC, Baltimore. And from there—"

"She doesn't have any ID, a credit card or a phone," he reminded her. "She has no money. So wherever she went, her first stop would need to be to get those things." Unless Beth had other plans for herself and her baby. For some reason all he could think of was Spencer's suicide plan—throwing himself off a bridge. Luka envisioned Beth and her baby sprawled at the bottom of a ravine. "You knew her better than anyone. Do you think she'd hurt her baby?"

Leah's eyes went wide. "No. No." If the first denial was vehement, the second was a little uncertain. "No. I don't think so. She seemed totally focused on the baby's safety. She was afraid someone was going to take him."

The buzzer sounded—the social worker waiting to be admitted. Leah saved Luka the pain of getting his crutches and went to let her in. "I'm Dr. Leah Wright and this is Detective Sergeant Luka Jericho." She made introductions as they all took seats in the narrow charting area.

"Lise Haywood." She sat hunched forward, hugging a binder to her chest. She was younger than Luka had imagined from her voice, but the expression in her eyes—that, he recognized; he'd seen it too many times in cops. Burnout. "I didn't do anything wrong. I did my job. That's all."

"You showed up for work and you'll get paid for your hours, but as to doing your job—" Leah snapped, surprising Luka. He caught her eye, reminding her that despite the unusual circumstances, this was still a witness interview. Funny, because he'd seen her face down a man with a gun without flinching or losing her calm. But the idea of someone letting down one of her patients sparked her fury.

"Look." Haywood's tone was one of aggrievement. As if she'd heard this before. Or maybe she felt guilty. "Talk to my supervisor, if you've got a complaint. You know how many—"

"All we want to know," Luka put in, keeping his voice low and friendly, "is about this one case. Your professional impressions. We need you to be our eyes and ears."

Haywood shifted in her seat, focusing on Luka, her back to Leah. She opened her binder, her gaze never raising from its scrawled notes. "Okay, then. I found her to be calm, attentive and caring for her infant, with no suicidal or homicidal ideation. No obvious cognitive defects or signs of delusions or psychosis. She simply refused to give any identifying information. I'm not sure whether that's not within her constitutional rights, by the way. I mean, if she was Amish, we wouldn't be hassling her for wanting to leave as soon as possible or even insisting on a home birth. And it's not my job to ensure that she is able to pay her hospital bill. So, without any further cooperation forthcoming from her, and no signs of any mental illness that might pose a risk to mother or child, my assessment was completed."

"No, it wasn't," Leah interjected. "What about discharge planning? Transportation? Money for food? Adequate housing? Were you planning to let her and her baby leave with nowhere to go?"

"No." Haywood ignored Leah, speaking directly to Luka. "My plan was, since the baby was being monitored for forty-eight hours for possible GBS infection, I was going to return later today and focus our next meeting on the infant's needs upon discharge. I had no indication that mother and child would abscond prior to that meeting." She stood, her grip on her binder white-knuckled. "I really can't tell you anything more and I have other clients waiting."

Luka waved her out. Once the door shut, Leah said, "Why weren't you tougher on her? She might have seen something that gave us an idea of where Beth went."

"No. She wouldn't have. I'll bet if we asked her to pick Beth out of a line-up, she wouldn't even know what she looked like. Probably buried her head in her notes, checking off everything so she could move to her next case."

Leah made a noise of disgruntlement that Luka sympathized with. He was used to less than helpful witnesses, but clearly she'd expected more from a fellow healthcare professional. He remembered when they'd first met and she'd been a suspect in her husband's murder. He'd interviewed the ER staff and the consensus had been that Leah pushed her team hard, striving for excellence. The only person she was harder on was herself.

"When'd you learn how to be such a good bad cop?" he asked, hoping to joke her out of her foul mood.

"From you and Ray when you interrogated me after Ian was killed."

He hated to tell her, but they'd taken it easy on Leah. "What's GBS? She said the baby was being monitored for it."

"Group B strep. A type of bacteria that can spread from the mom to the baby during birth."

"Is it serious?" His phone buzzed. A text from Harper that Spencer's autopsy had yielded a preliminary cause of death, asking him to call her.

"It can be. Can cause meningitis, sepsis. Most moms at risk get antibiotics before delivery to prevent it in the baby, but—"

"Beth delivered him before she could get any. So the baby needs medication?"

"No. From his chart, he looked so good that the pediatricians decided to monitor him clinically after checking cultures. If he's doing well and the cultures don't show any bacteria after forty-eight hours, the baby is safe to go home."

"Which means he's still in the danger zone."

She nodded, her expression grim. "Technically, yes. But I'm more worried about Beth's state of mind. The doctors and nurses would have all explained the risk to her baby, the need to monitor him. So what was so terrifying that she'd risk her baby's life by running?"

# CHAPTER TWENTY-FOUR

As Harper waited for Tierney to finish his exhaustive examination of Spencer Standish's body, she followed up with the CSU techs who were examining the SUV he died in.

"Double-check for any signs of blood or hair," she instructed them. "He died of a head wound and with the black paint and upholstery—"

"We know how to look for blood," the tech cut her off. "But we'll double-check. I'll follow up on the other samples from the garage as well."

"Thanks. Anything from the car's computer? It would help with calculating TOD." If she could tell Tierney the exact time the car was turned on, compared to Standish's carbon monoxide levels and the time his body was found, along with other variables like temperature, then she hoped he would be able to calculate a narrow window for their time of death.

"Yeah, sure. Hang on." The sound of computer keys echoed through the line. "Let's see. The engine was started at 8:04. Hmm, he must have been close to the car with his phone, because there's a call showing at that exact same time—maybe he was already on the phone and it switched to the car's Bluetooth when he got close to the car? If so, that would mean he started the car himself."

An image formed in Harper's mind. Standish in his garage, doors still shut, using his key fob to remotely start the car, walking toward it while speaking on his phone. But before he either got into the driver's seat—or perhaps he had gotten inside the car but left it again—he fell, breaking his neck. An accident? Or was he attacked by whoever moved him into the driver's seat and left him to die? Either way, there had to be a second person present, and that person's act of abandoning Standish constituted premeditated murder. "We're still missing his phone. Can you tell me who the call was with?"

"Yeah, it's listed in the car's contacts. Says he was talking to a Matthew Harper." He paused. "Any relation?"

"How long did the call last?" Harper asked. The Reverend had been the last person to speak to Spencer before he was killed? Why hadn't he told the police?

"Not sure. It wasn't dialed through the car, so he might already have been connected as he got into the car and started it? Anyway, it was disconnected four seconds after the engine started."

"Four seconds?" Long enough for someone to reach inside the SUV and grab the phone from Spencer. Had her father heard the killer?

"Does that help?"

"Yeah, thanks." She hung up and passed the information about the timing on to Tierney.

"Fits with what I'm finding," the medical examiner told her. "My guess is that he'd started the car, was hit on the head—or hit his head on something—and while unconscious he was placed inside the car, the engine left running. He breathed in a few minutes of exhaust, enough to raise his blood carbon monoxide to the levels we found, but not high enough for the CO to kill him before the lung failure from the cervical spinal fracture caused fatal asphyxiation. Now," he warned her in a stern tone. "That's a working hypothesis, only. I'll be repeating the calculations and need to complete my microscopic examination of the tissues before I rule for certain."

For Tierney to bend his rules and go as far as offering a hypothesis was a small miracle. One that Harper would gladly take. She turned to leave, then turned back, remembering her other case. "When do you think you'll get to Lily Nolan?"

"Who?"

"The girl found in the alley yesterday morning."

"Right." He glanced at the clock—it was almost eleven—then at the corpse before him. "Perhaps tomorrow? I saw Maggie's notes and the films; it looks pretty clear-cut. But I won't know for sure until I see for myself."

Harper blew her breath out in frustration. But then she had a thought. "Maggie said she died of a blow to the head. Her body was beaten—I thought to make it look like a robbery gone wrong. And Spencer Standish also died from a blow to the head, but his death was staged to look like suicide—"

Tierney glanced over his glasses at her, his expression stern. "Detective, I know you're new at this, but you can't go leaping to conclusions, not without evidence. And right now, I have no evidence that the two deaths are related."

"But—"

"Do you know how many people die of head injuries any given year?"

*Yeah, but how many of them were victims of homicide?* Harper had the urge to shoot back. But she kept her silence, knowing that Tierney was right; she didn't have any evidence to connect the two cases. In fact, the only real connection between Lily and Spencer was Harper herself—it was only because she knew the details from both cases that they appeared similar. Luka had warned her about that, had called it the "fallacy of confirmation bias."

She forwarded him the information about the time and cause of death. But she hesitated about adding that the Reverend was the last person to speak with Standish while he was alive. That particular tidbit seemed to require a conversation—as uncomfortable as it would be to tell Luka that her father might be more involved with the case than they'd suspected.

But she couldn't believe he'd bury evidence of a killer. What had he heard during Standish's final call? Maybe nothing. Maybe the call had been a simple follow-up after the Reverend had counseled Standish about his confession.

Except… it'd been Sunday morning. And the Reverend did not allow anything—legal work, family, breaking news, the house could be on fire—nothing interrupted his Sunday morning prayers as he prepared to preach his first service of the day. And yet, he'd taken a call from Spencer Standish.

She left the morgue, pausing at a vending machine to grab an energy bar before calling Luka. "The techs found something," she said. "Standish made a call that was cut off seconds after he started the car engine. Probably about the same time he was attacked and his phone taken. Well, maybe."

"Call to who?" Luka sounded distracted.

She swallowed. The good thing about the call between the Reverend and Standish was that it gave the Reverend a rock-solid alibi for Standish's murder. "My father."

There was a pause; she heard voices in the background. "Yeah, okay. I'll deal with him later. Right now, we've something more urgent. Are you still in the hospital?"

More urgent than finding a killer? "Yeah, I'm downstairs in the morgue. What happened?"

"A mother and her newborn child have disappeared from the hospital. I've locked down the area and am heading to security to review the tapes."

A critical missing person case took priority over everything. Harper spun on her heel and jogged to the nearest stairwell, not wanting to wait on the elevator. "What can I do?"

"I need you to help Leah. She suspects the mother might have been a victim of domestic violence, on the run from her partner, and she's going to start canvassing the shelters and outreach programs."

At first Harper was tempted to protest the assignment; it felt so minor, as if she was being sidelined again. If she wasn't going to play a role in finding the mother and child, then why not focus on her own case? She itched to follow up with Macy—who'd conveniently never mentioned that she'd gone with Lily to rehab. What else had she hidden? But then she realized that not only did Luka's assignment give her a way to search the streets for Macy, she also had the perfect person who knew every domestic shelter worker in the county and could coordinate them to help with the search for the missing patient.

"Tell her I'll meet her in the ER in five," she told Luka.

Harper ran up the steps and through the ER and found Leah Wright waiting for her at the CIC's entrance. "There's a long list of places she might have gone to for help," she told Harper, holding her phone up. "This might take all day. I think we should start at the Salvation Army's shelter and then try the one on Maple."

Harper smiled. It wasn't often that she held the upper hand when it came to Leah. But she knew exactly who might be able to shed light on where a desperate woman fleeing someone might go. Jonah's outreach mission. Finally, one of her family members who might actually do more than criticize her career choices or call her a traitor for not betraying her badge.

She told Leah, "We need to make a quick stop first." They reached Harper's Impala parked in front of the ER. "Trust me," she told Leah as they got in.

As Harper drove, Leah was on her phone to her mother, Ruby. "Did you get my text? Yes, I know it was only ten minutes ago, but this is important. Okay, ask Nate to send anything to my phone as soon as possible. Thanks."

"What was that all about?" Harper asked.

"I'm trying to get a photo of Beth. We don't have any to circulate and without even knowing her last name—"

"Gonna be hard to ask any outside agencies to help find her, much less make a public appeal."

"Exactly." Leah sighed. "But try explaining that to Ruby."

Harper's phone buzzed. Another text from Rachel. Now that Harper knew her father had been the last to speak to Spencer Standish, she understood her mother's sudden interest in Harper's career. She hesitated. She and Leah weren't that close. But maybe that was good; maybe that meant a more objective viewpoint. Especially as they seemed to share similar situations with their families. Yet, somehow Leah had made her fraught relationship with her mother work. "You two don't get along. I mean, you didn't talk to your mother for years, not until after your husband died, right?"

"She walked out on me when I was eleven, so I guess two decades of silence counts as not talking." Leah shifted in her seat, obviously uncomfortable. Harper was tempted to simply drop the topic, but she couldn't let it go.

"And yet you talk now, she's living with you, helping with your daughter—" Harper frowned, trying to sort out her confused emotions. "How did you make that happen? How do you make it work? Was it because she changed?"

Leah drew in a breath, glanced at Harper. "Ruby will never change. But she does occasionally bend a little—for Emily's sake, not mine. And I… well, I'm still angry with her, hell, I still don't trust her. She practically promised Emily she'd win a ribbon at the fair, but when that didn't happen—" She gave a quick, angry shake of her head. "Anyway, as soon as she lets Emily down, Ruby takes off and I have to pick up the pieces." She sighed. "But I guess we have enough common ground that we make it work, even if it's only baby steps."

"Baby steps," Harper mused.

"Is this about your father? Luka mentioned that he wasn't happy that you were working a case involving one of his parishioners. Is it hard for him, a minister, seeing his daughter become a police officer?"

Harper shook her head. "It's not that I'm a cop. We had problems way before then, ever since I was in college. Maybe even before. I think I've always disappointed him, never could live up to his expectations. But you're right, baby steps. Yesterday, he actually asked about my job. So did my mom—she seems more excited about my making detective than I am. As if suddenly I'm legitimate." She held back that Rachel's interest seemed mostly motivated by the Reverend's involvement in the case—that was too humiliating to share.

"Families are hard. Even if you know they love you. I always knew Ruby loved me; that was never the issue. But she made me somehow feel like I didn't deserve that love, like I hadn't earned it. As if that made it okay for her to leave."

"Try being the only daughter of a man whose three sons joined him in the ministry. Talk about feeling unworthy. Plus, I was adopted—something that I could never forget anytime I looked in the mirror. When I was a kid it made me work twice as hard to be good enough, but after I went away to college…" No need to expose those old wounds. "Things changed."

"You became an adult, started to think for yourself, make your own choices."

"Live with my mistakes was more like it, but yeah, something like that."

"So here you are, an accomplished professional—but your parents still see you as that little girl. And you feel like you have to prove to them that you are an adult, an equal." Leah blew her breath out. "Good luck with that. I don't think Ruby will ever see me that way. Only good thing I've ever done in her eyes was to give her a granddaughter."

"Well, my folks better not be waiting for that, because it's not happening anytime soon." Harper parked in a red zone across the street from Jonah's mission.

"Then keep working those baby steps." Leah glanced out her window. "The Pierhouse Mission? You think Beth might have come here?"

They left the car, the morning sun already raising waves of scorching air from the pavement. "If not, I know someone who can help us check the other shelters and programs in a fraction of the time it'd take us." Harper led the way across the street.

"Who's that?"

"My brother Jonah. He runs the place." Harper didn't bother to hide her pride—of all her brothers, Jonah was her favorite and, to her mind, the one doing the most to make a difference. You could preach all you want, but actions always spoke louder than words. Jonah was here every day, fighting to make life better for folks who had nothing and no one.

Folks like Lily Nolan. And Beth Doe and her baby.

# CHAPTER TWENTY-FIVE

Within a few minutes of meeting Harper's brother, Leah realized that the Pierhouse Mission reflected his energy and passion. When Harper explained about Beth and her missing infant, Jonah immediately leapt into action, sending a group text to fellow shelter directors and other resources Beth might have availed herself of.

The replies came in almost as quickly: no one had seen Beth in the past and especially not today.

"I'm sorry I couldn't be of more help," Jonah told them as he escorted them out. "But we'll all keep our eyes out."

"Thanks, I appreciate it." Leah gave him some of her cards while Harper gave him a hug. It was strange to watch—Harper never revealed anything personal, kept her private life firmly divided from her work. But it was nice to see.

They'd no sooner reached the door than both of their phones chimed. Harper had a call that she answered, stepping to the side of the foyer as she spoke, her shoulders hunching with tension. Leah, however had a text—from Emily: *Found where baby lady came from at fair. Come home and we can show you.* This was followed by a chorus of emojis including a carousel, baby, hearts, and a smiley face blowing a kiss.

Since Jonah and his associates had pretty much blanketed the city with alerts for Beth, Leah didn't have much else to do to help other than trying to find Beth's cell phone. She typed back: *on my way, good work!* And waited for Harper to finish her conversation. When the other woman hung up, a scowl filled her face.

"Something wrong?" Leah asked.

"No. Krichek's filling my inbox with scut work. He's sent me a list of license plates to trace, says he's too busy. It's not as if I don't have my own case to work on as well."

"Mind dropping me back at Good Sam so I can get my car? The kids reviewed their photos from the fair and think they might have figured out where Beth came from and where she threw her phone out. Maybe we can finally get an identification."

"Not to mention GPS tracking of where she was before the fair." Harper nodded. "Sounds like a better lead than anything I have. Let's go."

"What about your license plates?"

"They can wait."

A blast of heat hit Leah as they left the mission. The old building didn't have air conditioning, but its solid architecture and ceiling fans had kept the inside comfortable. She couldn't remember last summer being this hot, not so hot that the concrete sidewalks and the blacktop roads were shimmering with steam.

Despite wearing a jacket over her blouse, Harper seemed impervious, leading the way back to the car baking in the sun. Suddenly, she stopped, her hand dropping to her gun, gaze fixed on something down the block.

"Wait here," she told Leah as she took off at a stride that covered the ground faster than most people did while jogging.

Leah stood beside the car—she didn't have the keys, so there was nowhere else to go—and shielded her eyes from the sun to see what had caught Harper's attention. At the end of the block, a man was shouting at a girl he had pinned against a bright orange sports car. Leah couldn't make out any words, but when she saw him slap her, she set off after Harper, who had her phone out, talking to someone as she moved down the street.

"Darius, I'm sorry," the girl cried as Leah drew nearer, keeping behind Harper. "I couldn't help it—"

Darius raised his hand again, this time curling it into a fist. But then he caught sight of Harper, who'd stopped about ten yards away. "What do you want?" he demanded, lowering his hand and slipping it into his pocket. "This ain't none of your business."

Harper said nothing, merely shifted her weight so that her jacket slid open, revealing her badge and gun.

"Go away!" the girl shouted. "We're fine." Except, from the way her words slurred, Leah doubted that was true.

"Doesn't look that way to me, Macy." Harper's gaze never left the man's hands. "Come over here, Macy." Then she addressed the man. "Sir, I'm Detective Harper. I'd like to see your hands. You can wait right there while I speak with Macy about one of her friends."

Smart, Leah thought, applauding Harper's attempts at defusing the situation. Letting Darius know he wasn't the reason why she was there, trying to get Macy out of his reach, repeating the girl's name to forge a connection, while keeping things professional.

Unfortunately, Darius didn't see things that way. Instead, he grabbed Macy's arm, pulling her close to him. "She ain't going nowhere. Like she said, leave us alone, we're fine, don't need no police."

"Happy to," Harper replied. "Soon as I've talked with Macy. She's a witness in a murder investigation."

"Murder?" Darius' voice rose, both in pitch and volume, and his posture immediately shifted into an aggressive stance. His grip on Macy tightened. "What'cha tell this bitch, Macy? You tell the cops I killed someone?"

"No, I never—" Macy's words were cut short by a strangled cry as Darius pulled a knife and held it to her throat.

"I didn't kill no one!" he shouted at Harper. His eyes grew wide as a patrol car pulled across the intersection down the block, two officers emerging, weapons drawn. Darius dragged Macy across the sidewalk until his back was to the brick wall and she shielded him from the front. "You all got the wrong man! I didn't do nothing!"

he yelled to the patrolmen. Then he glared at Harper. "This bitch is trying to frame me! I'm innocent."

Harper realized her mistake and backed away, motioning for the other officers to hold their position. Leah saw the frustration cross her face at how events had escalated so quickly—less than a minute had passed since they'd left the mission. When she glanced over her shoulder, she saw a crowd gathering in the shade of the mission's awning, spectators using their phones to record the event, their faces filled with anger and mistrust.

As the crowd began to shout at the police, voicing support for Darius, several raising their own hands over their heads, yelling, "Hands up, don't shoot!" Leah realized that the police, including Harper, weren't going to be able to easily calm things. She glanced again at the girl, Macy. She was barely able to stay on her feet, her head lolling against Darius' shoulder. More than high—early stages of an overdose?

That made up her mind. She stepped forward to join Harper, making certain that she was on the opposite side of Harper's gun hand so she wouldn't risk crossing the detective's line of fire. "Let me try."

Harper shot her a glare but blinked and swallowed her reflexive distrust of any non-law enforcement professional. It helped that she'd seen Leah defuse a number of volatile situations during the six months that Leah had been working as a liaison between the police and the Crisis Intervention Center. "Okay, but don't get any closer. And don't block our line of fire."

Leah nodded and fixed her gaze on Darius. "Mr. Darius?" she called in a soft tone. If he was forced to listen harder, he'd also be focusing more on her words. "I'm Dr. Leah Wright. I'm not a police officer. I work at Good Samaritan's ER." As she spoke, she sidled away from Harper, not getting closer to Darius and his knife, but also distancing herself from the police physically as well as psychologically. "I want to help."

"Good. Get these cops away from me. Nothing here is any of their business."

"I'm worried about Macy. Do you think she's okay? She looks like she might need medical attention." Leah kept her voice low and steady, using an inflection that implied that Darius was in charge. "If you drop the knife, I can examine her, get her the help she needs."

"I drop the knife and these cops gonna shoot me dead."

"I'll guarantee your safety—as long as you put any weapons on the ground. Besides, you have all these witnesses."

"Like that's gonna stop them. Who they gonna blame for this? The stupid white girl?" He shook Macy, hard. Her eyes barely fluttered. "Or the Black man?" Someone in the crowd cheered at that and he glanced past Leah to his audience.

Leah needed to get his attention back on her. But before she could think of what to say next, Macy jerked her head up, her body shuddering. "Darius, I think she's going to be sick—"

Too late. Macy vomited all over herself and Darius, causing him to fling her away from him. She stumbled against the car, then sagged to the ground. Darius shook his leg, trying to shed some of the noxious liquid. He still held the knife, though, so the police maintained their alert posture. In fact, a second patrol unit had arrived, its red and blue lights bathing the scene from behind Leah.

"Darius," Leah tried again. "Is she breathing? I think Macy needs help. Would you please put down the knife so I can come over and check her?"

He frowned at his hand as if he'd forgotten the knife. Then he glanced at the crowd, but the newly arrived police officers were shepherding them back inside the mission. Macy's dramatic projectile vomiting wasn't exactly the fun they'd signed up to watch.

Leah inched forward, keeping the car between her and Darius. "What did she OD on, Darius? Help me, please. You don't want her to die, do you?"

"No," he muttered, and she wasn't sure if he was answering her question or simply responding to the overall situation. He took a step forward, leaning over, but Harper shouted, "Stop there, Darius! Don't take another step."

He jerked back, the knife at his side but still clenched in his fist. Leah tried again to regain the ground she'd lost. "Is she breathing?"

He shook his head. "I don't think so. I think she's dying." He raised his gaze to meet Leah's. "Can you really help her?"

"I can try. But only if you put the knife down. Can you do that for Macy? Can you save her life?"

He squinted at the knife in his hand like he was surprised it was still there. Then he stepped back and with careful, exaggerated movements, he lowered it to the pavement and backed away from it.

Harper and the other officers instantly swarmed him, tackling him to the ground. "Help her!" he cried out, his face pressed against the pavement, eyes pleading with Leah. "Save Macy like you promised!"

# CHAPTER TWENTY-SIX

After Luka did what he could to help with the search for Beth at Good Sam, he returned to his office at the police department, his plans for the day already delayed by several hours. He called Krichek and asked him to bring an update on the search for any footage surrounding Spencer's office, gathered what information he needed to prep for the interviews of Tassi and Dean Foster scheduled for later in the day, and finished his paperwork left over from the weekend.

Still, he couldn't stop thinking about Leah's missing patient. The hospital hadn't upgraded its security systems in decades, he'd learned to his chagrin when he'd stopped by before leaving Good Sam. The security chief, a retired cop from Pittsburgh named Ramsey, was working to organize the morning's security footage to make reviewing it as easy as possible. But it would take time before the hospital had the footage ready, and Luka had had other open cases that required his attention.

He glanced at his office clock: 11:48. Surely by now they'd found something.

"Because of patient privacy, there are no cameras inside the Labor and Delivery ward," Ramsey explained when Luka called to ask for an update. "And going through all the rest—we'll need to do it manually. Do you have a picture we can work off, yet?"

Thanks to Leah—well, actually Nate, and his curiosity and eagerness to try his portraiture skills—they had a photo from the fair where Beth's face was somewhat clear, although distant. Luka forwarded the image to Ramsey. "We need this as soon as possible." They had to consider every scenario. If there was any sign that Beth and her baby had been abducted, then precious time was slipping away.

"I already ran through the camera outside the ward and there's nothing unusual at all. Definitely no signs of a kidnapping or anything like that. And no single woman carrying a baby, only couples. My next step is to verify their identities with the nurses, but they were all accompanied by staff, so that shouldn't take long."

Luka was torn. If Beth left on her own and had no signs of mental impairment that might lead her to harm her baby, then he had no case to pursue. The most he could do was to file a missing persons report with the NCIC database so that any law enforcement officer who happened to come in contact with her would perform a welfare check, ensure that she was safe. As it was, Commander Ahearn would be incensed that Luka had wasted as much time as he had on something that wasn't even a real crime.

But… Luka trusted Leah's instincts. If she thought Beth and the baby were in danger, he owed it to her to follow up as best he could. It wouldn't be the huge manhunt that Leah would have liked—it almost never was, but civilians didn't understand that adults had every right to walk out of their lives; it wasn't a crime. And Amber Alerts for children required definitive information: detailed descriptions, makes and models of vehicles used, etc. All Luka had was Beth's first name and a blurry image. "You're sure, no signs of coercion?"

"Nope," Ramsey replied. "Which is why I canceled the code indigo."

"And there's no way Beth or the baby could still be on the ward?"

"My men and the nurses searched everywhere."

Luka glanced at the binders on his bookcase. All open cases, waiting for his attention. So many victims, the majority killed by people they loved—and who they thought loved them. "I hate to even think this," he said. "But what if Beth left on her own? Without the baby?"

"Told you, we looked—" Ramsey stopped himself. "Damn. You mean, what if she did something to the baby? Killed it?"

"Him," Luka corrected automatically. "Newborn. Tiny. Opens up a lot more potential search areas."

"We're on it. But I really hope you're wrong."

"Anything we could do to help?" A true search would mean closing down the hospital floor and anything accessed from it like trash chutes, drains, elevator shafts—it would be a time-consuming, logistical nightmare. "Perhaps a cadaver dog disguised as a service animal? A handler could take it on a quick stroll around the floor without attracting undue attention."

"Geez, and I thought I'd seen everything." Ramsey was silent for a moment. "Let me work with our people, see what we can do on our own. I've still got a dozen other cameras and hours of footage to review, but now that we have a photo, I'll also check the ward footage again, looking for a woman alone. Maybe we can get a handle on where she went." He paused. "But why? I mean, if you don't want your kid, just walk away, leave him with the doctors. It doesn't make any sense that she'd hurt the baby."

"We need to rule out every possibility."

"Well, I'm hoping like hell you're wrong." Ramsey hung up.

A knock came on Luka's open office door. Krichek.

"Got some good stuff from the Standish financials," he started. "Still working on the security footage from the strip mall and surrounding businesses. Generated an initial list of license plates. Sent them to Harper to follow up."

If Luka's attacker were any kind of professional, he would have made certain that his vehicle couldn't be traced back to him. Still, the job needed to be done if only to cross it off the list of possible leads. Scut work, Krichek called it, and the detective was obviously happy to pass it on to the newest member of their team.

Krichek swiped his tablet's screen. "I've sent the bank documents to you," he told Luka. "Bottom line is that, in addition to the funds Standish funneled through the charity to offshore accounts that we'll never be able to touch, there's also over six million missing. Cash."

"Any idea where it went?"

"I figured we'd never find it, not with Spencer's computers all wiped clean." He grinned, obviously pleased with himself. Luka nodded at him to continue. "But then Sanchez found a memory card in the printer/scanner. Kept a record of every document that went through it. Turns out Spencer's been converting the cash into gold."

Gold. The universal currency and in many ways more untraceable than cash or even Bitcoin. While actual gold was heavy and cumbersome, there were a variety of anonymous services that would exchange it for even more untraceable bearer bonds, which could be funneled into any financial account.

"Six million?" Luka repeated as he pulled up the summary report and squinted at it.

"And change. I'm guessing the wife has it—along with all the offshore account information for the rest of her payout. The stock fund and the foundation are both zeroed out." He pointed to Luka's screen. "Standish's last transactions, closing out all the accounts. On Friday."

"And then he meets with his pastor-slash-lawyer to compose his confession, making sure to exonerate his wife." The date on Spencer's confession was Saturday.

"You're thinking the widow did it?" Krichek's voice upticked. "She killed him for the money?"

Ray appeared in the doorway, not bothering to knock. "Is anybody invited to this coffee klatch?"

"What do you have?" Luka asked, noting his smile.

"Got the details on Standish's previous so-called death, the one he faked in Colorado three years ago. Did you know he was married to Tassi back then as well? Divorced her, gave her a pile of money, then a few months later Standish supposedly drowned during a fishing trip. Body never found."

"They were in it together." Krichek rocked on his heels, unable to contain his excitement.

"Only this time Standish ended up dead for real," Luka reminded him.

"Denver also confirmed that the Zapata crime family lost money in Standish's Ponzi scheme."

"Good reason to fake your death," Luka said. The Zapata family ran one of the largest crime syndicates in the United States. "I like how he protected his wife—excuse me, ex-wife—and his money at the same time; it set him up with enough cash to lay low until the heat was off."

"Then he re-emerged a few years later," Ray added. "New name, new town, same wife, same con. Guy should have quit while he was ahead."

"And alive," Krichek put in.

Luka's phone rang. Ford Tierney.

"You need to get here right away," the medical examiner said before Luka could offer a greeting. "I can't deal with these people. There's a widow demanding I not perform the postmortem I've already finished while also insisting on an expedited death certificate and some DEA guy wanting a photo of the deceased—"

"Are you talking about the Standish case?"

"Yes, of course the Standish case. I told security to keep them all in the waiting room, but I have work to do and this isn't—"

"We'll take care of it. Thanks, Dr. Tierney." Luka knew Ford would respond to his use of his formal title and a dash of politeness. "I very much appreciate your patience."

"See to it. We have grieving families here and important work that can't be disrupted with these—"

"I'm on my way." Luka hung up. Ray was sidling back out of the door while Krichek appeared intrigued. "Both of you, we're headed to the morgue."

"A hysterical widow and you need back-up?" Ray kidded him. Ray hated the morgue—although at least he didn't get queasy like Krichek did at the sight of a dead body. "Or is it Tierney you might need help with?"

"I'm thinking divide and conquer," Luka said. "We were set to interview Tassi and Dean anyway. Why not catch them while they're emotional, get as much out of them as we can before they calm down and start thinking?"

"What about Dr. Wright?" Krichek asked. "Could she help?"

Ray nodded his agreement. "After meeting the widow yesterday, I think she might get more out of her than either you or I could. I can't decide if Tassi Standish is complicit and the best actress I've ever met, or if she's as dumb as a load of bricks." That was Ray, never one to couch his opinions in politically correct terms.

"We can use the CIC interview rooms, if they aren't already booked." The Crisis Intervention Center was part of the ER and had interview rooms equipped with video and audio recording capacities. Using them would save bringing Tassi and Dean back here. Plus, Luka could see if Ramsey had found anything about Beth and her baby.

"What's Foster Dean want with a photograph of Standish?" Krichek asked.

"Proof that he's really dead," Ray answered. "And the only reason he'd need that—"

"Is if he's working for the Zapata family," Luka finished for him. Foster Dean intrigued him. Last night he'd gotten a few details from a phone call to a friend on the regional drug interdiction task force. It seemed Dean's retirement hadn't been entirely his own idea, from the rumors Luka's friend had shared. According to her, Dean had been suspected of feeding intel to the Zapata family, but nothing had been proven and he'd resigned under a cloud of suspicion.

If Dean was working for the Zapatas, it would explain why he'd been tenacious enough to follow Spencer from Colorado to Pennsylvania after Spencer had been desperate enough to fake his own death back in Denver.

Which made Tassi, as the only person involved with Spencer back in Colorado as well as his new life here, even more important as a witness. It was vital that Luka find a way to get her talking.

She hadn't responded to him or his team. Perhaps she really was too traumatized by her husband's death. If so, there was one person who could not only help ease the widow's pain but also help Luka get the answers he needed: Leah Wright.

# CHAPTER TWENTY-SEVEN

As soon as the uniformed officers had Darius restrained, Harper rushed to her car and grabbed the OD kit from the trunk. Leah rolled Macy onto her side and was monitoring her pulse.

"Heroin overdose?" Harper asked as she unwrapped one of the special nasal syringes of naloxone. She'd had to use the OD kits so many times while working patrol that she didn't even wait for Leah's answer, simply handing her the syringe.

"Definitely some sort of opiate," Leah said, shoving the reversal agent up Macy's nose and depressing the plunger. Harper kept back and noticed that Leah did as well. Naloxone immediately negated the effects of opioids, canceling an addict's high so fast that their first action as they woke was often to take a swing at whoever was closest.

Macy merely fluttered her eyes and released a groan. "Give me another dose," Leah ordered. "How far out is the ambulance?"

"Pulling up now." Harper prepped the second dose and handed it to Leah. This time they were rewarded with Macy jerking upright, looking around in confusion. But then she slumped back against the car, muttering incoherently.

"Are you guys seeing any fentanyl or carfentanyl?" Leah asked Harper as the medics took over. "I haven't heard of any cases from the ER, but she definitely took something higher grade than what we usually see."

"I'll ask, but the only cases of high-end stuff like that that I've heard of have been out of Philly and Baltimore." Harper stepped back so that the medics could push their stretcher past. "She going to be okay?"

"I hope so."

"Lucky you were here when it happened." Harper wondered how Macy had got enough cash to OD on high-grade junk—maybe that was what she and Darius were arguing about.

"I'm going to ride with her," Leah said, trotting after the medics.

"I'll be right behind you." Harper watched the ambulance leave, made sure the patrol officers were also taking Darius to Good Sam for a medical eval before they booked him, then walked back to her car. She used a liberal dose of hand sanitizer and made a note to replace the OD kit before signing the car back into the vehicle pool.

Jonah approached from the mission and rapped on her window as she was getting ready to head over to Good Sam. "I saw what happened. Is Macy going to be all right?"

"Hope so. Can you spread the word among your clients to be extra careful? Whatever she took, it was a lot more potent than regular street junk."

"Will do." He stood, then lowered his face again so that they were at eye level. "You did good today, sis."

As Harper drove to the ER, his words haunted her. Had she done good? Really? How could she have been so stupid? Stupid, stupid, stupid. She should have pushed the issue with Macy yesterday, brought her in off the streets. Now a girl had almost died because of Harper's carelessness.

The aftermath of adrenaline shook her almost as much as her guilt at her rookie mistake. She'd thought she was cultivating Macy, easing her into telling her what she needed to know about Lily's death. Should have known better. A street addict was going to do what addicts always did: chase their next fix, even if it killed them.

At least they'd gotten Darius. No way was he walking away from this. Kid was probably also high, reacting that way. The uniforms were taking him to get drug tested and cleared medically before booking him. Then it would be Harper's turn to see what Darius knew. Had he killed Lily? Maybe he thought she was trying to get Macy to go back to rehab, was trying to take Macy from him?

Too many questions, not enough answers and now one girl was dead and one almost dead.

It felt like Harper's first case as lead detective was going nowhere fast.

Harper pulled into one of the reserved parking spaces at the ER. She killed the engine, sitting in the sudden silence for a long moment, taking a few cleansing breaths. Macy was going to be okay—thanks to Leah. Darius was in custody. And soon Harper might have the answers she needed to bring Lily justice.

Those thoughts echoing in a reassuring cadence, she strode out from the car and into the ER, flashing her badge at the security guard to enter the inner sanctum.

"He give you any trouble?" she asked Miller, the patrol officer waiting at Darius' bedside.

Miller gave Darius a glare. Darius responded by closing his eyes tight and pretending to be asleep. "Nope."

"Everything by the book. Full medical eval, tox screen, and once he's cleared by the doctors and processed, call me."

"Sure thing, Harper."

Darius squinted one eye open. "Harper? That your name? Get ready, because I'm going to sue you all." He rattled his handcuffed wrist against the steel rails of the bed. "I'm going to take everything you have. This is false arrest, police brutality!"

"Shut up," Miller told him. "Save it for the judge, why don't ya?"

Not for the first time, Harper wished that Cambria City had the budget to be able to afford bodycams. But the patrol vehicles' dash cams would have caught most of the encounter—along with the civilians with their phones. There was probably already video streaming.

The thought brought her up short. Which meant Luka might at this moment be facing calls from the press—or worse, Commander

Ahearn. She knew Luka was shielding her from the commander's critical gaze, putting his own reputation on the line for her sake. And she'd let him down, big time.

Assured that Darius was in good hands, she moved down the hall to a quiet corner and called Luka. "Everyone's okay," she started, then explained what had happened. "If anything, this is good for the department," she finished. "No one fired their weapons, Leah did her crisis intervention thing, Darius is in custody—"

"How's the girl?" he asked, cutting to the heart of the matter, like always. She could tell by the background noise that he was in his car.

She glanced down the hallway to the resuscitation area. Macy wasn't in the major trauma area—a good sign, Harper thought—but rather in one of the nearby glass-walled rooms. Nurses swarmed over the girl in a well-rehearsed choreography, cutting off her clothing, covering her with a sheet as they applied monitor leads, drew blood, and inserted an IV.

"They're treating her now. I think she'll be okay."

He was silent for a long moment. "How's Leah?"

"Seriously? I think she loved it—maybe not so much the talking Darius down part. That was stressful, especially with us needing to be prepared to use force and the civilians cheering like Darius was some kind of hero. But you should have seen her, taking care of Macy. She's a good doctor."

"Listen. You're going to get questioned ten ways from Sunday about your tactics, about your motivations. Civilians and the press will ask why you didn't do something stupid like tackle an armed man, other cops might tell you you should have shot him as soon as the knife came out. But no one died today and, no matter what anyone says, that makes this a good day."

She slumped against the wall, the adrenaline that had sustained her earlier now totally dissipated. "Thanks, Luka."

"I'm headed over to Good Sam now. Tassi Standish and Foster Dean are causing some kind of ruckus in the morgue."

"Want me to leave, go down there?"

"No, you've got your hands full. Document everything, make sure it's all by the book. When you're done, let me know. I need to interview Tassi and Dean, so if the CIC rooms are open, I'll probably do it while I'm there."

"Okay." Usually she would have been pissed off, being excluded from an important interview, but now she was relieved. It gave her the freedom to see if she could get Macy talking about Lily Nolan. "Thanks, Luka."

He hung up. Harper saw the nurses had backed away from Macy, and several had left, so she took that as a sign that Macy might be stable enough to talk. She walked into the glass-walled room. Macy was on oxygen and in soft restraints, although she didn't appear to be fighting anymore. Her color was ashen, she reeked of vomit, and she barely stirred as Harper approached.

But she was alive. And from what Harper could interpret from the monitor, she was doing okay. The nurse turned to Harper, her hands full of Macy's clothing, shoes, and purse all collected in a clear plastic bag. "Detective, do you want to sign for her personal effects? I've inventoried them and found what could be drugs. The lab said her initial tox screen was positive for fentanyl, which explains why she needed multiple doses of Narcan."

Harper took possession of the bag, which was now evidence. "Are you testing for other drugs as well?"

"Yes, ma'am." Harper liked that—no one ever called her "ma'am." And the nurse wasn't even that much younger than she was. "We're running a complete tox screen."

"Thanks." She'd grab one of the uniformed officers to help her document Macy's belongings before taking them down to the station where they'd be logged into evidence. "When can I talk with her?"

The nurse shook her head. "Probably will be a while. Dr. Davidson is her attending, he can give you a better idea."

Harper glanced at Macy. She looked very small and very young, dwarfed by the medical technology surrounding her. Clutching the bag with Macy's belongings, Harper left the room and spotted Leah at the nurses' station talking with Dr. Davidson, the head of the ER.

"Any idea when I can interview Macy?" she asked them.

Leah started to answer but then stopped, no doubt remembering that Macy was no longer her patient. A quick look of yearning crossed her face and Harper realized she'd been right about how much Leah enjoyed—and missed—her life in the ER.

Dr. Davidson looked up at Harper, suspicion filling his eyes. "My patient needs rest, not an interrogation."

"I'm working a girl's murder." Harper didn't try to soften her tone or sugarcoat the facts. "And Macy OD'd on fentanyl, which means big problems for everyone—especially the ER. I need to trace her supplier." So far, Cambria City had been spared the stronger synthetic opioids smuggled in from China. Fentanyl wasn't only deadly to the addicts who inhaled or injected it; it also had the potential to be absorbed through the skin, placing every cop, EMT, paramedic, and first responder at risk.

"I understand," Davidson replied, the edge gone from his tone. "But Macy won't be ready to talk to anyone for a few hours at least."

Harper glanced at Leah, who nodded her agreement. "Thanks. I'll let you know when the lab definitively IDs the drugs we found on her."

"And we'll of course keep you apprised. I assume she's under arrest, so one of your officers will remain with her?"

"Yes. Don't worry, since she's in no condition to respond to her Miranda rights, no one will question her until she's medically clear."

"Sounds like an appropriate arrangement."

Harper swallowed a sigh of frustration and turned to leave, but Leah called her back. "Good luck, Harper."

Harper gave her a wave and walked past Darius' room on her way out. "Only thing he tested positive for was pot," Miller told her. "We're waiting for the discharge paperwork then we'll get him to the station, book him."

"Great. I have some evidence that needs to be logged in as well. Got a voucher?"

He took an evidence label from the rear of his notebook. They moved to the corner of the room where there was an empty stainless-steel table. Harper donned a pair of gloves and opened the plastic bag while Miller videoed her using his phone. They both recoiled at the noxious fumes from Macy's clothing, but Harper saw that the nurses had thoughtfully packaged her purse in its own bag. She slid that bag out, sealed the clothing bag shut, then opened the one with the purse.

The nurses had enclosed their own inventory and Harper verified it as Miller sealed each item in a separate bag: one small plastic baggie containing ten white pills consistent with OxyContin; two hand-rolled cigarettes, probably marijuana; an assortment of change in various denominations wadded up in a five-dollar bill; a syringe, tourniquet, lighter, cotton wad, spoon; a plastic bag containing unknown white powder—the fentanyl, Harper suspected, taking care not to disturb it; a cheap flip phone; a smartphone inside a glittery case; and a variety of condoms.

"Vice and Drugs are going to want to talk to her if this does turn out to be fentanyl," Miller said as he gingerly resealed the bag of powder. He hefted the bag in his palm. "Got to be almost dealer weight. Worth a pretty penny on the street if it's pure."

"If it was pure, she'd be dead." She couldn't see any dealer trusting Macy to hold such weight—and how could Macy have bought it herself? Even diluted, that much fentanyl would have cost a few thousand. Had she stolen it from someone?

She turned her attention to the two phones. The flip phone was charged and didn't require any security. She was tempted to "accidentally" access the recent texts and contacts, but anything she found could be ruled inadmissible if she needed the evidence for court, so she held off. For now. They'd be able to get a warrant easily; she just needed to be patient.

She examined the more expensive smartphone. How had Macy afforded this? A gift from Darius? Maybe the untraceable burner phone was for business and the smartphone for personal use? Whatever the answers, they'd need to wait since the smartphone was dead.

Harper turned to where Darius was snoring, sleeping the peaceful sleep of the guilty.

The overhead light glinted on a thin gold chain he wore around his neck. It was much too delicate for a man to have chosen for himself. She stepped toward him for a closer look. From the chain dangled a single calla lily.

"Call me after he's processed," she told Miller, excitement sparking through her. "I want photos of everything—including that necklace."

"No problem. Think he's got something to do with the drugs we found on the girl?"

"I think he has something to do with murder."

# CHAPTER TWENTY-EIGHT

Leah was finishing charting her involvement with Macy's resuscitation when her phone rang: Luka. "Meet me at the morgue?"

"Paperwork versus bodies? No contest."

"I'm serious. That widow I asked you to help interview? Tassi Standish? She's at the morgue along with an ex-fed who was investigating her husband. Anyway, it's too complicated to get into, but I need to separate them, get them out of the morgue before Ford Tierney refuses to do another case for us—"

"Ford does not enjoy complications, especially not ones coming from family members," Leah told him.

"I know. So can you help? I thought we could interview them at the CIC."

"Sure, no problem. Any word on Beth?"

"No." He paused as if considering. "But we can stop by security after the interviews, review their footage ourselves if you want."

She appreciated the time he was spending on a case that officially was no case at all. "Thanks."

The morgue was in Good Sam's basement. Leah took the stairs, and couldn't help but be reminded of the times after Ian's death when she'd taken solace in being surrounded by the stairwell's simple cinderblock, overwhelmed by her pain and sorrow. The seldom-used stairway had made for a good place to hide and regroup, compose herself to face the world once more. Thankfully, it had been a while since she'd needed to take advantage of its quiet comfort.

She passed the security desk in the lobby of the coroner's office, the guard jerking his chin to the visitors' waiting room. Luka leaned against the open door of the waiting room, balanced on his crutches, watching the people inside. He nodded to her as she joined him. The room held several seating areas, designed to allow families space and a bit of privacy while they waited to speak with the coroner investigators. There was a door on the side wall leading to a small meditation room and another room for private consultations.

The group gathered inside didn't seem at all interested in quiet reflection. A blonde woman sat in a chair that had been pulled to the center of the room, her face buried in her hands, although from her posture, Leah had the feeling that she wasn't actually crying. She wore a designer silk dress, black but definitely not tailored as widow's weeds with its short skirt and low neckline.

"Tassi Standish, wife of Spencer Standish—at least that was the name he used here," Luka told her in a low voice. He explained about the circumstances and questions surrounding Spencer's possible financial crimes and his death.

"And she's here because she's protesting her husband's autopsy?" she asked. "On what grounds? Religious?" She'd known the medical examiner to pursue less invasive methods in some cases, but only if they allowed adequate evidence collection.

"That's what she says. Loudly. But Ford said she also requested an expedited death certificate. For the insurance company, I'm guessing."

"The kind of woman who wants her cake and eats it, too."

"Or the kind of woman who understands how to create an emotional smokescreen and use it to her advantage," Luka replied.

In front of Tassi, in a protective stance, was a man who had the tan and muscles of a tennis pro. He wore crisp white linen slacks and a blue polo top that matched his eyes. He had his arms crossed over his chest and stood with his feet planted as if prepared for battle. The object of his fury was an even taller and more muscular man who, from his posture, had dismissed the second man's presence to focus on the widow, speaking to her in a low but threatening tone that was unmistakable even without hearing his words clearly.

"The Ralph Lauren model is Larry Hansen," Luka continued. "He's the neighbor who found Spencer's body. And obviously a very good friend to Tassi. Not sure exactly how good—that's one of the things I'd like to find out. Larry not only found the body, he also has no alibi and was an investor in Spencer's fund."

"So he was a victim. Which makes him a suspect," she surmised. Luka nodded. "Who's the wannabe Navy SEAL? He looks like he wants something from Tassi."

"Foster Dean. Former DEA, now works as an investigator for victims of Spencer's previous Ponzi scheme back in Denver. Back there Spencer faked his death, ran off with the money, and laid low until he showed up here almost two years ago and started up shop again."

"He's a good guy?" Her skepticism colored her voice. Any man bullying a widow—even if her husband had been a crook—was not a good guy.

"I'm not sure. All I know is that he left the DEA in a haze of suspicion for possibly feeding intel to the Zapata family. And, apparently, from what I've gotten from Denver so far, one of the investors in the Denver Ponzi happened to be a Zapata cartel money-launderer."

"Ah, making Mr. Dean our bad guy."

"Except he has a solid alibi—unless our time of death is way off. He was on a plane flying from Denver the morning Spencer died."

Leah's mind buzzed with the various ramifications and connections. Life in the ER was so clean and simple compared to Luka's work untangling the threads leading to a crime. And of course, his job was made more complicated by the need to be able to prove everything in a court of law.

Tassi raised her face so that Leah could finally get a good look. She was beautiful by any standards, but also had an elusive quality to her. The way, with a beseeching glance of her eyes, she compelled Larry Hansen to edge even closer to her, his body blocking Foster Dean. What had Luka called it? Emotional smokescreen. A woman like that, working with a husband who was a conman—were they partners in crime? "You think Spencer confessed to save his wife."

"Good call. Yes, I believe he did. Especially as she was also his wife back in Denver—before he faked his death, so how much does she really know about his criminal activities? How involved is she? She plays dumb, but I think she knows more than she's letting on."

"Clearly, Mr. Dean is as suspicious of her as you are." She thought for a moment. "How did you say Spencer died?"

"Ford was kind enough to share his preliminary impressions with Harper—" That drew a raised eyebrow of surprise from Leah. "I know, somehow he likes her. I'll need to start sending her to more autopsies. Anyway, he thinks Standish hit the back of his head, breaking his neck, which eventually caused enough swelling around the spinal cord to stop his breathing."

"But you found him in his car with the engine running. So someone put him there after he sustained the cervical spinal fracture? To make either an accidental slip and fall or an intentional blow to the head appear as suicide?"

"Even if he hit his head accidentally, it's still premeditated murder. It took him time to die, enough time for him to inhale some of the carbon monoxide fumes."

She cringed. "That's cold."

"Exactly. I wasn't expecting Hansen to be here, but I find it interesting, the way he won't leave the widow's side. Plus, he found the body—"

"Or says he did. You said Spencer had a broken neck—a chiropractor would know how to do that. He could be our killer."

"Any of them could. I wondered if you could get a preliminary statement from the wife. She was too distraught yesterday and I need to get her on the record. Which is especially dicey since Tassi's spiritual counselor is also her attorney. Reverend Matthew Harper."

"Harper? As in Naomi? I met one of her brothers today, he was very helpful."

"Well, the good reverend is her father and he's been anything but cooperative. Obstructive is more like it—it feels like this case is personal to him somehow. Maybe because he probably helped write Standish's confession. Not to mention, he's the last person we know who spoke with Spencer before he died."

"Isn't that a conflict of interest, if he's also Tassi's attorney?" Leah asked.

"Yes. And I plan to use that to convince him to find her another attorney and talk with me. Although I'm certain he'll hide behind attorney or minister privilege." He blew out his breath and leaned more heavily on his crutches. "Anyway, I'm hoping if Tassi talks to you, you can pull out a few threads of truth, enough for me to run with. Otherwise, I have nowhere to start."

Leah nodded. When she'd first taken the job as medical director of the Crisis Intervention Center, she'd been leery of working with the police. But not only did she and Luka work well together, she'd discovered that being able to console witnesses and victims, empowering them to tell their stories, was fulfilling, even if not as hands-on life-and-death thrilling as her old job in the ER.

She'd never admit it to anyone, especially not Luka, but even more exciting were times like this when her work with a witness might make or break a case, lead to justice being served. It was a feeling almost as good as saving a life.

"And if Tassi asks for an attorney?" She needed to tread carefully, given the legal minefield Luka had described. When Leah performed a forensic interview for the police, she was technically acting as an agent of the police, rather than a physician.

"Then we'll stop and find her one. But let's take it one step at a time."

Taking a deep breath, Leah stepped forward into the fray. "Mrs. Standish? I'm Dr. Leah Wright—"

Before Leah could explain who she was and why she was there, Tassi lunged past the two men to grab Leah's arms. "Please, you can't let them cut my husband up! Please, I need to see him. Please help me!"

# CHAPTER TWENTY-NINE

Luka watched in amusement as Leah handled Tassi's theatrics. She sat the widow back down, took a seat beside her and, after giving Tassi a few moments to vent her emotions, calmly explained why she couldn't see her husband—and why an autopsy was required. She was smart enough not to tell the wife that the postmortem examination had already been completed.

"But I don't want one," Tassi replied, pulling her lip in like a pouting adolescent.

"I'm sorry, that's the law," Leah said in a firm yet gentle tone. "And necessary before the coroner's office can issue a death certificate."

Tassi hid the sharp-edged gleam in her eye, but not before Luka caught it. So this was the real motive behind her visit to the morgue. Without the death certificate she couldn't cash in on Spencer's insurance. But why the theatrics?

Foster Dean gave him his answer. The former DEA agent stampeded past Hansen to loom over where Tassi and Leah sat. "We need to talk," he told Tassi, as if afraid she might be spilling her guts to Leah. Of course. If Tassi and Spencer were mixed up with the Zapata family's money-laundering, then Tassi might possess information she could use against the cartel. Plus, she was Dean's only surviving lead to the Zapatas' missing money. Which told him exactly where Dean's sympathies lay.

"Go away," Tassi cried. She turned to Leah, clinging to her arm with both hands. "Can you make him stop harassing me?

Everywhere I go, he's there, badgering me. All I want is to mourn my husband in peace."

Luka intervened. "Is that true?"

"I have every right to protect my clients' interests," Dean protested.

"That doesn't mean you can hound me, follow me everywhere," Tassi said. "Leave me alone, I don't know anything!"

"Ma'am, are you accusing him of harassment?"

"Stalking is more like it."

Hansen stepped forward, hovering protectively beside Tassi. "Can't you arrest him, make him stop?"

Luka would love nothing more, but he needed more probable cause to make an arrest. He could however leverage Tassi's accusations to force Dean into a serious discussion.

"I wasn't following her," Dean said. "I need a copy of the death certificate as well. And a definitive identification of the body. After all, Spencer faked his death once before. This time my clients need proof—"

"It was your clients who drove him to that. Otherwise they would have killed him," Tassi flared. Then she collapsed against Leah, her eyelids fluttering shut as if she was overwhelmed.

After losing her husband she had every right to be—except that Luka felt in his bones she was merely acting. It made him angry: Tassi faking her grief while sitting beside Leah, who had suffered such agony after her own husband's murder.

But Leah was a better person than he was. Instead of responding with contempt, she gave Tassi a quick hug of sympathy. "I also lost my husband recently."

Tassi blinked her eyes back open. "You did?" Tears reappeared and she swiped them away. "How did you—" She sniffed. "I can't, it's all too much…"

"I understand." Leah glanced at Luka.

He pivoted on his crutches to the two men. "I think we should give Tassi some privacy. And I'd like to speak with both of you."

"I'm not leaving Tassi," Hansen declared.

Dean planted his feet, signaling his own unwillingness to let the widow out of his sight.

Luka had no legal recourse to force them, but he did have bait to dangle. Thankfully, Leah picked up on his intentions. She stood and guided Tassi up. "Wouldn't you prefer a more private space to talk?"

Beneath half-lowered lids, Tassi eyed the men, then nodded to Leah.

Leah laid a hand on Tassi's arm, guiding her toward the door. "I'd like to make this as painless for you as possible. Sergeant Jericho has some details he needs, but I thought it'd be easier to talk to me? Get it all over with as quickly as we can. Then I can ask the medical examiner about the paperwork you need. Of course, we can also call your attorney, if you'd like us to wait for him."

Luka liked how she made the choice seem easy—talk to the mean policeman or the nice doctor who might get you what you want.

Tassi seemed to realize it was her best option as well, meekly walking with Leah past the men. "No, I don't need to call Matthew. Whatever it takes to get this all over with, that's what I need. Where are we going?"

"Not far. Just upstairs," Leah assured her.

Dean and Hansen seemed at a loss at first, but quickly fell in line behind the two women, both unwilling to let Tassi out of their sight. Luka hobbled behind the group as Leah escorted Tassi, Dean, and Hansen from the morgue, through the ER and into the secured CIC suite of interview rooms.

Luka was starting to see the new partnership with Leah and her CIC as his secret weapon. She'd personally facilitated a number of confessions, closing cases that he might not have been able to otherwise. He appreciated the way she treated every subject—witness, victim, or perpetrator—with the same care and consideration she'd given her patients in the ER, and as a result, interview subjects seemed willing to talk to her even when it wasn't necessarily in their best interests.

Waiting for him in the hallway outside the monitoring room between the CIC interview rooms were Ray and Krichek.

"Perfect timing," Luka told them. "Ray, can you take Mr. Dean into Interview Room One, please?" It was the room filled with toys and child-sized furniture, designed for their pediatric victims. Luka rather enjoyed the idea of the oversized former fed being forced into such an unfamiliar environment. Anything to knock him off his game. "I'll talk with Mr. Hansen in the waiting area while Dr. Wright begins with Mrs.—with Tassi," he amended after she gave him an admonishing glance.

"Me?" Hansen asked. "I'm here for Tassi. I'd like to stay—"

"Confidentiality issues, I'm sure you understand, Dr. Hansen," Leah interjected. Before anyone could protest, she led Tassi into the second monitored room, the lock clicking shut behind them.

Ray sized up Dean, the two exchanging the challenging grins of alpha males preparing for battle, and they vanished into the first room.

"Krichek, you can monitor," Luka told the other detective.

"Where's Harper?" Krichek asked impatiently. "Why isn't she here?" Usually mundane tasks like recording and monitoring interviews fell to the most junior member of the team.

"She's dealing with an OD victim in the ER. Unless you'd prefer to trade places?"

"An OD? Yeah, no thanks." He headed into the monitoring room where he could observe and record the interviews from the two rooms. Luka would have to improvise, relying on his phone to record his discussion with Hansen, but he didn't mind. His main objective had been to separate Hansen and Tassi. Dean and Tassi's objectives were easy to read, but the chiropractor's motives intrigued him.

"Right this way," he told Hansen, leading him around the corner to the small waiting room. Thankfully it was empty. They took seats in the vinyl chairs so that they were facing each other. Luka set his phone on the coffee table between them. "I'll be recording this interview. And, of course, you're free to leave at any time." One of the advantages of interviewing subjects at the CIC was that there was no issue of police custody—the CIC was a neutral, civilian-run location. He clicked the recording app, gave the date, time, and identifying information, all the while observing Hansen.

The chiropractor sat leaning forward, his gaze darting past Luka to the doorway as if searching for escape. Was he that desperate to be with Tassi? Was he afraid of something she knew and might tell Leah? Did Hansen have something to hide? Luka took his time, adjusting the phone's volume and positioning it in front of Hansen. A bead of sweat dribbled into the other man's eyebrow.

"I want to thank you for your help and cooperation," Luka started. "I know how upsetting it was, finding your friend's body yesterday. I'd like you to walk me through everything that happened. Take your time; no detail is too small."

Hansen stared at him, his knuckles white as they clenched his knees, the effort of keeping in his seat so great. "I already told you everything." He half stood. "I really should see if Tassi needs—"

"Sit down and let's start from the beginning," Luka said in a firm yet non-confrontational tone. "It won't take long and we'll have you back with Tassi. It's good that she has such supportive friends to help her in this time of grief."

"Thank you," Hansen murmured as he sank back into the chair.

"How long have you known Tassi? And Spencer?"

"Pretty much since they moved here—they hadn't even unpacked when I met Tassi at the club looking for a tennis partner. Then she introduced me to Spence later that night over drinks."

"And your wife? Is she also friends with the Standishes?"

He shifted uncomfortably. "My wife and I are separated—well, not physically, but emotionally. We don't spend any time together anymore. The house is in both of our names, and with the market the way it is, we'd lose too much money selling, so we each have our own wing, barely ever see each other."

"And is she acquainted with the Standishes?" Luka repeated his question.

"She knows them, sure. Everyone at the club does. But she has nothing to do with any of this—she couldn't have, she's been in Italy all month, isn't due back for another two weeks."

Nice of him to rule out his almost-ex as a potential killer, but Luka was much more interested in Hansen's own viability as a suspect. "You mentioned that you were invested in Spence's fund?"

"Yes. Not the first round, though. I got in on the second, thanks to Tassi putting in a good word for me."

"Were you ever concerned about the fund? Any irregularities? Any suspicions?"

Hansen seemed taken aback. "No. Never. Wait, you're not saying—is there a problem with the fund? I mean, even with Spencer's death there must be some continuity plan or the like. We can't lose all our money only because he's dead."

Luka glanced at his phone, scrolling through the financial summaries Krichek had collated. "Did you know that the fund had been cashed out?"

"What do you mean?"

"It's all gone." He held his phone out for Hansen to see. Hansen shook his head in disbelief. "We're trying to trace it—some of the money was transferred to overseas accounts, but a significant percentage was used to buy gold."

"Gold? Like physical gold?" Hansen's gaze turned cold and calculating—so unlike the overwrought emotional performance he'd exhibited yesterday at the death scene. "How much?"

Luka didn't answer, instead retrieving his phone as Harper texted that she was waiting in the hall. She knew he'd be in the middle of interviews and wouldn't have interrupted unless it was important.

"Excuse me a moment," he told Hansen, then stepped out into the hall, closing the door between them. "What have you got?" he asked Harper.

"I'm headed back to the station; I've got a suspect in the Lily Nolan case. But Dr. Tierney called. He ran some tests after not finding any signs of cancer during the Standish autopsy," she said in a breathless voice. "The lab confirmed it. Standish never had any cancer treatment and has no signs of cancer now." She paused. "I guess I'm not too surprised. The guy's a conman, lied about everything; of course he'd manufacture a fake illness to gain sympathy from his victims."

"You're right." Luka thought for a moment. "But follow that thought. Who told us he had cancer?"

Harper shifted her feet, then her eyes went wide. "The widow."

"Exactly. She told us that, *despite* knowing there'd be an autopsy and we'd find out if she was lying." He remembered Tassi's initial confusion yesterday when they'd found Spencer's body at the house. She'd said something about how he was meant to be somewhere else... the river.

At first, he'd assumed it was the natural product of shock and grief. But then, given that there were millions of dollars missing, he wondered exactly how much Tassi knew about Spencer's death. Had they planned to repeat another faked death, which had somehow gone terribly awry? If Spencer had vanished in the river, as Tassi had initially seemed to think he had, there would be no body, which meant no autopsy, so Tassi's story about Spencer's cancer leading to his suicide would have held up.

Although, if they had meant to fake his death to escape the Zapatas, then how had he ended up dead in their garage instead?

"But why? Once Tassi knew that Spencer had died for real, why would she have told us about the cancer unless she believed it was the truth?" Harper argued, echoing Luka's own thoughts.

"Maybe she actually believed he was sick? Maybe he was lying to her?"

"Because he intended to kill himself for real?" She shook her head. "And someone just happened to murder him before he could? No. Too coincidental."

"Back in Denver, Spencer gave Tassi all the money in their divorce *before* he supposedly died. It was a good plan—with her not claiming any life insurance or having anything to do with declaring him dead, no one could go after her for the money. But what if, this time, she wasn't in on it? What if Spencer was conning her the same as everyone else?"

"You mean, if she didn't know the cancer was a lie, then what else didn't she know about? So he was setting her up, but instead of faking his death like they'd done before and then returning to her, this time he was taking off for good?"

"Or he'd conned her into thinking he was going to commit suicide and leave her all the money. He might have faked the cancer so she'd believe him and not come looking."

"Either way, it leaves her holding the bag as far as the Zapata family and his other victims are concerned. If she figured out what he was up to, that he was planning to leave her behind—" Harper made a small sound of satisfaction. "Sounds like the widow has a perfect motive for murder."

# CHAPTER THIRTY

Leah escorted Tassi into the CIC's adult interview room. The subdued, intimate area held two loveseats facing each other with a coffee table between them. Leah settled Tassi onto the loveseat facing the two-way mirror, but instead of taking her customary seat across the table, she sat down beside Tassi and slid the box of tissues closer to the other woman.

It was always a difficult transition when she did forensic interviews for the police. She had to first make clear to the parties involved that she wasn't acting as their physician and that there was no patient-doctor confidentiality, how the recording worked and the fact that the police would be able to view the proceedings. But she also tried to use trauma-based interview techniques that would be somewhat therapeutic—her goal was to help the victim or witness she interviewed as much as she helped the police investigating their case.

This time everything felt different. Despite the fact that Leah understood Tassi's grief, she didn't understand the other woman's actions. Luka had implied that her melodrama was born of subterfuge, but Leah felt as if it might also be a way of masking her underlying emotions.

"How long have you and your husband been married?" Leah started out. She'd discovered that often simple questions helped people open up, making painful topics less difficult to broach, and she wanted Tassi to relax.

"A few years." Tassi sniffed. She leaned forward to take a tissue and dabbed her eyes. "This time." She turned abruptly in her seat, glancing at the door. "I can't bear thinking of him. Down there, all alone, what they're doing to him—"

"How did you meet?" Leah guided her back to more pleasant memories.

"I literally fell into his arms." A ghost of a smile crossed Tassi's face. "I was hiking on Mount Falcon and the ground was soft from rain and it gave way and I slid down a hill. And there he was, catching me before I could hurt myself. My Prince Charming."

"This was in Colorado?"

Tassi nodded, her expression growing guarded. Leah gathered her words carefully, knowing she was entering a minefield. "Sergeant Jericho said Spencer led a colorful life—that he even faked his death in Denver?"

"I wouldn't know." Tassi shook her head, her blonde curls sweeping Leah's words away. "We were already divorced when that happened. I don't know anything about all that."

"So you were married twice? I can't imagine—how did he find you again?"

"When I left him the first time—it was my fault, I was too young, naive." She shrugged. "Restless. Instead of alimony, he gave me a lump sum and I used it to travel the world. It was such an adventure, but I missed Spencer, more than I'd ever dreamed. Then, one day I'm on a beach in Portugal and a man's shadow falls over me, blocking the sun. It was Spence. Somehow fate had thrown us together again. So, when he begged me to marry him—again—how could I say no?" Her voice turned dreamy, as if reciting a fairy tale. But Leah caught a hint of over-rehearsal, as if the story had been practiced and prepared for an occasion like this.

"Did he have any history of depression? Or mood swings? Up one moment, dark and gloomy the next?"

Tassi sat up straight. "It's like you know him. Yes, that was Spence, through and through. It's part of the reason why I left him the first time. I couldn't handle his moods." She twisted the tissue between her fingers. "They say—the police think he did this—" She met Leah's gaze, a yearning for understanding in her eyes. "Was it my fault? Did I miss the signs? I mean, I'm his wife, I should have known he was going to, to do that, hurt himself." Fresh tears slipped down her cheeks. "It is, isn't it? It's all my fault."

For the first time the widow's grief felt authentic. Leah patted her arm, felt her trembling. It was hard to fake that kind of emotion. "Your husband, he never mentioned any problems?"

"No, no. I thought—" Another sob. "It wasn't supposed to happen. Not like this. He shouldn't be gone. He should be right here with me." She raised her face. "What am I going to do now? I'm all alone. What am I going to do without him?"

There was a knock on the door and Luka entered. He gave Leah a quick nod to let her know he wanted to take over. Leah felt a bit relieved—it was as if her conversation with Tassi wasn't between two people searching for answers but rather an audience and a performer. And yet, she had seen glimpses of genuine emotion. Of course, the best actors used their real emotions to enhance their performances. She sat back and let Luka ask his questions.

"Tassi," he said in a gentle voice as he took a seat opposite her, taking his time to arrange his crutches against the arm of the couch. "I just heard from the medical examiner, and I'm afraid we're going to need your help more than ever."

Tassi frowned at him. "My help? Why? What happened?"

"You know, we all want to find the truth about what happened to Spencer. So, there are a few things. First, we've discovered that all of Spencer's financial accounts have been drained—everything for his business and the foundation."

"But the rest, that's all right, isn't it? It should be—I mean the funds that are in my name, not Spence's."

"Yes. Your accounts seem to be fine."

"Oh good." She sank back in her seat. Leah glanced at Luka. The widow had just been told her husband's entire business had been wiped out and she didn't seem at all concerned. As if she had expected it.

"We're working on tracing the missing money," he continued. "But it appears some of it was transferred to offshore accounts that we might never—"

"Wait. What do you mean, some of it? How much? Isn't it all—" She caught herself, covered by sniffling into her tissue. "I mean, why would anyone take only some of Spence's money? If they were going to rob him, why not take it all?"

"We're not sure. His computers were all wiped clean, but our techs found data left on the memory card inside his scanner. That's how we were able to follow the money, at least in part. It appears that Spencer purchased six million dollars' worth of gold that is untraceable."

She blinked at that. "Spencer did? I don't understand."

"I'm afraid that's not all." Luka took a breath. "The medical examiner says that Spencer showed no signs of cancer."

"No. No. That's impossible…" She trailed off, her gaze searching the room as if seeking answers.

"Not only that, but Spencer shows no signs of ever having cancer. Not now or in the past." He leaned forward, elbows on his knees and Leah realized something big was coming— something he wanted to see Tassi's reaction to. "He lied to you, didn't he?"

She shook her head. "Spencer wouldn't, he didn't—" Then she nodded. "But he did, didn't he? He lied to me. But then, why? Why would he kill himself?"

"We don't believe that he did. Spencer was unconscious but still breathing when someone put him in the SUV and turned the engine on."

"Unconscious? Was he drugged?" She shook her head vehemently. "No. Spencer would never take drugs."

"No drugs. He sustained a head injury. That's what killed him, not the carbon monoxide."

Tassi gasped. She gripped Leah's hand, her entire body going rigid. "Someone killed Spencer? And stole six million dollars?" She shook her head, her mouth gaping, the expression so unflattering that Leah was convinced this was an honest emotion. More than confused or shocked, Tassi was utterly flummoxed. "Who?" she demanded. "Who killed him? And where's my money?"

Luka waited, gesturing for Leah to take over. "Did Spencer have any enemies?" she asked in a gentle tone.

"Sure, people didn't like him. It's one of the reasons why he left Colorado and changed his name after he moved here." Somehow she made it sound as if fleecing people out of their life savings wasn't a reason to want anyone dead. "But no one who would kill him—not like that."

"What do you mean, *like that*?" Leah coaxed.

Tassi's lips pressed together and she remained silent.

Luka gave her another minute but when she said nothing, he told her, "Tassi, we know about the Zapata family. We know Spencer stole their money back in Denver and was on the run from them. What can you tell us about that?"

"I—nothing. I don't know anything. Please, I just want to bury my husband in peace." Her words emerged in a plaintive wail. She stood, smoothing the skirt of her dress.

Luka grabbed his crutches and stood as well. That was when Leah realized he didn't have any proof of Tassi's involvement other than her own vague insinuations, and certainly not enough to arrest her. At least not yet.

As Tassi walked toward the door, Luka said, "Of course you're free to go, and please, feel free to not answer, but I'm curious about one thing."

Uncertainty crossed her face as she decided whether to push past him, but curiosity got the better of her. "What?"

"Why were you so surprised to see Spencer's body at your house yesterday?"

She stuttered to a stop. "Yesterday?"

"When we first saw you at your house, you said Spencer was at the river, he was supposed to be in the river." Luka shifted one crutch to casually block her path. "You were expecting us to have called you because we'd found his suicide note. Like in Colorado. A note but no body. You thought he was still alive, waiting for you with the money, didn't you, Tassi? You believed he really was dying of cancer, but Spencer wasn't the type to kill himself, was he? You thought you'd run away, to some tropical paradise where you could spend the rest of what little time he had together. And then, when he was gone, all the money he'd squirreled away, hidden in those offshore accounts, it would all be yours. So, where's the money?"

Her gaze turned steely, her eyes narrowed to slits. "I have no idea what you're talking about. My husband has been murdered and I need to go make arrangements for his body, if you don't mind."

Luka waited a beat, searching her expression, then moved aside. She stalked past him without another word or glance in his direction. He turned to Leah, leaning heavily on his crutches. "So, that went well. Got more out of her than either of the others. Hansen was useless and Dean stonewalled Ray."

"Were you telling the truth about the missing money and all that gold? Or was that to get a reaction out of her?" Leah asked.

"No, it was the truth. Sanchez really was able to recover data from a scanner at Standish's office—guess whoever wiped the computers didn't think to also erase its memory. And Krichek sent me the financials from the fund. It was wiped out on Friday. By Standish himself."

"You're thinking he was planning to fake his death and run away, but someone found out, wanted the money and killed him?"

"If so, then they didn't do a very good job of getting what they wanted. He was on the phone around the time he died from a single blow to the back of his head. No other injuries. No signs of torture. He was dead before he could tell anyone anything about where the money was."

"For what it's worth, Tassi seemed genuinely surprised to learn he was murdered."

"Or at least surprised that the money was gone. She seemed especially upset about the missing six million in gold."

"Who are your suspects?" Leah asked.

"Tassi's alibi checked out—we confirmed the time she left the Greenbriar and there's no way she could have gotten back here in time. Larry Hansen knows more than he's letting on. Plus, he found the body and doesn't have an alibi. It's possible he and Tassi were working together. Maybe he learned about Spencer's scam and tried to cash in? Not sure. Foster Dean has an alibi—he was on a plane from Denver at the time. But he might still be good for the break-in at the office. He'd have had enough time to get there after his flight landed, could have copied the information, wiped the hard drives so no one else could access the data, and have been the one I surprised."

"Then why return?"

"To insinuate himself in the investigation, stay one step ahead of us. Especially once he knew Spencer was dead; he realized that if the computer files couldn't lead him to the money, then maybe we could."

"You know, that scenario also works with Spencer erasing the computer files himself, covering his tracks," Leah pointed out. "Dean could have arrived and realized they were erased, a dead end—leaving you as his next best source of information, so he involved himself with the investigation."

"He's not interested in me, though." He pivoted on his crutches to glance out the door. "It's Tassi. She said he was following her."

"Luka. Shouldn't you warn her? You said he might be working for a drug cartel."

"She's not stupid, she already knows she's a target. And don't worry, I have Ray and Krichek following her and Hansen. That's why I wanted to stall her here, long enough for them to get in position." He frowned at his leg. "Wish I could go with them. I'd love to nail Dean, the smug SOB." He turned back to her. "Anyway, thanks. I know this wasn't the kind of interview you usually do for us and I appreciate you letting us tie up your facilities."

Leah was clearly out of her depth when it came to the twisted motivations of career criminals. But there was one woman in distress she might still be able to help. "You can pay me back by helping me find Beth and her baby. Didn't you say we could review the security videos?"

"I did." But he didn't move. Instead, he leaned heavily on his crutches. "I know you said you were certain Beth wouldn't hurt her baby, but when security reviewed the video, they didn't see anyone leave with a baby. So, just in case, I have hospital security searching."

"Searching? Of course we're all searching—" Then it hit her. What he meant, what he really meant they were looking for. "No. Luka, no. I don't believe it. You didn't see her, the way she clung to her baby, like she would do anything to protect him. C'mon. Let's go see the video from this morning; I'm sure there's another explanation for why they didn't see her and the baby leave. There has to be."

# CHAPTER THIRTY-ONE

Luka and Leah headed down to the medical center's security office. There they met Ramsey, the former Pittsburgh police detective who was head of Good Sam's security.

"Any news?" Luka asked.

"No sign of the baby," Ramsey answered. Beside him, Luka felt Leah's posture relax with relief. "And we've searched the entire floor. But I'm glad you're here. Once you sent that photo of the patient who absconded, I was able to track her, but only for a short while. Come, see for yourself."

"I'd also like to see the visitor log for this morning," Luka told him as he and Leah followed Ramsey into a darkened room. Even though Leah had found Beth alone at the fair, he had a hard time believing a woman who'd given birth the day before could make it out of the hospital with her newborn without anyone noticing. Unless she had help.

"After what happened in the spring, when Dr. Wright was attacked," Ramsey said, nodding to Leah, "we implemented new visitor procedures. Everyone has to show a photo ID and sign in to get a pass."

"Good," Luka said absently as he scanned the log. He wished the hospital took security as seriously as they did patient privacy. How was it they could computerize medical records but still used an outdated video system? A familiar set of names snagged his attention. Tassi, her neighbor Larry Hansen, then several minutes later, Foster Dean, all with the destination of the coroner's offices.

Then he spotted another familiar name. "Reverend Harper was here this morning? But it doesn't list his destination."

"The reverend? He wouldn't need to sign in, he has his own ID. He's part of the pastoral service, visits anyone who has a need, patient or family. Sometimes even staff after a rough case. That log just indicates when he used his keycard to enter."

"So he pretty much has the run of the place?" Luka asked.

"He's a minister," Ramsey said as if it explained everything.

"Your log shows when people arrive but not when they leave."

"They're meant to sign out but no one ever does."

Leah leaned past him to examine the log herself. "He signed in at six-forty this morning, right before shift change. That's an odd time, don't you think?"

"Why?" Luka asked, glad he'd brought her with him. Her intimate knowledge of how the hospital worked was proving invaluable.

"No visitors are allowed during shift changes because the nurses are tied up giving report, so the wards are short-staffed."

He nodded. "A lot like patrol officers and our watch changes."

"Exactly. And the reverend would know that, yet he arrived right before the day shift arrived on duty." She shrugged. "It's possible someone called him in that early, perhaps a dying patient and their family, but it seems odd to me."

Luka couldn't help but think how odd Matthew Harper's actions had been yesterday, at the Standish crime scene. He wondered if Harper had noticed anything strange about her father. He hated to get her personally involved, torn between her duties and her family, but if she had any insights—

"Here," Ramsey said from his position at the keyboard. "This is what I wanted you to see."

Leah had explained that the Labor and Delivery wing was divided into the labor area with mothers giving birth—including two operating rooms for C-sections—and the postpartum unit where the nursery was situated, along with the rooms for mothers who had given birth. Apparently staff went back and forth between them, but patients were sequestered in one at first, then moved to the other side.

"We don't have a separate camera inside Labor and Delivery," Ramsey continued. "Patient privacy issues. All we have is this one outside the main L and D wing." He pressed a button and the footage filled one of the computer screens.

The camera outside the locked labor ward also showed the elevator lobby, so it was a busy area filled with hospital staff, families, volunteers, visitors, along with patients. Ramsey fast-forwarded, stopping whenever anyone exited L and D. So far there were half a dozen women leaving, all wearing scrubs, most with their hair in surgical caps, some with surgical masks hiding most of their face as well. No civilians except for two discharged couples, the mothers holding their babies and wheeled out by nurses, both with fathers, hands filled with flowers and balloons and car seats, trailing behind. Luka had to smile at the expression of shock and awe that filled the men's faces.

Then Luka saw a familiar face. "Wait. Stop there." It was Matthew Harper leaving L and D. Luka checked the timestamp— twenty minutes after the reverend had entered the hospital and right during the change of shift when there were fewer nurses on the ward. Matthew carried a bag similar to the large diaper bags the discharged patients had with them.

"Go back twenty minutes, then forward another twenty after he leaves," Luka ordered, searching the faces of the women who had exited around the same time Matthew had. They all appeared to be staff members: scrubs, nursing shoes, ID badges.

"Stop!" Leah pointed. "That's Beth. I'm sure of it."

Ramsey froze on the film on the image of a woman in scrubs who had a surgical cap covering her hair and a mask over her face, head ducked low as if she knew a camera was there. But her shoes were wrong. She wasn't wearing the clogs or thick sneakers with extra support that the medical staff wore. This woman was wearing open-toed sandals.

It *was* Beth. She'd exited two minutes before Matthew appeared carrying the bag.

"He sent her ahead while he carried the baby out hidden in the bag," Luka said. Matthew Harper had orchestrated Beth's escape.

"Why would a minister take Beth's baby?" Leah asked. "They had to be working together."

How did Beth know Matthew? Luka wondered. Who was she running from that she had to go to such extreme measures, sneaking out, hiding her baby?

"Give me the elevator lobby," he told Ramsey. "Follow Matthew Harper as he exits."

Ramsey looked surprised but did as he was told, squinting at the time stamp and pulling up the other cameras. They watched as Matthew left the elevator and crossed the lobby, exiting out the door that led to the visitor's parking garage.

"Wait, keep rolling," Luka ordered. A few minutes later, the woman wearing the sandals emerged from the elevator. She must have stopped somewhere after leaving the OB floor because she now carried a plastic bag and held a Mylar balloon so that it hid her face. She followed Matthew's path although her pace was rushed, her stride urgent. "Okay, the garage, let's see him leave."

Ramsey switched cameras. "We don't charge ministers; his ID badge lets him in and out of any of the parking garages, even the paid ones."

A white SUV with the Holy Redeemer logo on it pulled up to the automated exit lane. Ramsey froze the image. Matthew leaned out the driver's window, swiping a key card. But no one else was visible in the SUV. The rear windows were tinted dark. Beth appeared nowhere else on the video; she had to have been in the vehicle, but Luka couldn't swear to it.

Which meant there wasn't enough for a warrant. But definitely enough for a serious conversation.

"Luka," Leah breathed. "They have to be in the car, with Reverend Harper. Where would he take them? Who are they running from?"

But Luka had an even greater question: What were the odds that Matthew Harper would be the last person to speak to both Spencer Standish before his death and their missing mother? A woman on the run and a man killed before he could run. That couldn't be a coincidence.

"I'm not sure," he told Leah. "But I'll find out."

He thought about calling Harper, then decided against putting her in the middle of a tug of war between him and her father. But he needed to know how and why Matthew knew Beth. And exactly how Beth was connected to Spencer Standish's murder.

# CHAPTER THIRTY-TWO

When Harper arrived back at the police department, the uniformed officers had Darius booked and waiting for her in an interview room.

She glanced through his possessions that they'd confiscated: the knife, a wallet, a belt, several cheap rings, and the chain that seemed much too delicate for a guy like him, a thin gold rope with a lily dangling from it. Exactly like one she'd seen Lily Nolan wear in her mugshots and when Harper had arrested her last year.

She called Sanchez in the cyber squad. "I had Miller bring in two phones found on a suspect. Did you get anything from them?"

"You mean the phones signed in twenty minutes ago that are at the bottom of a list that includes three full computer hard drives, six other phones, and—"

"I get it, I get it. You're busy. But I really need to know what's on those phones."

"Hang on. If I can get anything off them quickly—" The rustling noises of plastic evidence bags came over the line. "Warrants came through, so that's no problem. Let's see. The first one, the burner, has no encryption, no security, easy enough. Hmm... only two people on the contact list, a guy named Darius and someone named Lily."

Bingo. "Send me the call logs. How about texts? Can you send me those?"

"Yeah, sure. It'll take a few minutes. It won't be all of them, only the conversations she saved."

"Whatever you have. And GPS? Can we trace where that phone's been?"

"We can. But that's going to take longer."

She bounced on her toes in frustration. So close to nailing Lily's killer. "How long?"

"I'll have it for you by tomorrow. Soonest I can do," he said before she could protest.

"Okay. What about the other phone? The one with the pink glitter?"

"Can't get anything on that one until I recharge it—even then it might be encrypted or have security I can't get through."

"No such thing."

"Flattery won't change the facts. Give me until tomorrow and I can let you know if we can get anything from it."

"Okay. Thanks. But you're sending the text chats now, right?"

"Already done."

"I owe you one, Sanchez."

"Don't worry, I'll be collecting."

She hung up and logged into the secure cloud server that hosted the case management system for the department. Sanchez was true to his word; waiting for her were the text strings from Macy's phone along with her call logs. Almost all the calls were between Macy and Darius, except for a forty-two-minute call last week to Lily—which meant that now that Harper had Lily's phone number, she could get a warrant for all of Lily's data from her phone carrier. It would take a few days, though, and she couldn't wait. There were no saved text messages to or from Lily, which left her with very little ammunition.

Hopefully, though, it would be enough to get the answers she needed from Darius. Harper gathered her props, heaved in a breath, and entered the interview room.

"Hey again, Darius. Ready to talk?" The kid was only eighteen, a year younger than Macy, with no real record beyond some petty larceny. And given that he'd already refused a lawyer, telling Miller that he wanted everything recorded for the lawsuit he intended to bring against the department, Harper suspected he'd learned most of what he knew about being a criminal from video games and TV.

"Is she all right? Just tell me, is Macy gonna live?" Darius demanded before she got the door shut behind her.

"The doctors are working on her now. But they said she was stable."

He leaned back in his chair, breath whistling from him. He blinked and his expression morphed from worried to cunning. "Good. Then she can sue your asses, too. Assault, false arrest—"

"False arrest?" Harper swallowed her laughter. "You had a knife to her throat."

"Only cuz you all forced me to defend myself best I could. Yeah, add that one—excessive force. And, and police brutality. I'm gonna own your ass, my lawyer gets done with you all."

"If you're not in prison doing life for murder." Harper decided on a shock approach rather than something more subtle.

"Murder? What the hell you talking about?"

"When we booked you, I saw that chain of yours."

"What? My peace lily? It's cuz I'm a lover, not a fighter. My girl gave me that."

"Your girl? As in, Lily Nolan? I saw her wearing that same necklace last time I arrested her." She slid a photo of Lily's body, the most gruesome one she could find in the assortment from the coroner, and left it face down on the table before him.

"What's that?"

"Take a look and see. Nothing a tough guy like you can't handle."

He gave her a sidelong glance but then curiosity got the better of him and he flipped the photo over. "Nah-uh." He recoiled, pushing himself as far away from the table as the chair allowed. "You ain't pinning that bitch on me. Never saw her in my life."

"That bitch was a girl. She had her whole life in front of her. Why'd you do it, Darius? Was it because she tried to get clean? Was she going to steal Macy from you, get her into rehab and off the streets as well?"

He shook his head violently. "I'm telling you, I ain't have nothing to do with her." His gaze fixed on the photo again. He tapped his finger over the time stamp. "She died Sunday morning?" He slid a glance up to meet her eyes, mocking her. "You cops are all so stupid. Know where I was since Friday night? All weekend, until yesterday afternoon?" He slammed his palm down on the table, Lily's photo flying off the edge and onto the floor. "I was locked up. Check your records. Your own jail is my alibi. You ain't got nothing on me."

Harper hid her smile. Darius was wrong. She had him exactly where she wanted him: excited and talking.

# CHAPTER THIRTY-THREE

Despite his misgivings, as he drove up the mountain to Holy Redeemer, Luka called the district attorney's office and laid out his concerns along with what little evidence he had. The ADA practically convulsed with laughter. "You want us to try for a warrant on a minister and a church? A sanctuary? Based on what?" she'd asked. "There's no law against carrying a diaper bag out of a hospital or giving a mother and her baby a ride. Not that you even have evidence proving that he did that."

Luka hung up, more frustrated than ever. His leg throbbed and itched simultaneously, not to mention the brace and wrappings over the wound were hot and sweaty, and the damn crutches… He took a deep breath, gathered his thoughts, and turned onto the drive that led to Matthew Harper's church. Harper's father, one more addition to his list of aggravations and complications. Nothing about this case was easy—either case, Beth's disappearance or Spencer Standish's murder.

And yet, one man of God stood at the intersection of both. Luka always warned the others on his squad against the fallacy of connecting unrelated cases together—it was a human tendency; the mind was tempted to create order out of chaos. But in Luka's experience, all too often chaos ruled, and trying to force facts to fit an orderly theory led to wasted time chasing false conclusions.

But he couldn't deny the evidence here. Matthew Harper was the last person to speak to Spencer; that was a fact. And his presence on Beth's ward at the same time she walked away was too much of a coincidence to ignore, even if he had no physical proof that Matthew had helped Beth leave. There simply was no other answer that made any sense.

He drove past the church and its empty parking lot, then arrived at the house. It looked like a typical minister's house—white-framed, dwarfed by the church beside it, yet also mirroring the church's architectural lines. Despite the lack of rain, the exterior was spotless, placidly basking in the afternoon sun. And none of it felt like Harper—at least not the Harper he knew, the guarded, ambitious, highly energetic woman who'd climbed the ranks of the police force. The last adjective he'd ever associate with Harper was "placid."

He fumbled his way up the porch steps—he'd been tempted to leave the crutches in the car, but had decided that perhaps they might give him an edge, appeal to the minister's sympathy. He rang the bell and within seconds it was opened by a woman in her fifties wearing a sky-blue dress and an apron embellished with matching blue birds.

"Can I help you?" she asked.

"Detective Sergeant Luka Jericho." He held his credentials up for her to scrutinize. "I was hoping to find the reverend. Is he home?"

"Matthew is over at the church with my son. I'm Rachel, his wife. Come inside, please." She led the way into the foyer, which opened onto a large, formal dining room to the left and a living area to the right, as well as a hallway that continued to the rear of the house and a staircase leading up. "Wait here a second. Let me turn the stove off and I'll take you over, Sergeant Jericho." Rachel disappeared into the rear of the house, leaving Luka to be entertained by the wall filled with family photos: Matthew and Rachel stood alone in the first one, then two little boys stood with them, then three boys in another and in the furthest frames Harper finally made an appearance, first as an infant then as a little girl dressed in ribbons and laces. Luka smiled. The image was so very different from the Harper he knew, who even after her promotion to detective still wore Doc Martens beneath her dress slacks.

Rachel returned less than a minute later and held the front door open as he maneuvered his crutches over the threshold. "Luka Jericho? You're Naomi's boss," she said as they strolled down the drive to the church. "She's always talking about you, was so excited to join your team."

"She's a fine addition," Luka replied, trying to toe the line between polite conversation and professionalism. After all, he was here to discover what her husband had to do with one man's murder and a woman's disappearance.

When they reached the church, Rachel once again held open the tall, heavy door. Luka nodded his thanks and stopped inside, uncertain of which direction to go.

"They're in the office, behind the sanctuary," she told him, her heels clicking against the hardwood floors, the sound echoing up to the beamed roof above. "The original Holy Redeemer was founded by Josiah Harper in 1679—two years before William Penn received his charter from King Charles to form Penn's Woods. Back then it was a single-room log cabin, but each generation added to it until we now have this." She waved her hands at shoulder height, a tour guide gesturing. "We still use remnants of that original building for storage—Naomi and her brothers loved to play in there when they were kids."

Luka glanced around, hoping he appeared appreciative of her history lesson, when actually he was growing impatient. Was she mentioning her daughter as psychological leverage? And why had she brought him in through the main church when he'd seen a door at the rear when he'd driven past the parking lot? All this was meant to remind him to take care and tread lightly.

"And your addition?" he asked as she led him past the altar to a door hidden by heavy velvet drapes.

"You mean Matthew's. He and the boys have brought Holy Redeemer into the twenty-first century by spreading the gospel via modern technology. We now have congregants all around the world, an expansion that Josiah Harper could never even have dreamed of." She stopped halfway down a narrow hallway and knocked on a heavy oak door, then opened it without waiting for an answer. "Matthew? Sorry to interrupt, but Sergeant Jericho is here to speak with you."

She stood aside to allow Luka to enter the office. Matthew sat behind a desk that could only be described as regal, and despite sitting down he seemed to tower over the younger man who stood before him as if a supplicant. John, the youngest son. Luka recognized him from the family photos.

"Sergeant Jericho." Matthew managed to sound both surprised and dismissive simultaneously. "I wasn't expecting you. You know I can't discuss anything regarding Spencer Standish or his wife—"

"This is about another matter," Luka answered, mirroring Matthew's formal tone. He glanced at Rachel and John.

Matthew took the cue. "John, Rachel, please excuse us."

John took a step forward. "Father, you might need a witness."

Matthew pursed his lips in consideration. "If I do, I'll call you. Now please, leave us."

Reluctantly, John and Rachel left, closing the door behind them. Matthew sat in silence, polishing his glasses, waiting Luka out. Using one of Luka's favorite interview techniques against him. Without legal standing or probable cause for a warrant, this might get dicey, Luka realized. But Matthew was an attorney as well as a minister and he understood that even before Luka said anything. Suddenly the silence between the two men was more than a conversational gambit, it was a power struggle.

Luka's frustration simmered, threatening to boil over. He'd allowed Matthew to win the upper hand yesterday—he'd had no choice given the legalities—but now he was dealing with a missing mother and child and he wasn't about to cede the field of battle to Matthew.

"Sir—" Luka began.

"Reverend Harper," Matthew cut him off.

Luka ignored the other man's title. "I believe you accompanied a young woman and her newborn son from Good Samaritan Medical Center earlier today. I'd like to see them, ensure that they are safe. The physicians at Good Samaritan tell me that the infant may be at risk and requires further monitoring. If you could take me to them now…"

He stopped, waiting for Matthew to respond. The older man closed the open Bible on his desk with a heavy thud and stood. "You 'believe'? Meaning you have no proof of my involvement."

Interesting way to phrase it, Luka thought. Definitely not a denial, more like a sidestep. "If you won't take me to them. I'd like to search the premises," Luka continued. "And access the GPS on your vehicle."

"On what grounds? You have no warrant. Otherwise you would have led with that."

"Exigent circumstances," Luka bluffed. "A child's life is at risk."

Matthew stared at Luka, searching. Luka kept his face neutral, trying to not allow his anger to show. But Matthew squinted his eyes and gave a small shake of his head. "If you truly think you have exigent circumstances, you would have called for a search warrant on your way here, so clearly you don't have enough probable cause to act on any suspicions you may harbor. Not to mention, the church grounds are considered a sanctuary. I'd be happy to call a judge right now, if you'd like to obtain a ruling."

Luka could handle outmaneuvering a lawyer or a minister, but the combination of the two? "I'm not leaving without seeing them." He was certain that Matthew knew where Beth and her baby were.

"Then you're guilty of trespassing," Matthew snapped. He calmed down and relented. "However, given that my daughter holds you in high esteem, I'll forgive your transgression. Perhaps what you need, Sergeant, is less evidence from your own eyes, but more faith in the Good Lord and those He has chosen to do his work. There is a higher law that I obey, higher than man's."

Luka had been almost ready to back off, find another course of action. But Matthew's tone of smug superiority, his certainty that he knew better than anyone else, rankled so deeply that Luka gave in to his anger.

"I'll leave, then." He bit out the words. "But I'd like you to accompany me to the station for further questioning."

"Are you arresting me?" Matthew seemed almost amused.

"Perhaps. It won't stick, I know, and I'll look a fool, but I think you need to see evidence with your own eyes, Reverend Harper, of exactly how serious *man's* law can be." Luka threw the man's own words back at him. "Not to mention how serious I can be when a child's life is at stake."

Matthew appeared taken aback, and Luka thought for a moment that he might surrender, give Luka what he wanted: answers. But then Matthew shrugged and stood. "You're wasting your time, Sergeant, but I guess it's yours to waste." He walked past Luka and opened the door. "Let's go."

# CHAPTER THIRTY-FOUR

Leah couldn't remember the last time she'd felt this frustrated. At least in the ER, she could do something, anything to try to help a patient. Now she was relegated to the sidelines while Luka investigated—and he couldn't even do anything more than speak to Reverend Harper, since Beth's leaving the hospital wasn't a crime and there was no evidence that she or the baby were in any danger.

No evidence except Leah's gut instinct. Luka hadn't seen the terror that filled Beth's face yesterday. Plus, why would she leave the hospital if she hadn't felt threatened?

And all she could do was wait for Luka to hopefully get some answers from Reverend Harper. Maybe he helped facilitate some kind of underground network for victims of domestic violence? She could definitely see his son, Jonah, doing that kind of work with the people who came to the Pierhouse Shelter. Maybe Beth was in good hands, and Jonah and the reverend simply couldn't say anything because of confidentiality?

Except… wouldn't they have at least told Naomi? Keeping it a secret from a stranger like herself, she understood. But keeping it a secret from the reverend's own daughter? A police officer who could help protect Beth? That made no sense.

She returned to her office and tried to focus on actually getting some work done. Emily texted several times, each one more emoji-filled, but then came one final message, urging Leah to *HURRY HOME*. Leah had almost forgotten about back-tracking Beth's movements using the photos Nate had taken. Better than sitting in her office doing busy work, given that Luka hadn't called with any updates. She texted Emily that she was on her way, closed down her computer, and left for the day.

By the time she walked through the kitchen door it was almost six o'clock. Emily and Nate were gathered around Ian's old laptop on the kitchen table, their noses practically pressed to the screen, surrounded by neglected, forgotten bowls of congealing mac and cheese. The kids ignoring mac and cheese, one of Ruby's forbidden temptations that flew in the face of Leah's ban on processed foods? This had to be serious.

"Mommy!" Emily cried out. She hopped down from her chair and raced over, tugging at both Leah's arms. "We've found her! Nate took baby lady's picture and I made a map and she's here, she's here!" She pointed triumphantly at the computer screen.

Nate smiled shyly up at Leah. "Hi, Dr. Wright. How was your day?"

No matter how many times Leah told him to call her by her first name, he always began every conversation with her surname and title.

"My day was okay—better than your uncle's, at least. He's still at work."

"Poor Luka," Emily said. "Did he fall off his crutches? We should get him a wheelchair. Nate, we could build one, customize it, make it really cool!"

Two minutes in the door and Emily had used up a day's quota of exclamation points, making Leah wonder how much sugar Ruby had fed them. "Where's Ruby?"

"Living room," Nate said.

"Talking to her booooyfriend," Emily crooned. "Said it's private, grown-up stuff."

Leah wondered if it was the same friend responsible for Emily's fake ribbon. At least Emily seemed to have forgiven Ruby, even if Leah hadn't. Her stomach growling—she'd missed lunch—Leah grabbed her own bowl of mac and cheese from the stove and took the seat beside Nate. "Show me what you found."

He clicked a few keys, saying, "I thought we could try to retrace the lady's steps and see where she came from through the fair."

"Except she didn't come from the fair," Emily put in, nudging her own chair so she was between Leah and Nate.

"What do you mean, she didn't come from the fair?" Leah asked.

"No wristband," Nate answered.

"Wristband?"

"Like this," Emily chimed in without taking her eyes off the screen. She and Nate raised their hands in unison, revealing bright green plastic bands they still wore.

Leah thought for a moment. "Perhaps she was a vendor or a judge, someone who didn't come in through the admission gate. In that case, she wouldn't have needed one."

This time it was Nate who answered. "No, see, we've been going through all the pictures me and Emily took." He pointed to the screen as the images flitted past. "That yellow band, that's for the guys manning the booths. And the judges, they have red ones."

"So far we haven't seen anyone with no bracelets," Emily told Leah. "But we did find the baby lady in a few pictures." She reached past Nate to move the mouse and a new photo appeared. "Here she is walking out past the horse barn." Nate enlarged the photo and Emily pointed to a woman in the background. She had long dark hair, was wearing a sundress, and was very pregnant.

"Do you see?" Nate asked. "See how scared she is?"

"Were you able to retrace her steps? See where she came from?" Leah peered at the photo. No one seemed to be with Beth or following her.

"That's exactly what we did," Emily answered, excitement filling her voice. She brought up a map of the fairgrounds. "Here's where you and Nate found her at the judges' tent." She pointed.

"Then we followed her backwards and found her here, here, and here." Nate pointed out locations on the map that formed a path ending with the horse barn at the far edge of the fairgrounds. "And that's it. We haven't seen her in any other pictures."

"Show me all the photos with her. Can you put them in order? From the first time you see her?" Emily reached past Nate and clicked a few keys, the screen filling with a slideshow.

In the first few images Beth seemed upset, yelling at someone she was talking on the phone with, and in the final shot of the series she actually threw the phone onto the ground. It had to be more than anger, Leah thought. A pregnant woman in preterm labor wouldn't just toss away her lifeline. Was she afraid that someone was tracking her through the phone?

Leah inspected the map of the fair, pinpointing where the photos had been taken as she followed Beth's progress through the fairgrounds until the last photo at the judges' tent. Then she went back to the very first ones. Beth was behind the horse barn. Leah scrutinized the photo, then compared it to the map which showed an exercise ring for the horses and beyond that was a bunch of green swirls, indicating the state forest.

Craven Peak. It had cabins and a campground. The perfect place for someone to hide out.

"Do you have any more pictures of this area?" She wanted to see what kind of barrier someone coming in from the forest would need to climb over to gain entrance to the fairgrounds and the background had been too hazy to tell in the photos with Beth.

Nate and Emily huddled over the computer, scanning their photos with dizzying speed.

"Here, we found it!" Emily clapped her hands.

On the screen was a photo of two teenagers walking horses on leads, preparing for their event. Behind them was a wall of trees, too thick to see anything but shadows. And between the trees and the exercise area was a split-rail fence about four feet high.

Anyone could have gotten past the fence. Even a pregnant woman in labor, if she was desperate enough.

"She came from Craven Peak," Leah muttered, taking over the keyboard from Emily. A few clicks later and the state forest's page appeared. Craven Peak was considered a primitive wilderness area, so hikers and overnight campers had to sign in with a ranger. There was a page where you could make reservations for the cabins. Leah clicked on the cabin closest to the fairground. A calendar appeared, showing that it had been rented up until yesterday and was available any night this week.

Leah typed in her information, reserving the cabin for that night. A confirmation window popped up instructing her that she had to arrive at the ranger's office to check in by seven p.m. She glanced at the clock: it was almost seven already.

Nate watched her. "You're going, aren't you? Shouldn't you talk to Luka?"

Leah wasn't worried about running into any danger. And certainly she had no hope of actually finding Beth at the cabin. After all, it was where Beth had fled from—she wouldn't return there; it was too risky. If two kids with a computer could track her there, then anyone could. Leah's curiosity was overwhelming her. Who was Beth really? What was she running from? Maybe she'd left some clues behind in the cabin. Plus, if Leah could find Beth's phone, it might provide a treasure trove of information that could help her find Beth and the baby.

"I'll let him know if I find anything," she promised Nate. "But it looks like, if Beth was there, she checked out yesterday, so it's probably a dead end." Both kids looked disappointed. "You guys did great, though. Really good work."

"If it's a dead end, can we come with you? See for ourselves?" Emily asked. "After all, we found the clues like real detectives. And then we could stop for ice cream on the way home."

As if they needed another hit of sugar tonight. "Tell you what, you guys behave yourselves for Ruby and I'll plan something special for tomorrow night. Something we can all do, even Pops and Janine and Luka, if he's not busy."

Nate nodded eagerly but Emily was skeptical, always preferring the bird in the hand. "Promise?"

Leah grabbed her bag and kissed them both. "Promise."

She was halfway to Craven Peak when her phone rang—the Labor and Delivery ward. "Dr. Wright here."

"Dr. Wright, this is Vicki, the nurse who took care of Beth Doe yesterday. I wasn't sure who to call—" Her voice was taut with anxiety. Very unlike an L and D nurse—they were usually as calm and collected as Leah's ER nurses.

"What's wrong, Vicki?"

"Beth's baby boy. His blood culture came back positive for Group B strep."

Leah sucked in her breath. This was exactly why the pediatricians had wanted to keep a close eye on the baby. "He needs antibiotics."

"My charge nurse called the police, but I'm not sure they understand how dangerous it is. So I thought I'd call you, since technically you're the one who admitted her."

"I know the detective in charge of the hunt for Beth and her baby. I'll call him myself, make sure he gets the word out. Thanks, Vicki." Leah hung up, adrenaline sparking her nerves. There still was little that she could do to help—but at least now Luka had a good reason to make the search for Beth public and get more people working on finding her.

She'd just reached the ranger's office inside the entrance to Craven Peak, so she parked in the gravel lot in front of the ancient log cabin and called Luka. "Did Reverend Harper know where Beth and her baby are?"

"He's not talking. I'm going to send Harper in, hoping an appeal from his daughter might get him to open up."

"Everything's changed. The baby's sick—I got a call from the hospital. He has an infection in his blood; he needs antibiotics and to be back in the hospital."

"What kind of infection?"

"Group B strep. It can cause sepsis, meningitis. If it isn't treated, he could die."

He made a noise over the phone that was part frustration and part sympathy.

"Does this give you enough to go public? To call in the state police to help?"

"Yes. I'll start a PSA, get the networks involved, Beth's picture will be everywhere. Given how much time has elapsed, the staties will probably take over and go wider to New York, New Jersey, Maryland."

The amount of ground they had to cover to find one woman and baby was overwhelming. "They could be anywhere by now," Leah said. "What can I do to help? I'm actually at Craven Peak. Beth might have stayed in one of their cabins—it's the only one within walking distance of the fairgrounds, so I reserved it tonight myself. I thought there might be a slim chance she left something behind, even though it's probably been cleaned since yesterday."

She heard the sound of his keyboard clicking in the background—coordinating a public search over several states was a huge endeavor. "Call me if you find anything," he said in an absent tone.

"Luka—" Her fear colored her voice.

"We'll find them. I'll call you as soon as I know anything."

He hung up. Leah stared at the darkened phone for long enough that the screen saver came on. A photo of Ian and Emily, laughing and playing. She took a deep breath, closing her eyes in a silent prayer. They had to find Beth and the baby.

Before it was too late.

# CHAPTER THIRTY-FIVE

Now that she knew Darius had an alibi for Lily's murder, Harper relaxed her questioning, taking a more conversational approach. For a kid who liked to present himself as a hardened street thug—even to the point of threatening Macy with a knife—he was pretty naive. With a few gentle nudges, including a soda and a candy bar, he opened up and told her everything she needed to know. Well, almost everything.

No matter what she tried, he refused to acknowledge that he'd ever heard of Lily before that night and insisted that Macy couldn't have had anything to do with Lily or even met her Saturday night since she'd been busy getting the money to bail him out after his arrest.

"My girl loves me, would do anything for me, and that's all I've got to say." He backed up his statement by leaning back, crossing his arms over his chest, and speaking one word, the magic word that ended any chance she had of getting more from him. "Lawyer."

Harper glared at Darius, then pushed her chair back, retrieved Lily's photo, and stalked out of the room. Only to find Luka waiting for her, leaning heavily on his crutches, his posture one of disappointment.

A flush heated her cheeks as she realized that he'd been watching her interview on the video monitor. "I still think he knows something about Lily," she insisted.

"Forget about Darius," he said, giving her a look reminding her who was boss and who was the rookie detective. "He's not going anywhere anytime soon. Come with me."

Lily wasn't going anywhere either, she thought in resignation as she followed him to the conference room that the VCU used for meetings. Krichek and Ray were there already, laptops open, a map of Craven County spread out across the table between them.

"Leah Wright called," Luka told them.

"Is Macy okay?" Harper asked.

"Fine. They're keeping her overnight. But that's not why she called." He paused, waiting until each of them made eye contact. "It's the missing baby. His blood work came back showing a potentially life-threatening strep infection. If we don't find him soon, he could die."

"Damn," Ray cursed. He had two kids at home, Harper knew.

"Before, the most we could do was be on the lookout, since Beth hasn't committed a crime and left of her own volition," Luka said. "But now everything has changed. We have a critical missing person, so all hands on deck. Finding that baby takes priority over everything."

"What's our next step?" Krichek asked.

"I've got a call out to the staties and they're taking point, widening the search to a tri-state area. Ahearn is making a public appeal, but without a vehicle or even Beth's full name to go on, it's going to be difficult to find her." Then Luka turned to Harper. "Which leaves us with really only one viable avenue to pursue."

She tensed. Why was he staring at her like that?

"When I reviewed the security footage from Good Sam," Luka continued, "there was one man who could have helped Beth and her baby leave without anyone seeing her."

"Who?" she asked. Now both Ray and Krichek were staring at her as well; obviously they knew the answer.

"Your father."

"The Reverend?" Shock rattled through her, had her grasping her hands together below the table even as she fought to keep her face devoid of expression. "You think he helped Beth?"

"Take a look for yourself." He cued up video on the big screen. There was no audio, but there was a clear progression of events: Beth leaving alone, dressed like a hospital worker; the Reverend carrying a diaper bag out of the Labor and Delivery ward; the Reverend then Beth both leaving via the same exit; and finally, the Reverend driving away.

Harper sighed. "You want me to talk to my father?"

"I already spoke with him. At his church. He wasn't exactly forthcoming."

"I'm not surprised." It was so like the Reverend—he always had all the answers, never hesitated once he knew what needed to be done. If Beth came to him for help, he wouldn't even think of telling his daughter the police officer, much less answer Luka's questions. The Reverend was above questioning, his judgment final. "He would have been embarrassed, humiliated to be suspected of any wrongdoing," she explained. "Not to mention, the church is where he wields power—he would have felt in command."

Luka eyed her appraisingly. "So I learned. I brought him here for a formal interview. Beth didn't appear to be coerced when she left the hospital. But clearly they know each other, which means your father knows more than he's saying. We have no evidence of an actual crime—and he knows it. Legally, he could walk at any time. Which is why I need you—"

"To interrogate him? But if he tells me anything that points to a crime, it will never hold up in court."

"Right now I don't care about court, I care about saving a child's life." He paused, obviously waiting for her to defend her father. Harper was torn, feeling pulled in impossible directions. But Luka was right, a life was at stake. "I need you to get him talking, learn anything you can about who Beth is, where she might be going. You up for it?"

"Yes, sir." She swallowed and nodded, then scraped back her chair to return to the interview room. How to talk to a man she'd never been able to talk with? Would confronting him with the evidence loosen his tongue? Or reinforce his silence?

When she entered the interview room, she found the Reverend sitting at the scarred wooden table. His posture was rigid, and Harper could tell he'd lost his patience.

"So." He acknowledged her entrance with a scowl, as if disappointed that the police couldn't find someone better suited to the job. He'd arranged his body to sit on the very edge of the lightweight vinyl chair, to have contact with the least amount of contaminated atoms as possible. "They sent you—am I meant to crumble with sentimentality?"

He would be expecting her to hammer him about Beth and her baby, but Luka had already tried that so she chose a different tack. "Tell me the truth about Spencer. I know you're hiding something. Something that might help me stop a killer."

His lips tightened and once again his hands relaxed into his favorite position: clasped together as if in prayer. "It's privileged."

"Not everything you and Spencer spoke about falls under attorney-client privilege," she challenged him. The very fact that he didn't question her about her use of the word "killer" or Spencer's supposed suicide told her that he knew much more than he let on. He'd been on the phone with Spencer during the time frame of his death—had he heard the killer? Did he know who it was? If so, why was he protecting them?

"I can't tell you anything because it's privileged under the seal of confession. I won't betray that. I can't betray it. Not for you, not for anyone." He didn't seem apologetic—he appeared defiant. "Instead of trying to force me to betray my vows, you need to decide whose laws you're beholden to: man's or God's."

"This isn't about the law. There are lives at stake."

He shook his head, his expression blanking. "Did it ever occur to you, Naomi, to trust me? I know what the right thing to do is, even if you don't. By keeping my silence, following God's law, I'm saving lives. And that's more important than any of your laws."

"And what about Beth's baby's life? He could die—you know that, right?"

"Your sergeant said something. I'm not at all certain I believe him. You say that being a police officer is about finding the truth, yet you use deception and coercion to create your own truth. So how can I believe anything any of you say?"

They sat in silence as she considered her options. He shifted in his seat, frowning at the obscene graffiti carved into the table between them, covering it with his pristine handkerchief so that he would be spared the sight. Finally, he shook his head and scoffed, "This, this den of inequity, this is why you turned your back on your Church, your God, your family?"

The Reverend's trump card. She was surprised he had played it so soon. The leader of Holy Redeemer considered no sinner unworthy of redemption. No sinner except his own daughter.

That was what had kept her away for years. It was only recently that she'd started seeing her family again. Jonah had shepherded her way back to the family dinner table, but she still hadn't found her way back into her father's good graces. After yesterday, when the Reverend had appeared to show some interest in her job, she'd actually hoped that the wound was beginning to heal.

He pursed his lips—as close to a disdainful eye-roll as the Reverend ever got. "I'm sure you appreciate this irony."

"What? That a man of God is sitting in jail?" Harper asked.

"No. Of course not. I have many sins, but hubris isn't one of them." He folded his hands together on the table. "No. The irony that they sent you." He nodded to the door. "As if the agent of my redemption would be the child who was so willful and—"

"And unredeemable." Now it was her turn to shake her head, but in frustration, not disdain. "You never will forgive me for letting you down, tarnishing your image."

"My image?" His voice rose. "You think I was worried about myself? Did you even think about your mother? What your little drunken, lustful escapade cost her? How humiliated she was?"

His words were more forceful than a slap. She leaned back, putting space between them, space to think. Eleven years and this was the first time they'd spoken about what happened when she went away to college. Eleven years she'd waited to tell her side of the story, to face the pain, to be forgiven. Forgiven for a seventeen-year-old's naivety, for being stupid, careless, but not… "Drunken? Lustful? You have no idea what really happened, do you?"

"Of course I do. I spoke with the head of the college myself. And John, of course."

"You know those boys were John's friends."

"Yes, and he told them to look after you. A freshman at your first college party. You were lucky they were there to protect you before things went further—"

Further? She recoiled, ice filling her gut as she relived how far things had gone that night that had changed her life forever.

"That a daughter of mine would act so shamelessly—" Another shake of his head. "Your mother was inconsolable for months. And the fact that you refused to come home, that you left school and chose a whole other life, after we had such plans, such dreams… It broke her. You broke her."

"What exactly did John tell you I did?" she asked, every word a shard of glass to be swallowed. She knew what the boys had said, knew how the campus police had taken their word and written their report accordingly, even knew what the school officials accused her of when they suspended her: "crass and willful violations" of the Christian principles that the college had been founded on and engaging in acts that were "immoral, improper, and indecent." But what had her brother actually told their father?

He frowned. "We don't need to get into that here."

She glanced around the barren room. Where better? When better? Because in here, right now, she was the one with the power—unlike that night eleven years ago when she'd been the one trapped in another small room with no power and no means of escape. "Yes, Father. We do. What did they tell you?"

"They said you were drunk. They said you were acting like a wanton hussy, taking off your clothes and dancing, trying to seduce the boys—"

"Men, Father. They were twenty and twenty-one. I was the child, I was seventeen."

"Still old enough to know better. You should have never allowed yourself to get drunk—"

"I didn't." She crossed her arms over her chest, leaning back and waited.

"Of course you were drunk. The boys said—the campus police report said—"

"The report said whatever those three legacy students—all rich, white men with pulpits waiting for them to inherit—told the campus cop to write. I never took a drink of alcohol. To this day I still don't drink. You know that—I don't even drink wine at family dinner."

"I always thought that was because of your job. Or..." He hesitated, his gaze fixed on his folded hands. "Or that you refused to drink with us."

"Why the hell—"

"Language," he snapped. As if two adults couldn't handle a small, almost benign cuss word—or worse, that his almighty God wasn't strong enough to handle it. She'd never understood how a God prone to smiting and cursing entire populations, to the point of genocide even, could flinch at mere words.

Silence fell between them as Harper fought down the memories of that night so long ago, trying to sterilize them into something she could share with her father, something he might actually believe. Something that would heal this gaping abyss that had grown between them.

She had to get him to open up about the present. If revisiting the most painful night of her life helped, then it was worth it. "I was there, I know what happened. You need to accept my truth—or at least acknowledge that you might not know the entire truth."

The Reverend removed his glasses, rubbing them clean with his handkerchief, peering into her eyes, judging her worth. He replaced his glasses, carefully adjusting them, in no rush.

"The hospital really did call," she persisted, hoping to drive a wedge in the tiny crevice in his facade that she had created. "Beth's baby really does have an infection. He might die if he doesn't get medical help. Soon."

"You don't expect me to believe that, do you? Your Sergeant Jericho would say anything to force me to break my silence. Even use you as Satan's tool." He waved a hand in dismissal. "I thought I raised you better than that. Despite your sinful past, I had hoped—"

"All I care about," she interrupted him. "All *I'm* praying for is finding that baby before it's too late. Surely God would forgive you for breaking confession if it meant—"

"Stop it, Naomi. Give it up. If that's all you have to say for yourself, send your sergeant back in. At least he could mount a somewhat entertaining, if misguided, debate of the issues." He leaned back, closing his eyes, denying her presence as much as he'd denied the fact that Beth's baby was in danger.

Anger flashed over her, but she gritted her teeth and swallowed it raw. Outbursts of emotion never worked with the Reverend, would only serve to harden his resolve. After all, God had chosen him, spoke through him; who was she to challenge His authority?

She thought she'd broken through for a moment, but this was the same battle she'd fought and lost her entire life. Only now a child might pay the ultimate price for her failure.

# CHAPTER THIRTY-SIX

Luka was watching and listening to Harper's interview with her father via the video feed on his computer while also fielding calls about Beth and her baby. His team was no longer lead on the search, but he still needed to coordinate with the other agencies involved. He had sent Ray and Krichek back to relieve the uniformed officers surveilling Tassi and Hansen. Right now, patrol officers were more valuable out on the street searching for Beth than pulling overtime on a stakeout.

He was disappointed that Harper couldn't get her father talking—he'd really thought she had a chance when she challenged Matthew with the facts behind her assault when she was in college. Luka and her other supervisors on the force knew about the incident—she'd been required to report that she had been a victim of a crime when applying to the academy and it had come up during the psychological assessment, so it was well documented in her personnel record. He could see her pain as she related her side of the story. What he couldn't understand was Matthew's reaction. How could a man of God—how could any father—be so heartless in the face of his daughter's suffering?

His phone rang—the evidence garage.

"Look, it's not our fault, okay?" the impound officer started. "We just got the vehicle."

"What are you talking about?" Luka lowered the sound on the video.

"This Standish SUV. First, the CSU guys kept it for DNA processing and then they fumed it overnight for fingerprints. Then the cyber guys wanted to access its onboard computer, so it's only now arrived at our garage."

"And why is that an issue?"

"Because they don't inspect vehicles that are impounded as evidence, they only look for their own stuff, we're the ones—"

"What did you find?" Luka interrupted.

"Someone had a GPS tracker wired into the vehicle. Fancy one—a lot nicer than the ones the department uses."

"I'll need the serial number. And is there a way to track who was receiving its signals?"

"You'd have to ask the cyber guys. I told my guys to leave it as is, so it's still powered up. Figured that might help preserve any internal data."

"Good thinking. I'll send someone right over. Thanks for calling." Luka hung up. If not law enforcement, who would want to track Spencer's movements? Foster Dean was the obvious candidate, but he hadn't even arrived in Craven County until Sunday morning. Unless the Zapatas had sent someone else in addition to Dean. Or maybe the not-so-grieving widow had suspected her husband's plan to leave without her? Or perhaps another of Spencer's victims was searching for their stolen money? Someone like Larry Hansen?

He glanced at the video—Harper was wrapping up and still getting nowhere. He called Ray. "You said Larry Hansen brought Tassi home, right? Is he still there?"

"No one's come in or out since they got back from the hospital. Why?"

Luka explained about the GPS. "Could've been either of them who planted it."

"I'll take a run at them—unless you want them brought into the station?"

Luka considered. A familiar environment might relax them, help them to drop their guard. Of course, he'd thought that about the reverend as well when he'd gone to the church to speak with him. But somehow, he didn't think Tassi or Larry would be as difficult to get talking. He glared at the crutches leaning against his desk. That stupid piece of impaled glass was making his life much too complicated.

"Yeah. Bring them in. I want to see their reactions. Besides, so far they've been handled with kid gloves; let's show them how real criminals are treated." Ahearn wouldn't like it, but Luka was past caring.

"You got it," Ray said, sounding eager for action. "I'll call you once we're en route."

Luka hung up just as Harper tapped on the door. "Guess you saw," she said, hanging her head. "Sorry. I should've tried a different approach—"

"No. You did fine."

"Okay." Clearly she disagreed with his assessment. "What about my father? Are you pressing charges?"

"For what? Carrying a diaper bag out of a hospital isn't a crime." Not to mention that arresting a prominent clergyman without probable cause really would have Ahearn blowing a gasket. "I shouldn't have sent you in there. I wanted to throw him off balance."

She took a step inside, leaned against the bookcase. "No. It was the right move."

"You brought up what happened to you in college," he said in a gentle tone, giving her space if she didn't want to talk about it. "You never told your father what happened?"

"He never asked." She thought for a moment. "I really thought I could get him talking."

"Why don't you drive him home?" he suggested. "No questions, no judgments, simply listen. Maybe if you let him take the lead, give him back control, he'll tell you what really happened and where Beth and the baby are. Anything he says would be inadmissible, but seriously, as long as they're safe, and we can get the baby back to the hospital, I don't mind breaking the rules." He studied her. "That is, if you're okay with it."

"No, it's fine. If he had anything to do with Beth and her baby, or with Spencer's death, then we need the truth. If I can get it, I'm happy to do so."

"I don't want to put you in a position where you have to choose between your family and your job. But we need to make saving that baby a priority." He shook his head. "Explain it to me. He's a man of God; I can't understand why he won't talk to us, help us."

"Because that would mean admitting he's wrong," Harper said. "The Reverend has lived his entire life believing God works directly through him—"

"So how could he ever be wrong about anything?" Luka finished for her. Not for the first time, Luka wondered about Harper and how strong she was. Growing up in that environment must have been complicated. "I've no idea if that's a sign of a faith beyond my imagination or pure hubris."

"Don't ask me. I've given up trying to find those answers." She started to leave, then turned back. "Just so you know, boss. If it's between the truth and my family, I'm choosing the truth. Every time."

"I already knew that, Harper," Luka replied. "Now get going. Call me if you need anything."

The door had no sooner shut behind her than Luka's phone rang. Ray. "Got a bit of a complication, boss."

"What?"

"Tassi and Larry Hansen are gone."

# CHAPTER THIRTY-SEVEN

The Reverend said nothing as Harper led him out of the police department and to her car. They got inside, turned onto the street, and drove three blocks before finally he sighed and spoke. "Tell me the truth. About college. Everything."

Startled, she jerked her head up, eyes blazing as they met his. He couldn't handle the truth. At least that's what she'd told herself for eleven years, choking it back down every time she was tempted to set it free. No one in her family could handle the truth. They'd already judged her, cast her out without a word—she was the irredeemable, the prodigal. Not even the Holy Redeemer himself could find grace in her.

He reached his hand across the seat, covering hers with his in the same gesture he had made when she was a child and he wanted her to know she had his full attention. It was a gift, a blessing, an honor. The Reverend was listening. Finally listening. To her. "The truth, Naomi."

She hauled in a breath, staring out the windshield at the road—she couldn't face seeing his expression or it might break her entirely. "I went to the party at the house. John wasn't there but he'd told his friends to look after me. They were nice, real gentlemen. One of them brought me a Coke. We danced—everyone danced together, it was a big crowd. Nothing intimate, just letting off steam. Kids having fun. People were laughing, I thought maybe a few were drunk, but everyone was having such a good time." Her words caught; her throat felt raw. She swallowed twice. "Then I started feeling funny. Sick. Like the sounds were too loud and the lights too bright, everything was fuzzy."

"But you weren't drinking?"

"I hadn't even finished the Coke." She glanced over, met his gaze, making sure he understood. "The Coke he gave me."

His jaw tightened but he nodded for her to go on.

"One of them took me to a room to lie down—no, first he took me upstairs to a bathroom, in case I was going to be sick. I felt nauseous but nothing happened. I splashed some water on my face, drank a little, then he was holding me. Helping me, he said. And he took off my sweater and unbuttoned my blouse—so I could breathe easier, he said. And in the back of my mind I felt panicked but also I kept saying to myself, he's John's friend, he's looking out for me, he'd never hurt me." Her voice had tightened, no longer a grown woman's but the voice of that scared girl who was desperate to trust that everything would be all right, that there was nothing to be afraid of. Harper glanced at her father. His face was ashen, his hand abandoning hers to retreat to his side of the car, gripping his door handle as if they were hurtling toward an abyss.

"Then two more came in. They said I could lie down in their bedroom, where it was quiet and no one would hear us." She swallowed, bracing herself against the avalanche of memories. She almost shared them, but relented. He didn't need the specifics, the bits and pieces of sensory overload that formed the kaleidoscope of her nightmares. "And then they took turns."

The Reverend made a low groaning noise, deep in his throat.

"It was almost dawn when they let me go. They actually walked me back to my dorm but of course it was locked because it was after curfew, so the RA called security. I was so out of it, half-naked, incoherent. And they were three well-respected seniors saying they'd seen me act inappropriately at the party so decided to escort me home to make sure I got there safely and hopefully to mitigate my punishment. As if they were protecting me. After all, I was only a freshman, away from home for the first time, these things happen, right?"

Now her tone turned bitter, raw. "The guard actually shook their hands, told them they were gentlemen, a credit to the school. And later, when I tried to file a report, to tell the truth, the campus cops laughed. Then they got angry—how dare I tarnish the reputations of these three fine upstanding young men? So they called a disciplinary board and, well, you know the rest."

"The rest" being of course the lone young Black girl sitting across from a sea of white faces, including the three soon-to-be ordained ministers who painted her as an angry Black woman intent on destroying their lives because she refused to accept responsibility for her own poor choices. That John, the brother who was meant to watch over her that night, the brother who'd left her in their care, that he sat among those white faces, refusing to speak to her, humiliated even as his friends pitied him for his embarrassment, the embarrassment that was her, his adopted sister—that was the final straw.

Memories of the insults hurled in person and on social media, scrawled across her door or keyed into her car. *Bitch, slut, harlot, jezebel.* The death threats, the noose left hanging in her room. She'd left school, worked for a year, found a small state school that she could afford with the help of two jobs and decided that never again would she be a victim—and she'd found a career where she could stand up for victims who were silenced, as she'd been.

"So," she said after a long moment, her gaze fixed on the road. She couldn't bear to look at him, was too afraid of what she might see. Judgment, disappointment, shame? But no matter how he felt about what she'd told him, she was glad she had. Now that he knew the truth, maybe they could start afresh. Surely there was room for the Naomi she had become, the woman she'd forged herself into, so different from the daughter he'd lost after that night? Surely there was room for her in his heart? "That's everything. Now you know."

"I'm glad." The Reverend cleared his throat; still his words emerged slow, formal. "I'm glad you've finally told me."

As if she'd chosen to keep this from him for all these years. She swallowed her pride and pain. "Thank you for asking."

Then silence. Long enough for them to leave the heart of the city behind and start winding over the switchbacks that led up the mountain. "I have a confession to make."

She held her breath, nodding for him to continue.

"I know you feel excluded, not a real member of the family. It's not because of your race or you being adopted or even what happened to you in college. It's because you've never truly come to understand what it means to be a Harper, a custodian of a church that's survived for two centuries. We are the church and the church is our family. And we'll—*I* will do anything to protect that family."

How was that a confession? Confusion and anger flashed through her as she parsed his words. She'd shared her pain, her awful truth with him and it hadn't changed anything. She still wasn't worthy of his love, not even of the name Harper.

The church. It always came back to the church. She waited, but he didn't continue, so she asked, "Anything? Like what?"

"Bend written laws to obey God's law." He shifted in his seat. "That's the real reason why you no longer feel a part of our family, our church. You've chosen a profession that requires you to put your faith in men and their laws. Naomi, you need to stop pursuing this woman. She deserves sanctuary, God's protection. His will must always triumph."

Now it was her turn to embrace silence. The Reverend was so blinded by his faith that he couldn't even consider that he was in the wrong. Harper was certain that he knew where Beth and her baby were; he'd practically confessed it. To his daughter, the cop. And he knew that there was not a damn thing she could do. The realization was a gut punch that stole her breath. His almost-confession would never hold up in court, wasn't even enough to get a search warrant—not after the judge had already refused Luka's initial request based on the hospital's video evidence.

"Where is she?" she blurted out. The Reverend responded with an arched eyebrow. "Whether you tell me where she is or not, it's important that you get the baby to a doctor. Luka wasn't lying about him being sick, it wasn't some act to get you to talk. The baby needs medicine and you're putting him at risk if you're not getting him help."

"The baby will be cared for. You'll have to take my word for that." His tone implied the certainty of a man guided by a higher power. "Tell your sergeant to stop looking. Now. Before he gets someone else killed."

"Someone else?" She turned down the drive to Holy Redeemer. "Spencer Standish. You know who killed him?"

His lips pressed together so tightly they turned white. "Give your sergeant the message and leave us alone. I have a plan. God has a plan. You people play no part in it."

"I can't do that. You know I can't do that."

"For once, Naomi, why can't you do as you're told!" His glare blazed across the seat.

When she swallowed, she tasted tears. "Because it's my job," she finally said in a calm, steady voice. The voice she'd learned to use out on the street when a situation threatened to erupt. The voice she put on along with her badge and gun every time she went to work.

"Then you understand why you're no longer welcome here. If you can't obey God's will and mine, then that's your choice."

The Reverend's words swirled around in Harper's head. They mixed with words he'd spoken to her time and again: *Your choice, Naomi. Right or wrong. Make me proud.* And Harper realized that, no matter how hard she tried, she'd never win his pride, the ultimate gift, the only gift she'd ever wanted from him.

The church stood white against the backdrop of the towering evergreen forest and the darkening summer sky. It was a beacon of hope, but it was a beacon that had always been denied to her. She drove on toward the house, stopping behind John's SUV and Rachel's minivan. The Reverend made no move to leave the car.

Harper's mind buzzed with a thousand questions, but one was foremost. "Does she know?" She nodded to Rachel's minivan. "Does Mom know? What you've done? Kidnapping and hiding a woman and baby?"

"Your mother? Of course not, dear. It's nothing to do with her."

Harper almost didn't hear the Reverend as he opened the car door, humid air rushing in.

"But she won't argue with my decision. She never does. Goodbye, Naomi."

He closed the door and left, walking up the porch steps and into the house.

She'd failed. Again. Could you even call it failing when you never stood a chance to start with?

Harper considered her options. Exigent circumstances, a baby's life at stake. What was stopping her from searching the grounds on her own? Nothing, except she'd probably lose her job if the Reverend filed a complaint against her. She could call Jonah, explain the situation, ask him to search the house and church for her. And risk losing the one member of the family who accepted her for who she was. Maybe she should call Luka, dump it all on him, ask him what to do—and forever lose any credibility she had with him.

Or she could return to the station and do the work she'd been assigned. Krichek was still waiting for her to go through the list of license plates—

And then she realized something. She lunged for her phone from the charger on the center console, pulled up the list Krichek had sent her and that she'd barely glanced at earlier. Plate numbers from the strip mall where Luka had been attacked yesterday, waiting for her to connect them with registered owners. It was scut work, low priority, but now she frantically scrolled down the list. *No, no, no, she was wrong, she had to be wrong…*

There it was. Rachel's license plate. She'd been at the strip mall parked right next to Spencer Standish's office when Luka was attacked. And the Reverend had gone there with Luka—he had to have seen Rachel's van there.

Was all this silence of the confessional, unbreakable holy vow stuff merely an excuse? Was the Reverend covering for Rachel because she was involved in Spencer Standish's death? And somehow, so was Beth?

She left the car and strode toward the house. Her choice. Right or wrong. To hell with making anyone proud. She knew what she had to do and nothing and no one were going to stop her.

# CHAPTER THIRTY-EIGHT

Despite the fact that the official time of the sun setting was still more than an hour away, up here on the mountain, surrounded by ancient pines and towering hemlocks, it was already twilight. Leah left her car, inhaling the scent of the evergreens and embracing the cooler air compared to down in the valley below. She entered the log cabin that served as the state forest's office. The lone ranger on duty—a woman in her fifties who seemed resentful of human visitors intruding into the serenity of her forest—verified her reservation on the computer.

"Kinda last minute, isn't it? One night, right?" she asked as she ran Leah's credit card.

"What's your check-out process?" Leah asked.

"Return the key by noon and you won't get charged another night. If you leave a mess, we charge a cleaning fee."

"So the cabin has been cleaned since its last occupant?"

The ranger cast an irritated glance at a clipboard. "Should've been. We do a basic cleaning and linen change between guests, but the weekend guy didn't mark it down. Some guy had that cabin booked the past few weeks, but I don't remember ever seeing anyone there during patrols. Anyway, if you find a mess, let me know and I'll move you. Too late tonight for me to come clean myself; I've still got to make the rounds of the RV park and campground."

"I'll be fine, don't worry." Leah gave the ranger her best smile. "I don't suppose you could tell me who was staying in the cabin?"

"Nope." The ranger was rummaging through a drawer and didn't even bother looking up. "Can only find one key, that good enough?"

"Sure, no problem." Leah accepted the old-fashioned bronze key.

"There's two ways to get there. From here, this is the easiest." The ranger traced a route on the map. "Count your turns because once you're past the campground most of the roads don't have signs. If you're heading into town for groceries or the like, this other way is a more direct route—but the gates are locked at nine p.m., so you need to make it back by then. If you run late, come back here and use the call box, I'll come let you in."

"So there's not a check-in or guard booth anywhere except here?" She wasn't as much interested in security as the fact that the cabin could be accessed without anyone knowing. Making it perfect as a hideout for Beth. Leah suspected that if the baby hadn't come early, forcing Beth out of hiding, no one might have ever known Beth was even there.

"Guard?" the ranger scoffed. "Against what?" She squinted at Leah. "You do know you're entering a wilderness area—this isn't a Holiday Inn. You have camped before, right?"

"I know what I'm doing." Leah felt a bit offended. While in college, she'd often spent her vacations backpacking and hiking in places a lot wilder and less civilized than Craven Peak. "I grew up here, I've been all over these mountains."

Still, the ranger seemed doubtful. "There's no phone in the cabin and cell reception is iffy at best. Come back and find me if you change your mind."

"I'll be fine, thanks." Leah took her map and key and left.

By the time she found the cabin—a squat cube of a building, its dark-stained logs chinked with white caulking and a brown metal roof—the sun had almost completely vanished. Leah decided to start by retracing Beth's steps while she still had some light left.

She oriented her map. The fairgrounds weren't that far—a quarter of a mile—and there was a path leading to them from the road below the cabin. From the brochure accompanying the map it appeared that the meadow which had hosted the fair was also home to non-denominational Sunday services as well as other events including wildlife lectures and an astronomy star-gazing class. She made note of the latter for Emily and Nate as she walked down the dirt drive and turned onto the gravel road. A hundred feet up the road she saw a sign pointing to a trail labeled *To The Meadow* and marked by yellow blazes on the trees. Good thing because the foliage was so thick that she saw no signs of the fairground until she reached the old split-rail fence that formed its boundary.

At first she wondered at Beth's ability to climb the fence but then spotted a gate a few yards down. She crossed through it and put the map away, switching to her phone and looking at Nate's photos, orienting her position using trees with distinguishing features as landmarks. This had to be about where Beth had tossed her phone. Leah began pacing the area, scanning for any signs of the phone in the grass. Thankfully the meadow had been mowed before the fair.

On her second circuit she was rewarded with a glint of glass. She ran to it. A phone. It had to be Beth's. The screen was black and when she tried to turn it on it didn't respond. Hopefully all it needed was a fresh battery charge. Pocketing her prize, she jogged back to the gate and followed the trail to the cabin, using her phone's flashlight to guide her steps. It was completely dark by the time she climbed the cabin's rough-hewn porch steps and slid the key into the lock. The key turned but the knob didn't—she hadn't unlocked it, she'd locked it.

Which meant the cabin had been left unlocked—Beth may have been the last person to leave. If so, if the ranger had neglected to come to clean, then there might be some clues among Beth's belongings. Eager to test her theory, Leah reversed the direction of the key and the lock popped open. She turned the knob, pushed the door open, and reached in to snap on the lights.

The single-room cabin lit up, all its secrets illuminated. Including the woman's corpse sprawled face up on the floor, blood covering her body, her mouth and eyes open in a silent scream.

# CHAPTER THIRTY-NINE

Luka curbed his anger and mobilized what resources he could to search for Tassi and Larry. "Want to tell me how they got past you?" he asked Ray.

"Not us—they were gone when we went to bring them in. But don't blame the uniforms. This place is huge—you've seen it. Apparently, there's a service road around the back that isn't marked on the maps."

Damn. "Any sign of Foster Dean?"

"No. But Larry drove her back from Good Sam and both of their cars are still here. So, either they called a cab or someone picked them up. Could be another neighbor? Friend from the club? You know these rich people, they all stick together."

Luka's phone rang with another call. It was Leah. "Work the scene, find me a traffic camera, something, anything—"

"Rich people also like their privacy; there won't be any traffic cameras. And their houses are all too far back from the road for security cameras to help."

Ray was sharing facts Luka already knew and it wasn't helping his growing frustration. "We're monitoring Tassi's financial accounts; tell Krichek to find a judge and get us up on Larry's as well. Plus, phone pings and GPS records. I've got to go, Leah's calling."

"Hope that means they found the kid and he's all right. I'll let you know if anything breaks here." Ray hung up.

Luka switched calls. "Leah, sorry, I'm kind of in the middle of something."

"I found the cabin where Beth was staying." Her words were rushed but her tone was steady—the same voice he'd heard her use during emergencies. "It's in Craven Peak. Luka, she's dead. Murdered. I found her body."

"Beth? Is the baby okay?"

"Not Beth. Tassi. It's—" Her voice dropped. "Tassi's dead. Murdered."

Tassi? Killed where Beth had been staying? The implications were staggering, but his first priority was Leah's safety. "Get out. Now. Don't touch anything. We need to get you to safety in case—"

"I'm in my car driving to the ranger's station," she interrupted him. "I didn't want to risk it if anyone was still hanging around."

"Good, good." Of course, she knew the first rule of any initial scene response was ensuring that the scene was safe. "What did you see?"

"I think she was tortured." For the first time her voice sounded shaky. As if, now that the emergency was over, she'd allowed her emotions to finally creep in. "I could barely recognize her. Luka, what they did to that poor woman—"

"Ray isn't far, he's at Tassi's house. I'm sending him to meet you at the ranger's station and I'm on my way as well." Why torture Tassi? What did the killer want from her? The missing money? And then there was Beth; he couldn't forget Beth. She'd told Leah someone was after her, but the only intersection between the two cases that Luka could see was Matthew Harper's involvement with both women. Given his role as a pastoral counselor, there might be a straightforward explanation—if they could get the man to talk.

"I found Beth's phone," Leah interrupted his rampaging thoughts. "It's dead, though. But maybe once it's charged—"

"No. Hold on to it, the forensics guys will take care of it. We can't risk losing any data."

"Okay." Her breath was ragged. "Okay."

"Hang tight, we're on our way. I need to call Ray, get things rolling."

"Right. See you soon." She hung up.

He alerted Ray and Krichek and had patrol contact the state police—technically, the forest was outside of Luka's jurisdiction, but the staties were even farther away and they often cooperated on cases—as well as the forest ranger on duty. Even as he grabbed his coat, keys, and the damn crutches, and started out to his car, Luka couldn't help but feel as if somehow he'd lost control of this case. Things were spiraling in random, unexpected directions.

How did Tassi know about Beth's cabin? Why was she there? Was the killer looking for Beth and tortured Tassi to learn where she was? Or was Tassi the main target, taken there?

Tassi was last seen with Larry Hansen. Which immediately sent the tennis-loving chiropractor to the top of Luka's suspect list. Maybe he'd been the one faking all along—convincing Luka that he was a harmless fool, pretending to be in love with Tassi so he could stick close to her. All to get his hands on Spencer's money.

And then there was Foster Dean—if the former DEA agent really was working for the Zapata family, then torture would not be beyond the realm of imagination.

Luka made another call from the car: an attempt-to-locate alert for Foster Dean and his rented Tahoe. And he added a court order to the car rental agency for GPS tracking of Dean's Tahoe to Krichek's list of assignments. Odds were a judge would want more probable cause before granting it, but it was worth a shot.

If this was about Spencer's stolen money, the missing gold, then Tassi as a victim made sense. That kind of money was enough to motivate either Hansen or Dean into forcing her to talk. But why at Beth's cabin? And what did Beth and her baby have to do with any of it?

Too many questions with no damned answers. Time was running out for Beth's baby—he needed treatment quickly. Public service announcements and news stories were already filling the airwaves, asking the public for their help in locating mother and child. All featuring photos of Beth, broadcasting her image to the world.

But if a killer was also hunting for her, then had Luka just placed a bright flashing neon target on Beth and her baby?

# CHAPTER FORTY

Harper jogged up the steps to her parents' front door, but not even her fury and sense of betrayal could break habits ingrained by years of scolding. She paused to wipe her feet, then paused again to slide her paddle holster from her hip, where it was easily visible, to the small of her back. Partly because of her mother's rules against handguns, but also because she wanted Rachel to feel relaxed, hopefully enough to tell her daughter the truth instead of thinking she was being interrogated by a cop—as a suspect. Rachel's van being parked at a crime scene was no coincidence. And the Reverend hadn't said a word, apart from all his holier than thou talk of God's law being greater than man's. He'd willfully obstructed justice.

She unclipped her badge, dropped it into her jacket pocket, then went inside without knocking—because family shouldn't need to knock on their own front door. Voices sounded from the family room at the end of the hall, beside the kitchen. In the few seconds it took Harper to reach the rear of the house, she replayed the conversations she'd had with her mother over the past two days. What a fool she'd been, thinking Rachel was finally interested in her daughter's life. All those pleas for Harper to tell Rachel about her cases were merely an attempt to gain insider information on the Standish case. No wonder Rachel kept dismissing her every time she brought up Lily Nolan. All Rachel cared about was Spencer Standish's murder.

But why? There was no way Rachel could have killed Standish… was there? No. Her mother's faith was as strong as the Reverend's. Maybe he'd sent her to Standish's office while he'd been with Luka?

But why? What were they hiding? If only she could understand why they were involved and what exactly they were involved in, then she could try to help them before it was too late.

She reached the family room. It was open-plan, with the kitchen to the left, a small breakfast nook, then the larger living area with a fireplace, sofa, love seat and the Reverend's recliner. But the Reverend wasn't sitting in his favorite chair, not tonight. Tonight he stood in front of the fireplace, face florid, back rigid, glaring at his wife and youngest son. John and Rachel were also standing, Rachel nearest the kitchen—the center of her domestic universe—while John paced in front of the sofa.

Rachel caught a glimpse of Harper and made a tutting noise like a startled chick. John whirled on Harper while the Reverend simply seemed irritated by her arrival.

"Naomi, what are you doing here?" John said, stepping toward her as if hoping to shoo her back down the hall and out the door. "We're busy. Church business."

Everything fell into place. *John*, who always took the easy way out, even if it meant condemning his sister. John, always ready with a shortcut or excuse to get out of chores. John, who always won every game because he cheated—and was proud that he did it so well, nobody could ever prove it.

John, who would make the perfect mark for a conman like Standish.

"You were at Standish's office," Harper told him. "Why? No, wait. Let me guess. You invested the church's money in Spencer Standish's fund, didn't you? I mean, who could resist those double-digit returns, right?"

A rage of color crept up John's neck at her words. "How was I to know he was a crook?" He turned to the Reverend. "It wasn't my fault. I was going to tell you."

"What did you do, John?" the Reverend said in a low voice, his eyes boring into his youngest son's face. "Tell me. What did you do?"

"John only wanted what was best for the church," Rachel defended her youngest son.

"Think of all the people we could have helped if Spencer had come through with his promises," John added.

The Reverend's shoulders sagged as he turned away from his son. "How much is gone? How much did you lose?"

Harper held her ground, listening hard. The daughter in her was frantically trying to think of ways to save her father and his church, the little girl in her was seething at John's betrayal and cheering his fall from grace, while the hardened cop was wondering exactly how far a man in John's position might go to get his money back. Could John have murdered Standish?

"All of it," John admitted in a grudging tone. He jerked his chin up as if refusing to accept any blame. "But then, Mom overheard you and Spencer talking about the gold he'd hidden. And how if anything happened to him, you were to make sure his mistress got it."

That caught Harper's attention. "Mistress? What mistress? Who is she?"

John ignored her, his focus on the Reverend. "Why should some adulteress get the money when we could use it for the church and do so much good?"

"You knew about the missing gold?" Harper stepped between the two men so that John was forced to face her. "John, if you had anything to do with Spencer Standish's death, you need to tell me. Now. I can't help you unless you tell me everything."

John's haughty glare shot across the space between them, even as his lips tightened in defiance.

Rachel stepped into the fray, waving her hands like a school-teacher asking for silence. And it worked. "Let's all calm down. I'll make some tea, and we'll discuss this."

Everyone went quiet and stared at each other.

"I think it best if John comes with me down to the station. We can discuss it there." Harper broke the silence. She'd never get anything out of John with Rachel there for him to hide behind her skirts. "Please, you all need to let me help you. This is more serious than you know."

"It's not what you think, Naomi," Rachel told her in an admonishing voice. "There's no need for anyone to go anywhere. Now, come sit down like civilized adults."

As if Harper was the uncivilized lout barging in on the family gathering. How could Rachel be so calm, acting as if John had done nothing wrong? He'd admitted to losing the church's funds—and might be involved in much, much worse.

But that was Rachel, always overlooking her youngest son's faults.

The thought brought Harper up short and she turned her attention from John to Rachel. How far would Rachel go to protect her family? "The police know your van was at Standish's office," she said, watching Rachel for a reaction. She wanted to see shock or surprise, anything to suggest that she had no idea what Harper was talking about.

Instead, Rachel's face was an emotionless mask, her only giveaway the knowing glance she shot at John.

Before Harper could ask anything more, the doorbell rang. Rachel started, then rushed to the front of the house to answer it, the clack of her heels echoing against the hardwood floors.

Harper whirled on John. "What have you done?"

"Naomi," her father admonished. "Hush."

The sound of Rachel's heels came once more. This time moving more slowly. Harper backed away from both men, running through her options. She didn't want them to dig themselves in deeper, but she also couldn't ignore that they were involved in a homicide. She needed to know exactly what they'd done so she could minimize any further damage—to the case as well as to her family.

A few seconds later Rachel returned. With Foster Dean. Who held a gun to her head.

# CHAPTER FORTY-ONE

Ray and Leah were waiting for Luka on the cabin's front porch. He'd stopped to get directions from the ranger, who he'd left at the entrance to ensure that only the state police and their evidence recovery team were allowed access.

"Leah, why didn't you wait at the ranger's station?" Luka asked as he fumbled his way across the uneven dirt road to the porch steps.

"I wanted to talk to you," she answered.

"And I wanted her to show me anything she touched," Ray added.

"I ran out so fast when I found her. I had to come back, make sure she was dead." She focused on Luka. "I think Beth and her baby might be with Reverend Harper—he's the only link between Tassi and Beth. So I'm headed over there—"

"No," Luka told her. "I'll call Krichek."

"He's at the Standish place," Ray reminded him.

Luka was already dialing, thankful that he had any service this far up the mountain. "I'll have Harper relieve him there." That would keep Harper far away from anything connected with Matthew—and any potential conflict of interest.

"Boss," Krichek answered. "I was just gonna call you." His voice was tight with excitement. "I found Hansen."

"Great, where is he?"

"Here. Never left. We were sweeping the property and found him. Dead. In the pool house. It's bad. He's been sliced and diced and beaten and looks like a blow torch was used on him."

"Tortured." Luka swore under his breath. "Stay there. Did the judge come through on the warrants for Dean's rental car's GPS?"

"Haven't heard back yet."

"Call him, let him know Dean is now our number one suspect in two homicides. Add his phone and financials to the warrant." Luka hung up. Dean was trained too well, would dump both his phone and vehicle. But the GPS data was still valuable evidence and might give them an idea of where he was going. Did he have Beth and the baby with him? Or was Leah right and Matthew Harper was hiding them? Either way, they were running out of time.

"I'll go to the church if Krichek can't," Ray volunteered.

"No. I've got it. Ahearn will have a fit if we don't handle the reverend with kid gloves."

"I'm coming," Leah said, hoisting her knapsack higher on her shoulder. "If the baby's there, I have antibiotics, I can start treatment right away."

Ray frowned. "We don't know how involved the reverend is. Plus, if Dean tied Tassi to Beth, he might be headed there as well. You'll need back-up."

"I know. I'll call ERT." The Emergency Response Team was Cambria City's equivalent of SWAT. Luka turned on his crutches and headed back to the car, Leah walking alongside him, her stride and posture closing off any arguments about her joining him.

"You can't send ERT in, not with a baby there," she said as they reached the Impala. "Those guys are trigger-happy." During her six months working with the police with the Crisis Intervention Team, Leah had had a few run-ins with the ERT's commander, who hadn't embraced the department's new progressive stance on de-escalation tactics.

"Don't worry, I'll make sure they know about Beth and the baby." His left foot hit a rock, sending pain shooting up his leg.

"Want me to drive?" she offered.

He was tempted to take her up on it but driving helped him focus. "Against the rules."

Luka couldn't see in the dark, but he was certain she rolled her eyes at his response. She got into the passenger seat, waited for him to stow his crutches and lower himself behind the wheel.

"There's a faster way out, here, look." She held out a map, tracing a route that eventually came out on the two-lane road that led to Holy Redeemer. "Cuts our travel almost in half. The ranger said the gate is locked at nine p.m., so it should still be open."

"She's manning the front gate; I'm sure she hasn't gotten over there." He reversed the car and followed Leah's directions. Sure enough the gate was still open, allowing them to access the secondary road that cut across to their destination. He had her call Ray and tell him to remind the state police to close the gate and secure it.

Finally, they left the gravel track for a narrow two-lane paved road, Luka's leg sending a prayer of thanksgiving for the end of the jostling, bouncy ride. Luka's phone rang and he put it on the car's speaker. "Jericho."

"It's Sanchez. I ran the data on the GPS tracker found on Spencer Standish's SUV. He's been visiting a cabin out in Craven's Peak almost daily for two weeks. Other than that, it's all work and home. Oh, and a trip Saturday night, the night before he died."

Which tied Spencer with Beth. He was their missing link between the two women. "Where?"

"A church. Holy Redeemer. Then straight home and never left again. Does that help?"

"Sure does. Any idea who was tracking him?"

"Traced the serial number to the vendor. The tracker was purchased by the wife, Tassi Standish."

Tassi must have suspected Spencer was up to something, whether having an affair, stealing her share of the proceeds from the Ponzi scheme, or both. "Thanks, Sanchez."

Leah turned in her seat to face him. "I've got it," she said. "I know why Beth was so scared that she ran—she thought it was the only way to keep her baby safe."

"The missing gold," Luka replied. "The killer thinks Spencer gave it to Beth and she knows where it is."

"Exactly." Then she frowned. "Six million dollars' worth of gold—that's got to be pretty bulky and heavy. There definitely wasn't anything like that at the cabin. And Beth had nothing with her at the fair."

"She wouldn't need to. You can buy gold and have it held for you at a secure depository. If Spencer was planning to fake his death and leave with Beth, I'll bet he arranged for an offshore bank to hold either the physical gold or bearer bonds backed in gold."

"Then why go after Beth?"

"Some of those places don't need a physical key—a special code will do. Spencer probably has fake IDs for himself and Beth, along with anything needed to access the six million waiting at wherever he and Beth were headed. If I were him, I'd go south to a Florida port city, take a boat over to the Caymans or someplace like that."

"So Spencer hid Beth in the cabin until he was ready to make their escape. Tassi tracked him with the GPS but before she could confront him, he was killed—" She stopped. "You're sure it wasn't her?"

Luka shook his head, concentrating on the road ahead. "Her alibi checked out."

"Okay, Tassi didn't kill him. At least not herself—maybe she asked Larry to, promised to run away with him or something. And tonight, when Foster Dean caught up to them both, he tortured Larry and Tassi told him about Beth and the cabin. So Dean took Tassi with him and when he didn't find Beth and Tassi couldn't tell him any more, he killed her."

Luka frowned. The only good thing about the scenario Leah proposed was it meant that Dean didn't have Beth and the baby. Yet. "And now he's after Beth."

"But Beth might not even know what Spencer's plan was—she was hidden in the cabin for the past few weeks."

"If Dean's the killer, then he's desperate," Luka said grimly. "He can't go back to the Zapata family empty-handed, and he knows we're closing in. He'll do whatever it takes."

"And if it's not Dean? If he's getting close to finding the money, then the real killer might target him next."

Luka shrugged. Too many unknowns and too little in the way of hard facts. He turned into the lane leading to Holy Redeemer and cut his lights, slowing so that the car would make the least amount of sound possible. The church was dark except for a single dim bulb over the rear door, but the house next to it blazed with lights. Harper's car sat out front along with a minivan and two matching white SUVs with the Holy Redeemer logo. No signs of Dean's Tahoe.

Luka stopped and backed into the church's parking lot, placing the building between him and the house. He called in to dispatch. "What's the ETA on my back-up?"

"They're twelve minutes out."

Damn. "We need to wait," he told Leah as he texted Harper to ask for an update. He wanted Harper out of there but without knowing the extent of the reverend's involvement, he didn't want to give too much away in his message.

As he waited for her reply, a loud crack sounded. Luka grabbed the car's radio. "Shots fired, I'm going in. Repeat: shots fired."

He jumped out of the car, ignoring the pain in his leg. This was no time for crutches. "Keep low," he ordered Leah. "Stay here, help is on the way."

He left without waiting for her reply. One of his team was in that house. If Harper had fired the shot, she'd be calling in. Or answering his damn text.

Nothing. Only silence. Which made him run faster.

# CHAPTER FORTY-TWO

Harper cursed herself for being out of position to deal with the threat Dean posed. With no chance to reach her weapon, she instead eased a step back until she was positioned against the corner, the closest thing the room had to a blind spot for someone entering from the hall. She'd been focused on John, and years of parishioners ringing the Reverend's doorbell at all hours of the day and night had dulled her senses. Any other house and she'd have been immediately alert to danger.

At least those were the excuses that ran through her brain—another childhood-conditioned response, one that she thought she'd left far behind, this immediate search for quick and easy explanations for her failures. Because they were always hers to own, always the result of her inability to make the right choice. She'd been struggling so hard to make her father proud of the path she'd chosen that now, at the crucial moment, she'd let everyone down.

Harper edged sideways, her gaze meeting the Reverend's. To her surprise he widened both eyes, as if relegating any decision-making to her. She'd been angry that Luka hadn't given her more duties on the Standish case, but she now realized that it worked in her favor because Dean had never seen her, had no idea she was a police officer. Harper brushed at her waistband where her gun and badge usually were, and the Reverend gave her the tiniest nod of acknowledgment.

He stood tall, stepping toward the threat, bringing Dean's focus to him. "What are you doing here?" he demanded, ignoring the gun to his wife's head. It was all show, Harper knew, detecting the faintest quaver in his voice. He was trying to distract Dean, give her an opening. "How did you get here? I didn't hear a car."

"Left mine on a logging road, came on foot," Dean said in a jovial voice. "I'll be borrowing one of yours when we leave. But we'll figure all that out in good time. First, how about some introductions?" He pressed the muzzle of his semi-automatic hard against Rachel's temple and she gave a small yelp of pain. "This must be the missus, and you are—" He jerked his chin at John, who'd taken an aggressive step forward.

"My son," the Reverend answered. "John."

Finally, Dean glanced at Harper, who didn't meet his eyes, instead trying her best to appear meek and timid. "And who's this? Your deacon or some such thing?"

"My assistant, Naomi." The Reverend straightened, shoulders back. "Let them go and I'll give you what you want."

"Bit too late for that, Rev. Afraid my timeline has shortened drastically." He nodded to the Reverend's recliner, then eyed John, who clearly posed the greatest threat. Or so Dean thought. "You, Junior, have a seat."

John backed into the chair and sat down heavily.

"Push it all the way back, that's it, feet up high. Keep your hands on the arms where I can see them. Everyone else, stay still, don't make a move."

It was a good tactical move on Dean's part—short of shooting John—to eliminate the potential threat. And it also placed John out of Harper's line of fire. The Reverend was clear too, standing over near the fireplace. Now all she needed was to find a way to separate Rachel from Dean.

"Tassi told me about the mistress," Dean continued. "I mean, she was a bit reluctant at first, but aren't they all? In the end, she told me everything, even took me to the girl's cabin. Imagine my surprise when I see a picture—and it's the same girl who's been plastered all over the TV, the one with the sick baby."

"Please—" the Reverend tried, but Dean waved him to silence with his gun, returning it to Rachel's temple before Harper could do more than slide her hand behind her back, slowly inching her weapon from its holster. Still, the Reverend's interruption covered her movement and from the way he caught her gaze, she knew he'd planned it that way.

"Spencer trusted you, Rev. Tassi said he told you everything. She thought it was part of the con, to set you up to protect her after Spencer faked his death. As if the Zapata family would fall for the same trick twice. But I guess Spencer was conning Tassi as well, planning to run off with his sidepiece, dump his wife. He knew I was getting close, but I don't believe he killed himself, not for a second. So I gotta ask, was it you who killed him, Rev?"

The Reverend managed to look insulted by Dean's accusation. "No."

Dean shrugged. "Just a theory. But you have my money, right?"

"Your money?" the Reverend asked with an arched eyebrow. Harper needed Dean to drop his guard, even for a second. "I thought it belonged to the Zapata family."

"Seeing as how returning that money to the cartel is the only thing keeping me alive right now, feels like it's rightfully mine. Where is it?"

The Reverend pinched his lips tight. He was making himself a target—and yet, he was also the one person Dean wouldn't kill, since he had what Dean wanted.

Harper knew it, but so did Dean. He pivoted and, with barely a glance, shot at the recliner, the bullet impacting inches away from John's head, foam and upholstery spraying as John jolted upright.

"Freeze," Dean commanded, now aiming at John's torso. "Just a warning shot, to let your father know I'm serious." He kept one arm around Rachel and his weapon pointed at John, but his focus returned to the Reverend. Clearly, Dean had dismissed Harper as not posing any threat. "Now, then. Where's my money? I'm going to count to—"

Harper didn't give him a chance to finish as she drew and fired.

# CHAPTER FORTY-THREE

Leah hated waiting, helpless, as Luka raced into danger, but she understood the necessity of it. The last thing Luka needed to worry about right now was having to protect a civilian. Still, it rankled. After six months of working together, it felt as if he and his team were finally treating her as an equal, not an outsider.

She sat in the dark, not sure what she could do except be ready to help if needed. Her backpack held a field trauma kit, including a vial of ceftriaxone, an injectable antibiotic. If they found Beth's baby, she could begin treatment immediately. She opened the kit, fingering her supplies, taking mental inventory, ready to access them without needing to search. Then she zipped it closed again and went back to waiting.

Damn, this was worse than waiting for a trauma to arrive at the ER—at least then she'd be in communication with the medics, have some idea of what to expect and when to expect it. But this, not knowing… sheer hell.

Movement at the back of the church caught her eye. A woman was waving to her from the rear entrance.

Leah squinted.

It wasn't just any woman.

It was Beth.

Leah searched the shadows of the trees surrounding the church and parking lot. No one else was near; Beth seemed to be alone. Still, she remained wary as Beth crossed the parking lot heading toward the car. Leah kept her hand on her phone the whole time, ready to call 911 or alert Luka if she saw anyone else. But it was only Beth, still dressed in scrubs, otherwise empty-handed.

Leah opened the car door and stepped out. "Beth?" she called softly. "Where's your baby? Is anyone with you?"

Beth reached her, her face contorted with anguish. "Reverend Harper, he told me not to go outside, but the baby—something's wrong. When I saw the policeman leave and you here alone—" She grasped both of Leah's wrists. "Can you help him? Please, you have to help my baby."

Leah gazed at the distraught mother. Beth definitely wasn't acting. Leah raised her phone to call for an ambulance.

"No!" Beth grabbed Leah's arm with both hands. Leah shook her off and stepped back away from her. "No, please," Beth begged. "I can't risk them finding us. Can we take your car?"

Reluctantly, Leah pocketed her phone and grabbed her bag. Assessing and treating the baby came first. Then she would either convince Beth to see reason or call Luka to deal with her while she got the baby to the hospital. "Where is he?"

"Hidden. In the church." Beth led the way back across the pavement to the church door. They entered a small vestibule that opened up onto a corridor leading behind the worship area. There were several doors—offices and storage, and a changing room for the ministers, Leah guessed as Beth rushed her past them in the near-dark. Then Beth turned sharply and there was a deep step down onto rough stone, two more steps and they reached a thick wooden door. Beth opened the door, held Leah's hand, guided her inside an unlit room, far enough to close the door behind them, and finally, Beth flicked a light switch.

The room was much older than the rest of the building—possibly even original, given the white-washed curve of thick logs along the outer corner and the thick-planked, rough-hewn flooring. There were no windows, only a single, bare overhead lightbulb whose illumination was almost obscured by the dust motes that filled the air with a musty essence. Shadowy figures wearing bright-colored robes gathered along the outside wall, a life-sized nativity.

Leah glanced at Beth, who crossed to a set of shelves that held clear plastic boxes of Christmas and other holiday decorations. At the far side of the shelving unit was a tabletop hinged to the ancient plaster wall.

"Reverend Harper said this was the original church and they built a safe place to hide if they were attacked," Beth explained as she unlatched the table and raised it, exposing a horizontal support beam that was notched along the top, matching where the hinges protruded. Except for one notch that was empty, as if the corresponding hinge had broken. Beth slid her fingers inside the empty notch, releasing a mechanical click, and then she swung open a hidden door in the lower part of the wall.

"He's in here," she told Leah. "The reverend said no one would find us here, but I had to come out, get help when he got sick. He was fine, I don't know what happened, he was fine. Until I woke him a little while ago and he wouldn't nurse, felt warm." She ducked inside the hidden room and emerged with the baby cradled in her arms.

"Bring him into the light," Leah said as she dragged a plastic bin to the center of the room to use as a makeshift examination table.

Beth had swaddled the baby in several blankets. She set him down and carefully unwrapped him. "I thought he was just tired—I know I was. So I let him go back to sleep, but now he's so listless, I can barely keep him awake and he's still refusing the breast. The reverend was going to bring me some formula to try, but he hasn't come back…" Her voice drifted off, one hand caressing the baby's dark hair as Leah opened her bag and grabbed a stethoscope.

She listened—no heart murmur, good lung sounds—then checked the baby's fontanelle and reflexes. Responsive but drowsy, no signs of meningitis. "One of the blood tests they took after he was born showed signs of an infection," she told Beth, drawing up a dose of the ceftriaxone. "I'm going to give him a shot of antibiotic to fight the infection, but then we need to get him back to the hospital."

"No—you don't understand. I can't let them find us."

"I'm sorry, we really need to monitor the baby." Leah swabbed the baby's thigh and injected the medicine. He made a small squeal of pain, but went silent again.

"Can't you show me how to give him the medicine?" Beth pleaded. "If they find us, they'll kill us."

"He could get worse—sometimes this infection spreads into the lungs or even the brain. It's very serious, Beth."

Beth considered, her face tightening as tears seeped from her eyes. She leaned down and kissed the baby. "Take him. If I'm not around, they won't find him. Take him."

"We can keep you safe, Beth. Please let me—"

She shook her head. "No, no. I can't risk anything happening to him. I've already made so many mistakes." She clutched Leah's wrist. "Please, you have to promise me. You won't let anything happen to him. Please."

"We'll take good care of him." Leah glanced at the door. She hadn't heard from Luka and wasn't sure if it was safe to take the baby outside. She began to wrap the baby back up, debating whether she should call an ambulance—no, it would take them too long to get here. She could take Luka's car—he'd left the keys for her. It would be the fastest way to get the baby to safety.

The baby and Beth. They both needed protection. "The man you're afraid of, he works for the Zapata family, right?"

Beth tensed, her gaze going to the door as if getting ready to run. "How did you know?"

"He killed Spencer's wife and another man. We think he's coming to find Reverend Harper, that's why Sergeant Jericho and I came here."

"He's here? Now? Then there's no time." Footsteps pounding down the hall outside punctuated her words. "We need to hide."

"Quick, take the baby." Leah bundled the baby into Beth's arms and helped her back through to the hidden room. She didn't have time to lower the desk before the door to the hallway slammed open.

Leah whirled, her back to the wall.

# CHAPTER FORTY-FOUR

As Luka ran up the front porch steps, he heard two more shots fired in quick succession. He wrenched the front door open. His leg brace caught and he tripped over the threshold, slamming into the foyer wall and almost falling. Pain lanced up his leg but he ignored it, keeping his back to the wall as he cleared the front rooms, the dining room and living room, then followed the hall to the rear of the house.

Harper was crouched over Foster Dean's body, securing Dean's weapon.

Luka paused, assessing the situation. No other weapons or threats. Harper's mother was standing with her brother, John, pale and visibly shaken, while Matthew hovered near Dean. It was the first time Luka had seen the man of God appear uncertain or hesitant.

"Call an ambulance," he ordered John. "Then wait for me outside."

John nodded and escorted his mother through the kitchen. Luka turned his attention to Dean. The former DEA agent had a gunshot wound to his chest and a second to his gut. Harper was placing pressure on them with a lace doily she'd pulled off the back of the sofa.

"Dr. Wright's outside in my car," he told Matthew as he took over for Harper, who ran into the kitchen and returned with an armful of towels. "Go get her, tell her we need her trauma kit."

The sound of sirens echoed through the night. His back-up, about time.

"Wait," Harper said as her father turned to leave. "Luka, he knows where Beth and her baby are."

Luka nodded. "Harper, go with him. Leah needs to see the baby right away. The ERT medic can stabilize Dean until she's treated the baby."

Dean made a grunting noise of protest at this. Luka pushed harder, wadding the dishtowel deep into the wound. "Hold still, Dean. You're not getting out of this that easily."

Harper and her father left. Luka leaned closer to the former DEA agent. "Just us. For a minute at most. Want to tell me anything? Could go a long way to help you out."

Dean shook his head. "I talk, I'm dead," he gasped.

"You don't, you're dead. You know the Zapatas have the reach, they can get to you anywhere. Your only hope is the feds, witness protection." Luka hated himself for even making the offer. But he had little to no evidence to nail Dean for the murders and a wit-sec deal would include at least some jail time in addition to testifying against the cartel. Which might mean that instead of locking up one killer, they would end up getting several off the streets, not to mention putting a serious dent into the Zapata family's flow of money and drugs.

Dean considered it. Luka heard the banging of doors both front and back as the ERT made their entry. "Scene's clear," he shouted. "Get your medic back here."

"They'll know," Dean whispered.

"No. I'll make sure of it. I have a friend at the FBI, let me give her a call."

"How?" Dean's breathing had turned shallow and rapid, his color ashen. Shock, Luka realized. It was now or never.

"If I can, are you in? You'll give up everything you know?"

"Yes." Dean managed a nod. "But how?"

"Easy. We'll take you out in a body bag."

Dean's eyes went wide, either with pain or surprise, Luka wasn't sure. But then the wounded man managed a throaty chuckle. "Fake my death. Just like Spence."

The ERT's medic arrived, quickly assessing the situation and opening his trauma kit. "Just like Spence," Luka told Dean as he moved out of the medic's way. "Leave it to me."

# CHAPTER FORTY-FIVE

Leah braced herself against the wall as the door slammed open. To her surprise, it was a middle-aged woman and a man in his early thirties who charged into the room.

"Who the hell are you?" the man demanded.

The woman motioned to him to hush. She stepped forward. "I'm Reverend Harper's wife, Rachel. This is his church and this is his son, John." She took another step toward Leah, which blocked her view of John. "How can we help you?"

Did they know about Beth and the baby? Leah wondered. Surely the reverend would have trusted his own wife and son—but then she remembered how Luka had said the reverend refused to say anything, even to Harper, his daughter, after she told him the baby's life was in danger.

When Leah said nothing, the man, John, pulled a gun out from behind his back. "Told you we might need this," he said to his mother. Then he gestured to Leah. "Move away. I know my father stashed her in there. We just want the girl."

"We don't want to hurt you," Rachel added in a conciliatory tone that Leah did not trust, not for a moment.

"The girl can't help you," she tried bluffing. "She doesn't know anything about where the gold is. Spencer killed himself before he could tell her where it was."

John cocked his head. "See, now we know you're lying. We heard Spencer tell my father that if anything happened to him, he was to get the girl out and that the gold would protect her and the baby. Of course, at the time, he didn't expect the baby to be born right when he was leaving to fake his own death."

Leah frowned. "Wait. You heard—how? And how did you know he was leaving, much less what he was going to do?"

Rachel nudged John hard. "You talk too much."

"You were there," Leah said, shock flooding over her. "*You* killed Spencer?"

"It was an accident," John said. "Now open the door and get the girl. The police will be here any minute."

Harper appeared in the doorway, the reverend right behind her. "The police *are* here. Put the gun down, John."

She held her own pistol aimed at John, but in such a small room, that also meant it was aimed toward Leah. The reverend didn't help matters as he pushed past Harper to confront his son. "You were there when Spencer died? You need to tell the truth, John. What happened?"

"Don't say a word," Rachel snapped, squaring off with her husband. And blocking any shot Harper had, Leah couldn't help but notice. She scanned the area closest to her, searching for a weapon, but the only things close to hand were the life-sized sheep clustered among the other nativity figures.

Despite the fact that John's attention was diverted by his parents' argument, he still held the gun aimed at her and was far too close for her to have any hope of his missing if he pulled the trigger. She patted the wall behind her, judging its thickness. In the ER, she'd taken care of civilians caught in the crossfire when bullets had gone through apartment walls. At this range even if a shot missed her, could it pass through to where Beth and the baby were hiding?

"Rachel," the reverend said in a patronizing tone. "Don't meddle in affairs you know nothing about. You can't coddle the boy; he needs to take responsibility for his actions."

"Maybe you two can take this outside," Harper suggested.

They ignored her. "You push him too hard," Rachel told the reverend. "Besides, you're the one who knows nothing about it. John didn't kill Spencer. I did."

"You? No." The reverend suddenly seemed smaller, taking a step away from his wife and sagging against the metal storage shelves.

"John and I went there to get the money John lost. Spencer was on the phone with you, ready to get into his SUV when he saw us. I couldn't let him tell you what had happened, how John had lost all that money—there was no need for you to know since we were going to get it back anyway. I grabbed at Spencer's arm as he was stepping up, climbing into the driver's seat and it pulled him off balance. His feet went out from under him and he twisted and fell, hit his neck on the edge of the running board." She grimaced. "There was a snapping noise and he didn't move after that."

Leah noted that Harper's free hand was in her pocket and she wondered if the detective was recording her own mother's confession. She wasn't sure what to think about that, although she was certain Luka would approve. But she also saw that Harper didn't have a clear shot—they needed to stall until Luka could arrive to help. "Did you know Spencer was still alive?" she asked Rachel.

The older woman flushed—with anger or shame, Leah wasn't sure. "We had no choice. John put him back in the car and we let nature take its course. It was God's will, that's all."

"God didn't leave the car running or shut all the windows and doors," Harper snapped. She edged past Rachel to focus on her brother. "Put the gun down, John. Now. Last warning."

"Don't you dare threaten your brother," Rachel screeched, lunging and pushing Harper into the life-sized Magi. Harper stumbled and fell off balance, but quickly righted herself, putting her back to the nativity characters, facing her family and covering them all with her gun.

"You listen to me, Naomi Harper," Rachel continued. "You're going to go out there and tell the police that there's no one here, that you have no idea where the girl is. Or better yet, send them on a wild goose chase, buy us some time."

"I can't do that. You just confessed to murder."

"Fine, then arrest me. But it wasn't murder, it was a mother protecting her son, remaining loyal to her family. Not that you'd know anything about that."

A stricken look crossed Harper's face as if her mother had physically slapped her. "Don't make me choose. John, put down the gun and both of you come with me. Now."

"Me?" John protested. "You can't arrest me!" He whirled away from Leah to face his sister straight on, raising his gun.

Leah shoved his aim away from Harper, but he still pulled the trigger. The shot went wild, pinging against the metal shelves. She threw her weight on John's arm, but he flung her away. Then Harper was there, twisting his wrist behind his back, until he dropped the gun into her hand and ended up on the floor, crying in pain.

"Now, stay down," Harper told him as she handcuffed him.

"What have you done?" Rachel cried. Both Leah and Harper whirled away from John to see Rachel on her knees, cradling the reverend in her arms. "What was he thinking?" she said, tears streaming down her face. "He could have stopped you, saved John. But instead he jumped in front of a bullet. A bullet meant for you." Her face contorted with hatred as she spit the words at Harper. "You made John shoot his own father. It's all your fault!"

# CHAPTER FORTY-SIX

Leah gently disentangled the distraught woman's arms from where they'd wrapped around the reverend's head. There was blood, a lot of it. But when Leah palpated his skull, a shard of blue metal rattled from the back of the reverend's jacket onto the floor.

Not a bullet, a piece of shelving. And it hadn't penetrated the skull, merely grazed it. Probably a ricochet. The real damage had been caused by Matthew's fall—his head had hit the floor hard enough to stun him, possibly also causing a concussion. The reverend's eyes blinked open, confirming her diagnosis.

His wife didn't even notice. She lunged at Harper as Harper handcuffed her brother's wrists and hauled him to his feet. "He did nothing wrong," she screeched. "Arrest me, not him."

Harper's cold, expressionless stare stopped her mother in her tracks. "Believe me, we will." Two ERT officers swarmed through the door and restrained Rachel.

"What the hell happened here?" Luka asked as he limped through the door behind them. He stood aside as the ERT men dragged John and Rachel out. They were quickly replaced by two more, crowding the doorway, guns still drawn.

"Rachel—" the reverend moaned. Then he slumped back. "My God, what have I done?"

"Stay still," Leah told him in a soft voice. "You'll be okay."

"But, my son, my wife…" His voice trailed off.

Harper opened the hidden door and beckoned for Beth to come out. "It's okay. Everything's okay. Dr. Wright is here to look after your baby."

Beth emerged, her eyes wide with fear, face ashen as she clutched her baby to her chest. Leah left the reverend to check on the baby—he was awake and sucking on Beth's finger. A good sign.

"Leah, we need you at the house," Luka said. "Foster Dean has been shot."

Suddenly Leah had four patients to triage, one critical. The reverend was stable, as was Beth's baby—although with kids, you never knew, they could go downhill fast—Luka's leg was bleeding, probably torn stitches, leaving Foster Dean as her most urgent priority. But one good thing about having the ERT squad here was that they were all trained in basic trauma care.

Leah nodded to the two ERT men. "Put pressure on his wound and call for an ambulance—he has a scalp laceration and probable concussion." She turned to Beth. "We're going to get your baby to the hospital as fast as possible. Harper, can you drive them? It will be faster than waiting for the ambulance."

Harper nodded, then looked to Luka for confirmation. "You'll need my statement and—"

"Exigent circumstances," he told her. "We'll deal with the formalities later. Go. Stay with Beth. Whatever you do, you don't leave her side, not until I say, understand?"

Tears streamed down Beth's face and Leah could tell she was so frightened she might run. "Beth, this is Detective Harper and Detective Sergeant Jericho. They're going to keep you and your baby safe, understand me? You're safe now."

Beth shook her head. "No, no. They'll find me."

"No. They won't." Leah wrapped an arm around the trembling woman. "We're going to take care of you and the baby. Go with them, now. We need to get your baby back to the hospital. I'll meet you there, I promise."

"Leah, we need to go," Luka urged.

She grabbed her kit and followed him into the hall. He was limping badly, moving slowly. "Go ahead. The ERT medic is with him, I'll catch up," he told her. "But Leah, don't mention his name. As far as anyone is concerned, he's a John Doe."

"Why?"

"My friend at the FBI, the one who got me the info about the Zapata family's dealings with Spencer back in Denver? I just got off the phone with her. She said if Dean will take it, she'll offer him witness protection if he talks. She's on her way here to make him a deal."

"Wait. Dean killed two people that we know of, and he gets witness protection? Why not Beth? She's the innocent here, the one really in danger."

"You don't get wit-sec unless you have something to trade for it. I have no idea what Beth knows—she hasn't been around to interview," he snapped, obviously also frustrated by the idea of a killer making a deal.

"Then go with Beth," she urged him. "You need that leg checked out anyway. Talk with her, see if you can help her."

They'd reached the back door of the church. Behind them, Harper was already leading Beth and the baby out.

Luka nodded. "I will. Now hurry. I need Dean alive."

# CHAPTER FORTY-SEVEN

Once again Luka found himself stranded, lying on a stretcher in the ER, forced to manage his growing Hydra of a case from flat on his back. Beth was under guard while the doctors treated her baby; Harper was giving her statement to the state police officer-involved-shooting team; Ray and Krichek were booking her mother and brother; while he'd heard from the nurses that Leah had called for a LifeFlight to transport Dean to Good Sam and he was currently in the operating room.

The highlight of his night so far was the fact that Leah had been able to keep Dean alive. Hopefully the surgeons would do their job as well and soon Dean would be able to talk. Because neither he nor Harper had been able to get anything out of Beth during their drive to the hospital—not even a last name, forcing them to admit her son to the hospital as Baby Doe.

He'd just gotten off the phone with Ray—both Rachel and John had lawyered up—when a rap came at the exam room door. Leah. She'd changed into scrubs, so he hoped that meant she had news about Dean.

"How is he?" he asked.

She sank onto the stool beside the bed. "Hanging in there. They removed his spleen, but his liver is also damaged and he's lost a lot of blood."

Luka blew his breath out in frustration. All this death and destruction—he dearly wanted someone to pay. Not only Dean but the people who'd sent him to Cambria City as their enforcer.

She glanced at his wound that he was waiting for the nurses to dress. "You know that's going to scar."

"What do I care?"

"Did you call Nate? Let him know you're okay?"

Luka focused on the far corner of the ceiling. He'd been tempted to wait until morning to call home, but the memory of the look on Nate's face yesterday when he'd seen Luka in the ER had forced him to interrupt the phone calls and details of his case that he was juggling to take the time to call Nate. "Yeah. Woke him up. He was upset, but better than yesterday. Even thanked me. I felt like it was the first time anyone had ever taken his feelings into consideration, put his needs first."

Son of a junkie, raised mostly by the foster care system, it was no wonder Nate was insecure and anxious. But what really overwhelmed Luka, what had him now blinking back tears as he thought of their conversation, was how, despite all that, Nate was already turning into a damn fine human being. Eight years old and he was a better man than most people. Including men of God like Matthew and John. Poor Harper. She'd be dealing with whispered innuendos and the fallout of her family's actions for a long time to come.

"You know, if it wasn't for Nate and his photos, we'd never have found Beth's cabin," Leah interrupted his thoughts. "Tassi's body could have remained undiscovered for days and Dean could have gotten away with everything."

"Nate and Emily." Luka hesitated. "He's a good kid. Talented."

"More than that. Special—he's so good, the way he treats Emily. Like he understands what she's feeling more than she does herself."

"The judge at the fair? She teaches art at Cambria Prep. They're offering Nate a scholarship." There, it was out. He kept his gaze on her face, bracing himself for her reaction.

"You mean—" She swallowed, looked down at her hands, then nodded and glanced back up at him. "Luka, that's wonderful. Nate deserves it. It's a fantastic opportunity."

"But—"

"But, I can't help but think of how it will impact Emily, not having him with her at school. She doesn't have any other friends and is always in trouble—she'll be miserable."

He straightened as best he could, lying on the gurney. He couldn't help but notice that she didn't mention how Emily's behavior had often gotten Nate in trouble with their teachers. Of course, she was focused on her daughter and what was best for her, but Nate had no one but Luka to stand up for him. "I need to put Nate's needs first. I hope you understand that."

She took a long time before finally nodding, her expression still troubled. Before he could say anything more, her phone rang. It was a quick conversation and when she hung up, the look on her face was not a happy one.

"What happened?" he asked.

"Dean died. The surgeons did everything—"

"Damnit." He grabbed his phone. "I need to call the FBI, tell them not to bother."

"Hold off. Let them come."

He glanced at her in surprise. "Why?"

"I stopped to check on Beth and the baby. I told her about Dean. And I told her that if she had something to offer the FBI, we might be able to get her witness protection."

"Leah, you had no authority—you can't make promises like that!"

"Dean tortured two people—and who knows how many more—for the Zapata family, and it's okay to get him a deal, but not an innocent victim in fear for her and her baby's lives? How's that justice?" Her face was flushed with indignation.

"It's not. It's not justice, it's the system. It's how we get bad guys to roll on even bigger, badder guys so we can get them off the street." He sighed and pushed himself upright so he could meet her gaze. "It's not a perfect system, not even a very good one, but it's the best we have."

"Your FBI friend, she's after the Zapata family? Why not DEA? Aren't they drug dealers?"

"They're into everything. Drugs, weapons, human trafficking, money laundering, you name it. The FBI was actually hoping Dean could tell them who the money guy in Denver was, the one who made the mistake of investing in Spencer's Ponzi scheme. They figure if that guy is still alive, he could tell them about the family's finances."

"What makes you think the Zapatas haven't killed him? They don't seem like the forgive-and-forget types."

"Except that the only people they allow to handle the money are members of their own family. So there's a chance, a slim one, that the guy isn't dead." He sank back against the pillow. "Not that we'll ever know."

A strange expression crossed her face. Part smirk and part consideration. "Tell your FBI friend to come. She'll have someone to talk to when she gets here."

"Wait, what? Who?" Then it hit him. "No. You can't be serious." He lowered his voice to a near whisper. "It's Beth?"

"They met at a charity gala. Beth invested her own money with Spencer—she wanted a way to leave the family, but that meant cash for a new identity, a new life. She had no idea Spencer was running a con, not at first. But then, they fell in love. Spencer knew he couldn't just leave Tassi—not without protection, which also cost money. So he made a deal with Beth. She'd funnel her family's money through him, he'd squirrel away enough for all three of them, Beth, Tassi, and Spencer, to start a new life, and he'd divorce Tassi and then run away with Beth."

"Didn't exactly go to plan, then," Luka said.

"No. Her family got wind of the Ponzi scheme and went after Spencer, so he had to fake his death. The plan was for Beth to wait until things cooled down and they'd reunite, but then Tassi found Spencer and began to blackmail him, forcing him to run another Ponzi—this time with the money going to her—or she'd tell the Zapatas where he was."

"Explains Tassi's reluctance to cooperate with us—she was as much behind the Ponzi operation as Spencer was." He thought for a second. "Why did he write the confession exonerating Tassi?"

"They were going to fake his death again, but that would leave Tassi behind to face the consequences, even if he did actually plan to run off with Beth. Maybe he was trying to protect Tassi? Maybe he still cared for her at least that much?" Leah shrugged. "Guess he must have loved her."

"Just not enough to play it straight with her. Conman to the end. Both of them."

"In a way, Beth was the only innocent victim—well, her and her baby. Don't they deserve a second chance?"

"With Dean dead, there's a chance Beth's family has no clue she's here." He nodded as he thought it through. "It could work. She tells the FBI what she knows—"

"And she knows everything," Leah put in. "But she wants full immunity in addition to witness protection."

"Yeah, yeah. It could work. It could actually work." He met her gaze with a smile. "Leah, if you hadn't gotten her to talk—"

"All I did was my job. But you'd better do yours and make sure that FBI friend is true to her word."

"No problem." Then he sobered. "I still need to prep the case against Harper's mother and brother."

"How's she doing?"

"Hard to say. You know Harper, she keeps her personal life private."

"Fat chance of that once the press gets hold of this."

"Yeah. But I'll hand it to her—last thing she told me before she left to check on her father was that she knows who killed Lily Nolan and she's determined to get them to confess."

"Solved her first big case. You must be proud."

"I wish it wasn't in the middle of all this other mess. She deserves a chance to shine."

"What about her father?"

"I don't think the DA is going to bring any charges—the most might be obstruction of justice, but I'm not sure he had any clue about what his wife and son really did." He shrugged. "Or maybe he did and decided it was more important to protect his family."

"He did try his best to protect Beth, like he promised Spencer he would."

"Doctors said we can interview him tomorrow. But he said he'll only talk if Harper's there."

Leah grimaced. "Could be the worst conversation of her life—"

"Don't worry," Luka told her. "I'll be there with her, to protect her as best I can."

# CHAPTER FORTY-EIGHT

The next morning, Harper met Luka at the station and drove him to Good Sam where the doctors had kept the Reverend overnight to monitor his concussion. She'd talked Luka into interviewing him at the hospital rather than the station in the hopes that he could avoid being seen by the media and creating more bad press for the church. It seemed the least she could do after disappointing him in every other way possible, including arresting her own mother and brother. What did he always say, *life is a choice*? Well, she guessed the whole world now knew what her choice was: her job over her family.

Jacob and Jonah were both at the Reverend's bedside when they entered. Jacob jerked up from his chair, taking a step toward Harper as if planning to block her from seeing their father. "Haven't you caused this family enough pain?"

But Jonah interceded. "Let them do their job," he said, ushering Jacob out. Harper was stricken at the thought that Jonah might never forgive her, but as he crossed the threshold, he looked back and gave her a fleeting grimace of understanding. Close enough. She hauled in a breath. Now for the hard part.

The Reverend was sitting up in bed, already fully dressed in his usual clerical garb. Staples bristled through his hair—hair that for the first time Harper realized was actually more gray than blond. When had that happened?

"I did it," he told them before she or Luka could say anything. "I confess, take full responsibility. I'll take any deal you want if you let my wife and son go."

Luka tapped his way to the chair beside the Reverend and dropped into it heavily, setting his crutches to one side. "I think we're past that, sir," he said, adopting a respectful tone. "Do you really think one more lie is going to make things right? Lies and secrets began all this, maybe it's time to trust in the truth?"

For some reason both men stared at Harper. Finally, the Reverend sighed, somehow becoming smaller as the exhalation escaped him.

"You've got a smart boss here, Naomi. Make sure you learn everything you can from him." He fussed with the bed controls, getting to a more comfortable position. Then he frowned, turning to Luka. "She's not in trouble, is she? It's not her fault—she did the right thing. It was me, a stubborn old man, blind to my own weakness, assuming my family was above man's law. You can't blame her."

"She's not in trouble," Luka assured him. He nodded to Harper, who pulled out her phone and set it on the table above the bed.

"Fine then," the Reverend said. "Let's get started. I'll tell you everything."

"Did you know Spencer was going to fake his death?" Luka asked after providing the formal interview language to start things.

"Yes. He knew the Zapatas were closing in and enlisted my help to ensure both Tassi and Beth's safety. I guess I failed them both. I knew nothing about the Ponzi scheme. Spence told me that the fund he ran back in Denver had a down quarter, that he hadn't even known one of the investors represented the cartel, until they came and demanded their money and that he'd been on the run ever since."

"When did you know your wife and son were involved in Spencer's death?"

"I had no idea. I saw my wife at Spencer's office. Then she drove off and picked up John at the far end of the parking lot. I assumed John was the one who pushed the dumpster at you in the alley. After that, I couldn't say anything, I had to protect him—assaulting an officer is a serious charge."

Harper leaned forward, itching to press him for more details—he'd been on the phone with Spencer; how could he not have heard anything?—but Luka caught her eye, reminding her that she was only here as a courtesy.

"Did you ask them why they were there?" Luka continued.

"John said that he'd learned of the Ponzi scheme and missing money, and since the church had been the recipient of some of the charity foundation's funds, he wanted to see if there were any records that might reflect poorly on Holy Redeemer. But everything was already erased—Spencer had taken care of that before he came to see me Saturday night. I had no idea John had invested the church's money."

His chin dropped to his chest and his glasses slid down his nose. Harper couldn't believe the change one night had wrought in him—gone was the haughty authority figure she'd known her entire life. In his place, all that was left was an old man, made vulnerable by shame and guilt.

"I guess I was a fool not to suspect anything. I honestly thought Spencer was trying to protect his family—both of them." The Reverend looked up again, this time not at Luka but at Harper. "That's all I was doing as well. Please, can I speak with my daughter? Alone? Then I'll write out a complete statement, tell you everything I know."

Luka glanced at her, asking her permission. She felt a bead of sweat slip down along her spine, and it had nothing to do with the heat and everything to do with facing her father's wrath. But she swallowed her misgivings and nodded.

"I'll be right outside," Luka said.

The Reverend beckoned Harper to his side. He placed both his hands over hers, his lips moving in silent prayer. "I only need to say one thing to you," he said when he looked up. "All your life

I've tried to teach you right from wrong. And despite my being blind to what was right, you still made the correct choice. You make me proud. I want you to know that. Whatever happens, you make me proud."

Harper's words vanished, the way they always had when she was a little girl, waiting for the Reverend's judgment. So instead, she gave her father a hug.

"Go now, do your job. It suits you," he told her as he released her. She smiled, nodded, and obeyed him. But as she left him behind, her step felt lighter, her shoulders broader, her spine straighter.

Luka and Harper still had one final stop: Macy's room. This time Luka gave Harper the lead. She squared her shoulders, tapped her bag where she'd printed out everything in preparation, then went in, Luka following behind her.

Macy was pale, her cheeks hollowed out, hair matted with sweat, but the doctors had cleared her for the interview. When she saw Harper, a wistful smile actually crossed her face, as if Harper was the only friend she had left, but even Macy knew that was a fantasy. Harper wasn't here as a friend.

Still, Macy slid to one side and patted the bed for Harper to sit as Harper took her statement. The biggest difference this time was that, unlike the Reverend, Macy was under arrest, although she waived her Miranda rights without hesitation. Harper took that as a good sign as they began their dance, circling the unspoken, painful truth.

"Tell me about Lily," Harper started. "You two were close?"

"Neither of us had family, you know. Not really. Guess we were each other's family. She used to say I was the sister she never had. Used to say…" Her voice drifted off.

Harper had planned to lay out her case, but instead took another tack. "Losing family, someone you're that close to—it's difficult.

I'm still trying to reach Lily's family, let them know she's gone. Can you tell me anything about them?"

Macy sniffed. "Her mom kicked Lily out after she got pregnant."

"Lily has a child?"

"Her stepdad's. She was only fifteen, but her mom didn't believe her, kicked her out instead."

"Where's the baby now?"

"Lily's aunt. On her dad's side. Hagerstown, I think. Lily said she tried to make it work—go back to school, take care of the baby, but it was all too much and she started using, then working the streets for money, so she left. Said she'd rather die than let her baby girl see her mom let her down like that, so she came up here for a fresh start." Macy swiped tears from her cheeks. "You gonna go tell her aunt she's gone? Don't bother with her mom, she's still with the bastard. But Lily's aunt and her baby girl, they need to know."

"What's the aunt's name? Got any contact info?"

"Lilian. Lily was named after her. That's all I know. But it will be in Lily's phone."

Harper nodded, appreciating that Macy was inching toward the truth that Harper already knew. She waited a beat, then asked, "Lily's little girl—"

"Grace. Gracie is her name. She turned two last month. Lily showed me a picture." Macy closed her eyes. For a moment Harper thought she'd drifted back to sleep but then more tears seeped out from under her eyelashes. "Two. That's too young to remember anything, right?" She opened her eyes and stared at Harper, desperate for a lie. "I mean, she'll never know what her mom was like, what happened—"

"She might not remember, but she'll still know. That kind of pain, it stays with you, shapes your whole life." Harper thought of her own mother—not Rachel, her biological mother. Maybe it was time to get answers to the questions that had haunted her all her life?

"Yeah, you're right," Macy said, pulling Harper's attention back to the interview. "I went into foster care after my folks OD'd when I was only a baby, just crawling, but sometimes when I close my eyes, it's like they're here with me." A sob escaped her, but she cleared her throat and swiped at her cheeks. "But look at me. I mean, she'll be all right, Gracie will. She'll be fine." She turned a pleading look on Harper. "Right?"

"It'll be hard." Harper glanced at Luka, who gave her an encouraging nod. Time to apply a little pressure. "Harder still if she never knows the truth about how Lily died."

Macy pulled the sheet tighter around her, her fingers twisting the fabric into tight knots. Harper continued, "Macy, you know we inventoried your belongings. We found the cash, the drugs—enough meth and fentanyl to charge you with intent to distribute. And we have Lily's necklace. The one you gave Darius after you bailed him out. We'll find her prints and DNA along with yours on it. And we found two phones. Yours and Lily's." She rested a hand over Macy's trembling ones. "Can you tell me what happened, Macy? Why'd you kill Lily?"

Silence for a long moment. Had she pressed too hard, too fast? Harper wondered. Was Macy about to invoke her Miranda rights? Had she blown her last chance at getting a confession?

But then Macy nodded, her head bobbing as she sobbed. "I called, told her I wanted to get clean, that I was ready for rehab. We'd gone once before—she stuck with it, got her life back, had a job, was getting her GED, had her aunt and Gracie. Her life was so good. But I quit, started using again and my life was—"

She cleared her throat and started again. "Lily, she was like my sister. My only family. When I called and asked her for money for rehab, she grabbed all the cash she could, came right up to take me. But it was Saturday, I told her we needed one last chance at fun—no drugs, just good food, some dancing, you know, fun—and that she could take me Sunday morning. And it was fun, so much fun…"

More tears, these silent. Harper slid the tissue box closer, but Macy ignored it, instead wiping her face on the shoulder of her gown. "What happened after the dancing, Macy?"

Macy's expression was one of pure anguish. "Lily didn't know it, but I scored some meth at the club, smoked it when she thought I was in the bathroom. Then we left and we were crossing through the alley, the one beside the Towers, the one where—you know. That's when Darius called, said he needed bail money, that I was the only one who could help him, that he loved me and if I loved him, I'd get him the money."

She went silent. Harper again marveled at the way girls like Macy were manipulated, love and family twisted into a macabre fantasy by men like Darius. "Then what happened?"

"I told Lily I didn't want to go to rehab after all, I needed the money for Darius instead, and she said no. I tried to grab her purse, but she pulled away and I… I, oh God, I hit her, so hard that her lip split and her nose spurted blood. And she was so shocked she fell down and just looked at me, like she didn't even know who I was. That look, it was awful—"

Macy broke off, buried her face in her hands. "She was my only family," she wailed. "And now she's gone."

Harper gave her a moment. No wonder Macy had used Lily's money to buy enough drugs to keep her so high she might forget. But no high lasted forever. "Macy. What happened next?"

Her face still hidden, she continued in a voice so low Harper had to lean forward to hear it, "I couldn't take it, I had to stop her from looking at me like that, and there was this chunk of wood and it was in my hand and…" She choked back a sob. "And I hit her. Hard. I grabbed her necklace, and she didn't even fight, just lay there blinking at me, whispering my name. I had to shut her up, shut out the sound of her saying my name like she loved me, like she cared, like she was surprised. I hit her again, to stop her from saying my name. Over and over and over. I couldn't stop. She had everything and I had nothing and I was so angry at her for being strong enough to get off the streets and escape, but she left me, she left me behind, I was all alone and I couldn't stand it anymore and I wanted to die and I wanted her dead and, and, I did it. I killed her. And now I have no one."

Later that afternoon, Harper hesitated, then knocked on Luka's open door to get his attention. He glanced up from the small mountains of paperwork that formed a barricade on his desk. She never understood where all the paperwork came from—their case management system was computerized.

Luka followed her glance and grimaced. "Ahearn. He's decided we're not busy enough and wants us to review these cold cases."

Now it was her turn to frown. Cold cases? Sounded like work that the rookie in the unit would be assigned. "I found Lily's family."

"Good work. Where?"

"Her aunt lives in Hagerstown. She has custody of Lily's baby."

"Did you call Hagerstown PD to make the death notification?" Usually, the locals made out-of-town death notifications—or at least sent someone to be with the family while they called Cambria City for details.

Harper shifted her weight from one foot to the other, suddenly feeling like the rookie detective she was.

"You want to go yourself," Luka said, immediately understanding her silence.

"I know it's not protocol, but I can be back by—"

"I should go with you."

His offer was a kindness she hadn't expected. And a relief. She'd done death knocks before as a patrol officer, but this felt different.

She knew things about Lily that no one else did, maybe not even her own family. How much to tell them? What to hold back? No one taught this in training.

Luka's gaze drifted back to the stacks of dusty files. "But it'd mean I'd need to miss Ahearn's meeting."

Her shoulders slumped. Then, despite his words, Luka stood and grabbed his suit jacket, then his crutches.

"But—what about the meeting?"

"Yeah." He smiled. "A trip to Hagerstown means I'll need to miss the meeting." He moved past her out the door to the bullpen. "Ray, Harper and I are taking a road trip. You'll need to cover for me with Ahearn."

Ray rolled his eyes. "You know, you keep missing his meetings, sooner or later he's gonna think I'm the one in charge of this unit."

"Fine with me. The paperwork is all yours, as well." Luka glanced at Krichek, who was sitting with his feet on his desk, chair tilted back, sipping the noxious brew he called coffee. "Krichek. Got a case for you—actually four cases."

"Four? Boss, I can't carry four open cases!" His feet dropped to the floor. "It'll ruin my batting average."

"Not just four open cases, four open *cold* cases. Files are in my office."

"Cold cases?" Krichek protested, his glare aimed at Harper. "Shouldn't that be the rookie's job?"

"Not today they aren't. I want case summaries and action items on my desk by the time we get back." Luka hobbled past them, heading to the door, Harper following.

As they waited for the elevator, she caught sight of his bemused expression. "You enjoy that, don't you? Making his life hell?"

"It's what the kid needs. The swift-kick-in-the-pants style of motivation is the only thing that works for Krichek. On his own, he'll sit around all day wondering what to do next. Give him a challenge—"

"And he'll rise to the occasion." She thought about that. "You know, it's really because he doesn't want to let *you* down. Has nothing to do with clearance rates or looking good."

He said nothing, so she asked, "And Ray? What's his motivation?"

"Ray doesn't need any motivation. He does what he does out of love. For the team, to get bad guys off the street. Most of all, for the victims."

Ray? Always ready with a jibe or devil's advocate argument? "I can't see him as any kind of crusader for justice."

"Ask his two ex-wives or the kids he never gets to see. Why do you think he refuses to take the sergeant's exam? Because it would mean time off the street and behind a desk."

"And me?" she asked as they reached the door leading to the parking lot. "Where do I fit in?"

"You? You're the rebel, the pesky little sister who never stops asking questions or finding new ways to think and do things." He grinned as he held the door for her. "A lot like how I was when I was young and naive."

She laughed at that—Luka was only ten years older than her and most of the brass still thought of him as a rebel. A rebel who got the job done and brought the department good publicity, so they mostly left him to his own devices. "Guess I could have worse role models."

Neither of them said it, but she knew they were both thinking it: role models like her family.

"Maybe it's because I never married or had kids," Luka said, "but it always seemed to me that we may be born into one family, but what counts is the family we choose when we grow older. Who we love, who we're loyal to, who we'd lay our lives on the line for."

"And who'd lay their lives on the line for us," she said in a low voice.

"Exactly." They reached the car and he threw her the keys. "Welcome to the family, Harper. You drive."

# A LETTER FROM CJ

Thank you for choosing to read *Save Her Child*. If you did enjoy it, and want to keep up to date with the latest Jericho and Wright thrillers, just sign up at the following link. Your email address will never be shared and you can unsubscribe at any time.

*www.bookouture.com/cj-lyons*

People often ask why I set my stories in the mountains of the rust belt of Pennsylvania. Not only did I grow up there—and most of my family still lives in a small city very like my fictional Cambria City—but during my career as a physician caring for children and their families, transporting patients in medevac helicopters, as well as assisting police and prosecutors, I've learned that these tiny "forgotten" corners of the country are a microcosm reflecting the world at large.

These are areas surrounded by wilderness where you can literally get away with murder. But, like larger urban centers, there are also families in crisis, leading to a population of "throwaway" children who find new, more dangerous "families" with the predators on the streets who convince them that they love them like no one else can. The disparity between the "haves" and "have nots" grows with each passing year and yet the families who have deep roots in the history of these small, forgotten mountain towns with their exhausted coal mines and shuttered steel mills, they refuse to leave, unable to turn their backs on their ancestors and traditions even as they fear for the next generation's legacy.

Rust-belt cities like Cambria City make for great storytelling, because they reflect so many of our own real-life stories. Stories of courage and honor and sacrifice and most of all, stories of communities building hope for the future.

These ordinary, average working people trying to make it through a day as best they can… they truly put the "heart" in my thrillers, more so than any serial killer or cunning criminal I could invent. I hope their stories have provided much more than a mystery to puzzle through or spine-tingling suspense to steal your breath; I hope that their stories offer solace in rough times along with a glimpse of a universal truth that I witnessed with every shift in the ER: heroes are born every day.

Which is why I believe we're never alone when lost in a good story.

Thank you for getting lost in one of mine!

I hope you loved *Save Her Child* and if you did, I would be very grateful if you could write a review. I'd love to hear what you think, and it makes such a difference helping new readers to discover one of my books for the first time.

I love hearing from my readers—you can get in touch on my Facebook page, through Goodreads or my website.

Thanks,
CJ

www.cjlyons.net

cjlyons

@cjlyonswriter

cjlyons

Printed in Great Britain
by Amazon